THE LAST MOON BEFORE HOME

Also by Barbara J. Dzikowski

Searching for Lincoln's Ghost
The Moonstoners

THE LAST MOON
BEFORE HOME

BARBARA J. DZIKOWSKI

WIARA BOOKS

Designed by Vince Pannullo
Cover art, copyright@ Deposit Photos stock imagery
Printed in the United States of America by One Communications LLC

ISBN: 978-0-9840305-6-9 (paperback)
ISBN: 978-0-9840305-7-6 (ebook)

To my family.
And
to caregivers everywhere.
"Greater love has no one than this …."

"Life can only be understood backwards;
but it must be lived forwards."
-- Soren Kierkegaard

CONTENTS

The Last Moon Before Home

ONE

1973: The Moment

THE suspension of time has a way of revealing the truth; the kind of truth that's bigger than one person, one lifetime. And there are certain things that have the power to still the world long enough to see truth in all its clarity before the mirror returns to dim. Things like a river, a cemetery, the moon and the stars, like fire in the night. Or that stark, edifying moment when your body first reveals its mortality.

△△△

That was how it was for Noël Trudeau as she reached for something high in the kitchen cupboard that Saturday morning and a horrible pain seized her belly—horrible enough to warn her that something was wrong with her pregnancy and to force her to call the doctor who called the ambulance. Within the next few hours, she was lying in a railed bed in the emergency room of the nearest hospital thirty miles away, awaiting test results.

Doctor Wharton had already come into the curtained cubicle to see her twice, his dimpled grin a sharp contrast to the antiseptic hum of the emergency room, casting a thin net of hope to harness her fears. But later when he entered the room grim-faced, she braced herself to receive the verdict.

"We need to terminate the pregnancy as soon as possible." He allowed the sting to soak in before continuing. "You and your baby cannot both survive this birth."

Time stopped for her right then. She couldn't feel her own body, let alone absorb his words. Like a distant spectator hovering over the scene, she was stunned into that truth-bound place of her own mortality.

"You're not strong enough to carry her a full nine months."

Her? She was struck by the revelation that her baby was a girl. "Are you saying there's a choice?" she asked. "Either she lives, or I do?"

Doctor Wharton sat down on the stainless steel stool and rolled it closer to her bedside, stroking his chin with the tips of his fingers the way his grandfather, her first doctor, used to do. "It'd be very difficult and would require complete bed rest. But, yes—the baby might survive, though very likely premature. There are a lot of 'probablys' on the baby's side of the equation. But not on your side." She watched his demeanor sink, his shoulders slump. "This birth will kill you."

She tried to digest the information, layer by layer. She wasn't afraid of death, no, only of the thought of leaving her children behind. Growing up motherless herself, she understood the unfillable void of abandonment. "What about a C-section?" Her voice faltered.

"That wouldn't change the outcome for you. I think I know where you're going with this, but don't. You have a son who needs you." He leaned toward her and touched her arm, an uncharacteristic personal gesture. Was he trying to comfort her or plead for her sanity? "Listen to me, Noël. The internal damage you sustained before your pregnancy is compromising things now. Your blood pressure is sky high, and you're bleeding internally, which has led to anemia. You're a prime candidate for PPH."

"PPH?"

"Postpartum hemorrhage. But if we end it right here and now, *you* can live." His eyes were drenched in sorrow. "Make the wise choice."

His words rolled past her like black clouds over a silver lining he was somehow missing. The original Dr. Wharton had told her years ago that she'd never be able to conceive another child after Adam and she'd lived with that painful truth until one winter morning when out of the blue, miraculously, she'd found herself pregnant again. Her baby, her daughter, *their* daughter—Leon Ziemny's and hers—had a chance, that was the core of what she was hearing; this baby who was the sum culmination of the best she knew about life, this baby who, at conception, had already defied all odds. Weren't some things worth dying for?

The image of Leon's grandmother stirred her senses, a hazy, half-formed vision of a courageous, brokenhearted woman, a cotton headscarf tied beneath her chin, blowing a kiss at a departing steamer with her only child onboard. It was a vision Noël had carried around for years to get through the toughest times.

△△△

Once the decision was made, she couldn't look back or second guess it; it was already too late in the pregnancy for that. Two weeks later, she wrote a letter to Leon who had remarried three months prior and who had no idea she was pregnant, and she slipped it into an envelope, sealed it, and mailed it to the last address she had for him in Langston, Indiana. She hoped it was still a good address, but maybe not, maybe he'd already moved into a new home with his new wife, but even if he did, they forwarded mail for up to a full year. The clerk at the post office had told her as much.

Her hope sunk in slow motion. Every morning, she listened for the sound of the mail dropping through the slot in her front door … but only a pile of bills and junk lay on the floor. Every time the phone rang … but it wasn't him. Drip, drip, drip. Her hope faded away like a melting candle. She tried to comfort herself. After all, she had been the one who'd urged him to start a new life and never look back. A month later, she knew she had to make other plans. From the confines of her bed, she contacted her brother Steve in California, her only living relative, a fundamentally good man and a strong one too, soon to be the lone survivor among them.

"What about their fathers?" Steve asked.

She assured him that neither father would be claiming her children. Adam's father was long out of the picture—and Leon?—well, he was newly gone, but out of the picture just the same.

After a few days contemplation, Steve committed that he and his wife would take both children, both Adam and the new baby, and raise them like their own. Later, Steve and Betsy flew from California to visit her, found an attorney, and they put it in writing to make it legal.

Finally, Noël could rest. She spent the remaining months of her pregnancy in a warm bed, having every conversation imaginable with nine-year-old Adam; visiting with her dearest friend and former neighbor, Theckla Chavis, who despite advancing age came all the way from Alabama to tend to her; and writing in a diary to her yet unborn daughter, whom she named Willow after the graceful trees she loved. Weeping willows had all kinds of legends associated with them, both joyous and sorrowful, but their resiliency—by far their most important attribute—was unsurpassed. When one of their branches became disconnected, it easily grew into a new tree, if it found the right soil.

On a steamy afternoon in July, a month before her due date, Noël's blood pressure soared like the outside temperature, and her baby was taken from her failing body by Caesarean section. Upon awaking from the anesthesia, she was able to cradle her newborn in her arms and pray to a merciful God for the right soil. Seconds later, filled with certainty that bringing Willow into being was the fulfillment of her destiny on this earth, Noël Trudeau died.

TWO

FEBRUARY 1997:
THE DIAGNOSIS

WALT Ziemny gave the mahogany bar a final swipe with a damp cloth, then glanced down at the confusing array of little digits on his gold watch. A few minutes ago—or was it longer than that?—his wife, Mary, called to remind him to hurry home to get ready for his appointment with Doc Podemski. "You didn't forget about it, did you?" she'd said, her voice hardening with that now-familiar icy tone.

"Hell, no, I didn't forget about it!" That's what he'd told her, but the truth was, it had totally slipped his mind. Now he had to hurry home to put on clean pants and underwear, and whatever else Mary insisted he do before they left for the appointment. Lately, she was always nagging at him to make himself cleaner, the same way she used to pester their boys when they were small.

He gazed around the warm, windowless room where he'd found refuge since he was old enough to hoist a brewski over a half-century ago. He loved the Mazurka Inn. Oh, the stories he could tell about the hours spent here with lifelong friends, living and dead, through thick of laughter and thin of tears; about the changing cast of characters who occupied the upstairs apartments over the years—a cacophony of wanderers, drifters, men in transition without a home to call their own. In this neighborhood, the Mazurka Inn was the next best place.

Walt owned the tavern along with his younger son, Ricky, having purchased it a few years back, long after Walt had retired from the steel mill. Ricky was mostly a silent partner who floated the money to help Walt buy it, but he had agreed with his father when it first came up for sale that they couldn't allow it to get boarded up like so many other businesses up and down Pulaski Street or get turned into some taco joint that'd go belly-up within a few months. The Mazurka Inn was a neighborhood shrine, a landmark, a harbor that had sheltered them and four generations of Polish-Americans, and it had to be preserved.

The first day he took ownership, he asked Ricky to help him hang a gallery of framed photographs on the inside brick walls— of those friends and neighbors, their parents, their grandparents, in various stages of life. And pictures from *Life* magazine too, including one of Walt's favorites—Chief Petty Officer Graham Jackson, squeezing out "Going Home" on the accordion, tears streaming down his cheeks as President Roosevelt's flag-draped coffin rolled by. Walt created the wall to remind his patrons of the power of history, of ancestry, the astonishing way that genes were jumbled up and passed around to live on. That was what the Mazurka Inn was all about: the unseen bonds that held us together in spite of ourselves.

As he reached for his coat, he was distracted by the sound of Gus' cowboy-booted footsteps on the stairs. The current occupant of the largest second floor apartment, Takoda "Gus" Sultanski was half-Cherokee, half-Polish, a former policeman newly retired from a long string of southwestern cities only to resurface in his original neighborhood six months ago. A gentle giant, Gus stood to a height of six foot four. Most days he restrained his wild silver

mane in a thick braid that hung halfway to his waist. Grizzled and
pock-marked, his skin was tough as a well-worn saddle.

In Walt's estimation, Gus was by far the most interesting tenant
in the Mazurka Inn's history. Not only his looks, but the sound of
his voice—deep baritone, the way an ancient tree might talk. But
what made him fascinating was his assertion (after packing away
too many whiskeys late one night), that Lee Harvey Oswald was
a maligned, framed man. Gus held him spellbound when telling
his tales about working as a Dallas cop when JFK was assassinated,
and he claimed to have first-hand knowledge, even photographic
evidence, to back up his allegation. After "foolishly" (Gus' word)
mentioning his photos to a steely-eyed Dallas detective one night
who demanded Gus surrender the photos the next morning or
else, Gus had spent years on the run.

"Morning, Walt." Gus nodded when he reached the bottom
of the stairs. "I thought you had a doctor's appointment today."

"Oh, shit." Walt stared down at the coat draped over his arm.
"Thanks for reminding me."

△△△

As Walt walked back home, he stuffed his hands in his pockets
to keep them warm. He'd forgotten his gloves. Thank God, their
house was only couple blocks away, otherwise his fingers would've
frozen over with frostbite, and Mary would give him holy hell for
leaving his gloves on the ... or in the ... where *did* he leave them
this time?

He couldn't really blame her. Walt Ziemny knew there was
something going wrong inside his head. He couldn't hold on to his
thoughts anymore; he'd be thinking about something and when he
tried to form it into words, the whole thing dissolved like a fizzing
Alka Seltzer tablet.

For a while, he could fool Mary. Just change the subject or

start yawning in the middle of the sentence. Half the time, she wasn't really listening to what he was saying any way, and vice-versa. When you'd been married to the same person for sixty years, there wasn't much new to hear. Ricky was the first to catch on. "Don't you remember?" he'd ask Walt about some picayune little thing.

"Hell, no, I don't remember," Walt would say. "I just remember the important things."

Not only was it a good answer, it was a truthful one. Going through his day was like rummaging through the attic by the light of a flashlight, a tiny little spotlight on one thought at a time, and the best ones at that, not who said what to who. Without all that extra junk floating around in his noggin, he was able to focus on what mattered. Mary, Leon, and Ricky could take a lesson from his playbook instead of running around like headless chickens half the time. "Slow down!" He'd tell them. "Stop and smell the roses."

△△△

Ricky was already parked in the gravel parking lot, covered under an icy layer of freshly plowed snow, waiting behind a sign that read: *Doctor Zigmund S. Podemski. Se habla Espanol. Private parking. Violators will be towed.* His truck was filled with bags of groceries on the seat beside him. Weather conditions being as they were, he'd decided to make a run for the grocery store in between the heavy snowfalls.

"The milk is going to spoil sitting there in your truck," Mary admonished him. "I don't know why you insisted on doing the grocery shopping before you have a chance to unload them at the house. You're throwing good money away."

"It's five degrees outside, Ma. The milk will be okay."

Walt slapped a gloved hand against his son's back. Ricky was a good boy, skinny as a flag pole even under his bulky coat, an artist who'd made enough on his paintings to quit the steel mills, and a talented one too, better than Vincent Van Dyke or whatever that crazy guy's name was, the one who chopped off his own ear. Walt couldn't remember exactly how old Ricky was, but he knew he could more than afford to live on his own if he wanted to; he *chose* to live with him and Mary. Ricky was the kind of kid who needed people around him, and Walt was grateful for his company. A few years back, Ricky had the courage to join A.A. and give up the booze, once and for all. His boy was doing pretty good now; a sober, yet sadder, man.

Doc Podemski's office was housed in an old red-brick building that used to be the Red Apple restaurant, a popular Polish eatery back in the 1950s and 1960s that served traditional food from the home country. The three of them headed up a long wooden plank, inclined to accommodate wheelchairs, and entered the building through the back door. "This place still smells like sauerkraut," Walt said.

"Shhh." Mary put a finger to her lips before smiling at the receptionist, safe behind Plexiglas.

"Why're you shushing me?" Walt asked. "It's not my fault this place stinks."

Before Mary could check in, Doc Podemski emerged from a side door. "You're one-hundred percent right. It *does* smell like old sauerkraut in here." A fringe of shiny black hair rimmed his balding head, his long doctor's coat stretched across his bulging stomach. As he held the door open to allow them to pass through into the small examining room, Walt gave the doctor's belly a friendly pat.

"Let's have a look at you, Walt. Get up on the table here."

"Aye-aye, Sarge." Walt saluted, but he couldn't quite manage the climb onto the stainless steel examining cart on his own steam.

With Ricky on one side and Doc on the other, they hoisted him up.

"Now, what seems to be the problem?" Doc looked straight at Walt.

"Other than being an old coot, I don't have any problems."

Doc shifted his expressionless gaze to Mary, who opened up her purse. She retrieved a lined tablet and flipped it open. "Walt's not himself lately," she said, examining the bulleted list in front of her. "He's having trouble figuring out the remote control—the same one we've used for years. He can't remember things from minute to minute. He forgets to take baths. He couldn't think of our daughter-in-law's name the other day. He keeps repeating himself, the same stories, over and over. And he couldn't remember this appointment no matter how many times I reminded him."

"You've been writing all that down?" Walt shifted his weight on the examining table. "I didn't know I was living with Sherlock Holmes."

Mary ignored him, kept her attention focused on the doctor. "But the thing that made me finally pick up the phone and call you is that, last week, Walt got lost coming home from K-mart. He was gone over five hours, and Ricky had to go out looking for him."

"I didn't do that!"

"Yeah, you did, Dad." Ricky nodded gently.

"I did?" How come he didn't remember a thing like that? "Well, big tragedy!" He flailed his arms toward the ceiling. "Like no one else ever got distracted and forgot where they hell they were going."

Doc listened to all of it, jotting things down in his chart, his face still deadpan. "There are a lot of things that might cause those kinds of problems. Why don't you put this on?" He handed Walt a thin white gown, "and we'll just take a few tests to see what's going on."

"Since when do you need to strip down to your skivvies to have your head examined?"

Doc Podemski chuckled, his facial features realigning for the first time since they'd arrived. While Ricky helped his father undress, Doc rattled off his own list of questions. "Have you been under any extra stress lately, Walt?"

"Besides this, you mean?"

"No," Mary replied. "We're not under any stress out of the ordinary. We have a good life. Don't we, Walt?"

"Yeah, yeah. We've got a good life."

"Are you taking anything new over the counter, or vitamins, on a regular basis?"

Mary answered again. "Nothing besides our usual multivitamin. But he eats an awful lot of candy lately. He especially likes Werther's. He eats them like they're—."

"Like they're candy?" Walt interrupted.

Doc smiled again, scribbling more notations on his chart. "How long have you been noticing problems?"

"She's been noticing problems since the day I married her," Walt said, as Ricky tied the strings to cover his backside. "But I don't see any goddamn problems." He turned around to look at his son. "Do you?"

Ricky grinned, his eyes distressed. "Just relax, Dad, and let the doctor do his exam."

Doc Podemski shined a light into Walt's eyeballs, his nose, ears, and then mouth. His nurse entered the room with a blood pressure cuff and slapped it around Walt's upper arm. "It's high—170 over 97," she announced.

Doc Podemski made more notes. "Are you taking your pills every day?"

Walt glanced at Mary, who looked as befuddled as he did. "You're taking them, aren't you, honey?" she asked.

"Sure, I'm taking them!"

"You might need to start helping him with that now," Doc said to Mary. "Are you eating okay, Walt?"

"He eats like a horse," she replied.

"But you're not gaining any weight, are you? Ricky, help me get your dad off the table and on to the scale."

"Up and down, up and down. Make up your cotton pickin' mind, Doc."

After Ricky steadied him on the scale, the doctor slid the steel bar until he achieved the final result. "One-hundred and sixty pounds. That's pretty good. You're down only two pounds from your last visit six months ago."

Mary sat near the edge of her folding chair, her eyes big as blimps as if waiting for the other shoe to drop.

"I'm going to put in some lab orders," Doc said. "Blood tests, lab tests, tests on your neck arteries. You could have a deficiency somewhere or a blockage." He wrote some more on his chart. "How old are you now?"

"Old enough."

"And exactly how old is that?"

Walt scratched the top of his head. "I'm sixty-nine."

"No, you're not sixty-nine," Mary said. "He's going to be seventy-nine this year."

He shot his wife a startled look though he dared not challenge her.

"Can you tell me today's date, Walt?"

"What kind of silly question is that?" He stalled as he searched the small room for a calendar. There were posters of bent spines and bad hearts and bunioned feet but not one calendar to be found. What kind of set-up was this? He turned to Mary, her head bowed to the linoleum floor. Ricky was no help either. He just kept grinning at him with that frozen smile. "Just wait until you're an old geezer and see how good you can remember one day from the next."

"It's the tenth, Walt. What about the month? Do you know what month this is?"

Fortunately, that one was easy. Christmas was just a little while ago, and shortly after that, Leon had left for Florida for a few months, like he did every year around that time. "January."

"Pretty close. It's February. How about the year?"

"Nineteen—" Walt tried to calculate in his head. "We just had a presidential election, not too long ago …"

"That's right, we did."

"1990?"

"Just a few years off." Doc nodded. "It's 1997. Can you tell me who that newly re-elected president is?"

"For gosh sakes." Walt sighed. "You must think I'm some kind of nincompoop." He closed his eyes; he could see the President's face clear as day in his mind—a big clump of hair on top of his head and a great big smile—but … *what the hell was his name?* The harder he tried to retrieve it, the further it slipped away, like a kite on a string. He opened his eyes, glanced at Mary again; she was looking down at her shoes. Finally, it came to him. "Kennedy!" he blurted out. "Yeah, John F. Kennedy."

Mary tugged a Kleenex out of her purse, sniffled into it. "Oh, Walt!" she cried. "The President's name is William Jefferson Clinton!"

Clinton? The name rang a bell. Why the hell didn't she tell him the answer when he needed it?

"I'm going to give you a list of three words now, Walt. Try to remember them because I'll ask you to repeat them a few times before you leave. Ready?"

"As ready as I'll ever be." He rubbed his sweaty palms against the paper-thin gown.

"Apple, table, penny. Can you repeat them to me?"

"Of course, I can. Apple, table, penny."

"Good."

After that, Doctor Podemski made him lie down flat on his back, and he felt him all over for lumps and bumps or whatever the hell else he was feeling him up for. When Walt was upright again and Ricky was helping him back into his clothes, he was hit with another barrage of questions, one right after the next, in a span of time that made Doc seem more like a gestapo than a family physician. Stupid questions like "can you spell WORLD backwards?" Hell, he wasn't even sure he could spell it forwards. The anxiety on Mary's face was making him so nervous that he could barely remember his own name, let alone President Jefferson's.

"What were those three words I asked you to remember?"

"What three words?"

"Apple ..." Doc curled his fingers back and forth in a *come-on-and-spit-it-out* motion, but Walt had no clue what he wanted him to spit out, so he only stared at him. Doc made another notation on his chart, a checkmark or something, the kind the old nuns used to make in red ink on Walt's arithmetic tests. Slipping off Walt's wristwatch, Doc handed him a pencil and clipboard with a blank paper. "I want you to draw the face of a clock."

"I'm no artist. Ask my son to do it."

"I'd like you to do it, Walt."

Reluctantly, Walt drew a circle, put the twelve up high and the six down below, but after that, he got confused about how they hooked up. He clumped the numbers close together as he counted them off in his head, jamming the *one-two-three-four-five* right before the six, then did the same at the top, squeezing the *seven-eight-nine-ten-eleven* just before the twelve. But it didn't look right; there was a helluva lot of empty space in between. When Doc asked him to insert the time "ten after eleven", he couldn't fathom where to put the hands.

Doc's face turned dour as he looked at Mary. "We've still got to take the tests, but based on Walt's pattern of forgetfulness, I'm fairly certain that it's Alzheimer's disease."

Alzheimer's disease? Walt tried to absorb the diagnosis. The room seemed suddenly smaller, the four walls caving in on him like they were made of cardboard. *Alzheimer's disease.* How could that be? He felt pretty much the same as always, except for some flubs, but a diagnosis like that meant that everything was going to be different from then on, that he'd start shrinking away like the walls. It was happening already. Doc was talking to Mary instead of him, as if having Alzheimer's disease made you invisible.

"You think I have Old-Timer's?" Walt interrupted.

"No, Walt. It's *Alz-hei-mer's.*" Doc pronounced the word as if he were some kind of moron, without bothering to look at him.

"I know that's not the way you're supposed to say it! Geez, give me credit for something! I know it's called Alzheimer's—but only old cows like me come down with it, so *old-timer's* seems a better name for a disease that's gonna make my light bulb go dimmer by the day."

"Please don't say that, honey." Mary whimpered into her hanky.

"Why not? That's what it does, doesn't it? Just ask Ronald Reagan. If you can find him, that is. He announced his Alzheimer's to the world, and nobody's seen him since."

"We'll know better, Mary, after the tests. I want Walt to get an MRI. I'm also going to write him a prescription for a medication called Aricept."

"A medication? Oh!" Her face flooded with hope. "Will it help?"

"It's not a cure. There is no cure. But it might help a little. ... Do you have any questions?"

Mary and Ricky glanced at each other. Their expressions looked unnatural to Walt, like marionettes with their wires drawn up high and tight so that their mouths wouldn't flap open by mistake. Silently, they rose from their seats, Mary heading straight for the door, while Ricky came over to assist him off the examining table. "Hey, Doc," Walt said. "*I've* got a question. Or doesn't that count?"

The three of them froze in their tracks like scared rabbits. "Of course it counts." Doc cleared his throat.

"After this thing eats up my brain, is it gonna kill me?"

"Eventually." Doc nodded. "But not for a long, long time. It's a very slow disease."

"So I'm gonna die in slow motion, huh?"

ΔΔΔ

On the ride home, Mary insisted on driving, even though Walt was the one who had gotten them over to Doc Podemski's in the first place without a hitch. His dear wife was a terrible driver— he'd taught her himself, way back when they were teenagers, but she'd never gotten any better at it—and it was hard to believe, Alzheimer's or not, that he was suddenly a worse driver than she was. At least it gave him time to process the news.

It was starting to snow. Mary's hands gripped the wheel, her knuckles turning white. She was driving too fast for the weather conditions, skidding on the ice at intersections, and she kept asking him if he was all right. Already, she was treating him as if he was made of glass or ripe for the booby hatch.

The familiar businesses and homes blurred by through the car window. Walt could name every neighbor on every block, except for some of the newer ones, the Mexicans who were swarming in like picnic ants. Good people—Catholics, just like them—with tons of little kids running around the neighborhood again, like it used to be when Leon and Ricky were small. Besides that, their peppy Mexican music reminded him of polkas. He didn't get twisted into a pretzel the way some of the old Polacks did, bellyaching that two out of the three Sunday masses at St. Stan's were now in Spanish, the all-Polish mass completely kaput. "So what?" Walt told them. "Just sit, stand, and kneel when the rest of them do." Whether in Spanish or Polish, it was the exact same mass every single Sunday. Did they think Father Burton was gonna stick in something new for the Mexicans? But they never listened. People weren't happy unless they had something to complain about.

The diagnosis didn't really surprise Walt all that much. He'd known something wasn't quite right for a long time. The only difference was he had a name for it now. *Alzheimer's disease.* A German name too, just like the goddamned Nazis he fought against in World War II. Now the Nazi was inside him.

But he wasn't ready for the booby hatch. Not yet, anyway. He still had plenty of marbles rolling around inside his old noggin, plenty of stuff to figure out before he left this earth, and there was no way in hell he was going to just clam up and fade into the sunset until he was good and ready.

THREE

FEBRUARY 1997:
TAMPA BAY

STELLA Ziemny liked to take her longest beach walks on Monday afternoons just before dinnertime, the least crowded time of the week. She'd walk two full miles, up and down the shoreline. Further down from their time-share, the sand was cluttered with sharp stones and jagged rocks, and she'd learned the hard way that she had to wear something substantial on her feet, despite the fact that pairing Nikes with a bathing suit was a fashion misstep.

She was already out on the back patio headed straight for the shore when the phone in their condo started ringing. Knowing Leon was sitting in his usual spot at the kitchen table with his nose stuck in the afternoon paper, she rushed back inside to answer it. "Stella, thank God you're there!" She heard her mother-in-law's voice.

Leon barely looked up, even when he heard Stella gasp, "You don't say!" After that, it was a good minute or two before she was able to shush Mary long enough to hold the receiver out to her husband. "Your father went to Doc Podemski today, and your mom wants to talk to you."

He dropped his newspaper to take the phone. "What's up, Mom?"

She watched him as he listened to his mother's second telling of the bad news. Nothing on his face moved, except a muscle in his cheek, the one that always throbbed when he heard something unpleasant. "Doc Podemski is wrong," he said. "He's getting old, that's all. All old people forget." Stella used to hate the sight of that throbbing muscle but it fascinated her now; it was the only part of him that betrayed his innermost emotions. As his mother talked on, his eyebrows knitted in irritation. "Well, then, you're lucky you don't forget things too."

The extended conversation gave Stella the chance to scrutinize her husband of twenty-four years in a way that normal life rarely afforded. The Florida sunshine had bronzed his skin, making it appear tauter than it did back home. Soon to be fifty-four, he remained a handsome man. When they were first married, she used to take him in like this in the moments before he awoke in the morning—waiting, just waiting, for his olive eyes to crack open for the first time that day. Back then, his hair was nearly black. Now his thick mane was tangled with more salt than pepper— long enough (since his retirement last month) to fall slightly out of place whenever he turned his head. Only his trim trademark mustache and eyebrows remained pure black.

Her thoughts returned to what his mother was telling him: Walt had been diagnosed with Alzheimer's disease today. No big surprise. Everyone except Leon had noticed the changes in him for over a year now, maybe longer. Last summer Walt didn't have a clue how to start his own lawn mower.

"You're making a mountain out of a molehill," Leon was saying. "We have the condo for another month. We can't come back right away." After a few more minutes of enduring his mother's latest soliloquy, he cut the call short by lying to her that someone was at the door.

"So the diagnosis is official," Stella said.

"Official, my ass." He picked up the local section of the newspaper from the table and rolled it up like a diploma. "He's just a little forgetful, that's all."

"Doctor Podemski obviously thinks it's more than that."

"Doctor Podemski doesn't know shit! I wish they'd get a real doctor." He sat back down at the table and pressed the newspaper flat again before raising it to conceal his face.

She took a seat beside him. "Honey, we've seen signs of this coming for a while now."

"I haven't seen any signs. For Christ's sake, the man is nearly eighty years old! Give him a break. What do you expect?"

She reached out her hand to lower the newsprint wall between them. "I expect him to remember my name, for one. I expect him to know how to find his way home from K-Mart. I expect him to remember how to start his lawn mower."

"Alright, alright," Leon snapped. "You're all doctors now, and I'm the crazy one. By the way, aren't you the one who forgot to take your keys with you during your walk yesterday and got locked out of the house?"

"Come on now. That's different. We all have our moments."

"Exactly."

He pretended to read the newspaper, but his eyeballs weren't moving; the muscle in his cheek still was. She watched him light up a cigarette.

"You're not supposed to smoke in here, you know." Airing the place out before they left and saturating it with sanitizer was a ritual that got harder to pull off each year.

"Oops. I forgot. Maybe I have Alzheimer's too."

"Hardy har har. Very funny." She decided not to push the point. Hearing the word *Alzheimer's* was shock enough for him to process, she imagined, and Leon was not a talker. His emotions burned down deep, a campfire in some remote location no one else could find. Oddly enough, his reticence to share himself was one of the qualities that first attracted her to him. Back in the day, her most fervent desire was to crack Leon Ziemny's mysterious code or die trying. Now, a quarter century later, the dying part was long over with.

"Sure you don't want to join me for a walk today?"

He gave his head a quick shake, then pushed the hair out of his eyes before turning the next page of the *Tampa Tribune*.

Stella stepped outside the patio door. The sun felt warm on her skin, soothing as a bubble bath. She was wearing short shorts over her one-piece bathing suit; the long daily walks kept her fit enough to pull off beach attire in a way the other aging women who lived down the shoreline could no longer manage, their pot bellies and crepey flesh jiggling as they cavorted along the sand in seeming oblivion. When the ravages of time finally caught up with her, she hoped she'd have the good sense to notice.

It was just past four p.m., and the beach was empty. She glanced at Gene's villa next door to see if he was out doing his afternoon push-ups yet. He wasn't.

She and Leon co-owned this time-share with three other couples who took turns using it for two to three months each throughout the year. It was an extravagant purchase, but they'd bought it anyway, back in 1984.

As Stella moved toward the surf, the sea breeze gently lifted her hair away from her face. Last year, she had dyed it auburn, and the girls in the office told her she looked like some movie star whose name escaped them. She untied her Nikes and removed them. Closing her eyes, she perched her body on top of the hot sand, digging her fingertips into the coolness underneath. The walk could wait; she felt too good to move an inch.

This condo community, a series of individual villas right on the bay, had been a real find. The one thing not so perfect about their villa was that it wasn't personal to them. Being shared by others, its furniture was sparse, simple, generic enough to please, but not offend, any of the investors. The artwork that hung on the walls was no different—soft, muted colors and nondescript scenes. It never felt quite like home.

Right after they bought the place, Leon used to walk with her on the beach. Now he strolled alone along the bay long after dark, smoking an endless chain of cigarettes, explaining that it was his *thinking time.* "Everyone needs some time alone," he said, and she wondered what that meant. Physically, he'd been with her every day for twenty-four years, but was he ever really there?

The young woman from the condo two doors over approached the shore in the distance along with her new husband, giving Stella a wave. She and Leon had known Jenny Sue since she was a child, and here she was, all grown up and married. The newlyweds looked adorable in their tiny swimsuits; they couldn't keep their hands off each other. Stella smiled as she watched them frolic toward the waves, screaming and howling as they dove into the water. By the time they rose together like synchronized swimmers, their lean, tan arms were wrapped around each other in a bliss Stella couldn't begin to imagine.

Even when Leon used to stroll with her along the beach, he never took her hand as they mulled things over, discussing their life and their future as if it were a business plan. Stella had suffered a miscarriage in her second trimester five years after their marriage, and both had decided there would be no more trying for children. They filled the void with nice cars, beautiful furnishings, good jobs at the steel mills—where Leon had been a supervisor and Stella was administrative assistant to the head of personnel.

"Want to join us?" Jenny Sue called out to Stella while her husband clowned around on an inflatable raft.

"Thanks, but I'm okay here." Stella grinned. Lying back on the hot sand, she closed her eyes, soothed by the sounds of the waves lapping against the shoreline as her thoughts drifted. By the time she married Leon, he wasn't the same man she'd fallen in love with years before. Any passion he'd had for life had dissolved to dust. He didn't hoot and cheer for the Chicago Bears, like the other guys who came to their house on Monday nights to watch football on their big-screen TV. Music used to be his mainstay, but to this day, he never touched his record collection; his big LPs stood silently on four shelves near the stereo back home, alphabetically arranged like legal papers.

When she'd first met him, he exuded a muted, beneath-the-surface kind of tension vented only during his lovemaking. He seemed like he was trying to work out his unspoken demons during sex and, as his partner, she had a major stake in the endeavor. She'd outlasted all his other girlfriends, and she was the one who could save him. And then Noël Trudeau came along and ruined everything, including him.

The last time he initiated sex was Thanksgiving night. He'd had too much to drink when he reached out for her under the sheets, and she'd tried the best she could to excite him, but it was a restless, extended lovemaking that he couldn't complete. When he finally stopped trying, he turned his face away from her, toward the bedroom wall. "Honey, maybe you can talk to Doctor Podemski," she'd suggested, but he didn't stir. His only response had been to give up completely.

The honeymooners were far out into the water, their two little heads bobbing up and down like buoys. As he tried to balance Jenny Sue on top of him, her husband's slippery shoulders couldn't sustain her, and Jenny Sue toppled into the waves, roaring with delight.

"There's nothing like young lovers, is there?" Stella recognized the voice behind her as Gene Henke's, the man who owned the condo on the other side of them. She thought he resembled Charlton Heston, but Leon scoffed whenever she drew the comparison. "That old *dziadzia*?" Leon would say. "You only think that because he's got a thing for you."

Maybe he wasn't far off. Maybe she embellished Gene in her mind because he made her feel desirable. She tried to ignore Gene's balding head with the five-strand comb-over, or the way he had to squint to see up close, even with his reading glasses. One evening last week they invited him over for supper, and he flirted with Stella all night long right in front of Leon—refilling her wine glass, helping her with the dishes, directing his dinner conversation almost entirely to her—his small, dancing eyes fastened on hers with barely a blink.

"Mind if I join you?" Gene smiled.

She patted the sand beside her. As he settled himself into a comfortable position, his eyes grazed over her body from top to bottom. Pretending not to notice, she soaked up the attention, even puffed herself out to feel worthier of it. She was ashamed how exquisite it felt. She gladly accepted the cigarette he held out to her. Holding the burning match, he glanced back toward their condo. "What's Leon the Lion up to today?"

"The *Tampa Tribune*. Same as always."

Gene made an exasperated expression. Pulling his sunglasses out of the breast pocket of his polo shirt, he slipped them on before looking out at the beach in the direction of the young couple. The glasses concealed his most aging feature—those small, brown eyes hidden in a nest of wrinkles. Other than that, he had a rugged face, strong, square jaw, muscular build. At seventy, he continued to operate a successful real estate firm, though a team of agents pretty much ran it for him while he raked in the profits and soaked up the sun.

Stella hadn't cared much for his ex-wife—the third of three—when she was still around, a younger woman, a little older than Stella. Her name was Bonnie, but Stella used to joke to Leon that the little diamond "B" necklace that shimmered around her neck didn't stand for "Bonnie." Gene treated her like a full-fledged queen, and Bonnie pranced around like one.

Neither Stella nor Gene spoke for a while; he was sitting, she was lying down. Being alone with him always made her a little uncomfortable at first, mostly because she realized she was stoking his attention to fill up her own voids. Shame and pleasure clunked around inside her until one or the other won out, depending on her mood.

"Your husband seems to be packing up the car," Gene said. "Are you leaving already?"

Stella sat up, shifted her body to look at their carport. Sure enough, there was Leon, carrying their baggage and placing it into the trunk. "Apparently so." He must've decided to go back to Langston like his mother was begging him to do this morning, but it would've been nice to discuss it first.

As Leon emerged from the condo with another load, she noticed Gene's visible disappointment at the prospect of her premature departure. "Your husband isn't a very sociable fellow, is he?"

Stella shrugged.

"He's a bit of a cold fish, I'm sorry to say. ... He'd have to be to neglect a woman like you."

His boldest declaration yet. She wasn't much of a blusher, but she could feel her face turning red, not from modesty, but guilt over what she was thinking about doing. Extinguishing her cigarette in the sand, she gazed at her husband with defiance. When he finally looked over at the two of them, she scooted closer toward Gene and searched Leon's face for a reaction. Even a *twinge* of jealousy would be enough. She watched Leon go back inside the condo and close the drapes, her heart sinking down that familiar slide. "He's just a private man," she said.

She lay back down in the sand, its warmth no longer comforting. Leon didn't have strong emotions about anything, except maybe his family, including his father's misdiagnosed dementia. He went through the days of their marriage, good and bad, like one of the guardsmen at Buckingham Palace. They'd seen those guardsmen up close; nothing could crack them. After her miscarriage and throughout the years, Stella and Leon had taken trips to England, to Ireland, Venice, and Spain, and all over the United States. Traveling was his preferred way of vacationing from himself, and from her too. When they traveled, they were absolved of the pressure to communicate in more intimate ways— they could converse about the best routes, the places they were touring, what they would visit the next day—and they felt like two different people, voyagers with alien frontiers to engage them; an escape from what they'd become. Even at that, the thrill of escape sometimes left her longing for more. On a moonlit gondola ride in Venice, she listened to him drone on and on about what an important transport corridor the Canals of Venice were, with their four hundred bridges connecting one hundred and eighteen islands.

How had Leon been able to remember those dreary details? Had he even noticed the moon?

Rising from the sand, Gene gazed down at her. She was hoping he wouldn't remove his sunglasses, but he did. Leon was right; Gene was an old man. "You've still got the condo for another month. Will you be coming back?"

"Probably not until next year. Leon's retired now, but I'm not."

"I can't imagine retiring at his age." He shook his head. "What on earth is he going to do with himself?"

"He just found out this morning that his father has Alzheimer's, so taking his dad off his mother's hands should keep him plenty busy."

"Alzheimer's? Oh, gee, I'm sorry." Gene folded his glasses into his breast pocket and looked out toward the water. "That's a tough diagnosis. … No wonder he seems so much more distracted today."

His sudden sympathy for Leon annoyed her. "Oh, I wouldn't worry too much about him—he doesn't believe it. He thinks the doctor is crazy." She stood up, brushed the sand from her clothes. She wished the condo had an outside shower; she hated to track sand inside, especially if they were getting ready to leave.

"So I guess you'll be heading back north tomorrow morning?" he said.

"Probably." Hands on her hips, she stared at the closed drapes. "I doubt if we'll be leaving yet today. We've got to clean the place up and all."

"Can I give you a good-bye hug?"

Ancient or not, Gene was sweet and considerate. He knew how to treat a woman. "I wouldn't have it any other way." Moving into his outstretched arms, she lingered inside their warmth longer than she knew she should. When his hands began to stroke her bare back, she felt a tingle of something else; wonderful and self-indulgent. A yearning.

"You're beautiful, Stella," he whispered in her ear. "Don't you ever doubt it."

She squinted back sudden, embarrassing tears, a betrayal of vulnerability. She didn't care whether Leon was watching or not. In fact, she nearly prayed that he was standing behind the generic curtains cursing Gene Henke's name. More to punish Leon than to encourage Gene—or was it for her own sake?—she brushed her lips over Gene's, the way a lover might.

"Stay here," he urged. "Let him go home without you this time."

Hearing the newlyweds' laughter off in the distance jarred her back to reality. "Oh!" She pulled away. "I'm so sorry!" Running through the sand, back toward the condo, she didn't look back, not even once.

FOUR

March 1997:
Hail Mary

WHEN Ricky Ziemny had purchased the Mazurka Inn with his father a few years back, he had his own plan in mind after surveying the upstairs. There were three apartments up there, a large one-bedroom that Gus now inhabited, and two spacious studio apartments. Ricky's first order of business had been to give the bigger of the studios a fresh coat of off-white paint and install track lighting. The next thing was to pull up the carpet, refinish the squeaky old hardwood floor, and install two larger windows to let in the natural light. And with that, he finally had it: his own art studio. Tearing down the wall between the two smaller apartments would have to wait until he sold more paintings.

That Tuesday evening, he stepped back to observe his current work—an abstract, impressionistic oil painting with short, intense brushstrokes of brown swirls moving downward into a deep vortex. True to the cliché, his life imitated his art. Lately, he was using one predominant color in each work, and this was his Brown phase— an exploration of primal, earthy tones.

He heard the door opening behind him and turned around to find his brother standing there, right on time, dressed in a jacket and black trousers, his Florida tan fading away. "Well, let's get this thing over with," Leon said.

"That's a great attitude." Ricky wiped his hands with a turpentine-soaked rag, tossed it on a table beside the easel.

"I just don't see the point. Who wants to sit around and listen to other people whine about their problems when we have enough of our own?"

"Oh?" Ricky raised his eyebrows. "So you finally admit Dad has a problem?"

"Sure he has a problem. He's *old*." Leon was pacing around the room, hands clasped behind his back, surveying the array of hanging paintings.

"Yup, he's old—and he has Alzheimer's." Though he wanted to say more, Ricky held his tongue. Why tempt fate when Leon had already agreed to the implausible: to accompany him to a caregivers support group. "You want to drive, or you want me to?"

"I'll drive." Leon tossed his keys in the air and caught them. "That way I can make a quick getaway." Raising his eyebrows, he gave Ricky a look that was as close to a smile as he got.

△△△

All the way there, Leon was wondering what had possessed him to actually go through with this escapade, reminding him of that awful weekend a few years back when Stella had dragged him to some touchy-feely marriage retreat sponsored by St. Stan's. The caregiver support group met in the basement of the United Methodist Church downtown, an old limestone block structure with a side entrance off the parking lot. Even before they went into the building, he could feel a tension headache coming on.

Upon entering the small, must-smelling meeting room, the sight of the facilitator cinched his dread. Pale enough to join the walking dead, she was a wispy, gray-haired woman with watery blue eyes as ooey-gooey as the icing on Stella's cinnamon rolls, so sweet they made his teeth ache. "Hi, Ricky." She hugged his brother timorously, like his bones might break. "I'm so glad you came back again this month."

"It was really helpful last time," Ricky said. "And so I brought along my brother, Leon, tonight."

"Oh, good, I'm glad it helped," she sing-songed as her eyes shifted to observe him. "Welcome, Leon. We're happy you're here." He was afraid she was going to hug him too, but instead she extended her palm, and he hesitated—a handshake meant you were sealing a deal and Leon wanted no part of this—he was already selling out his father by coming here. But she kept dangling her fingers out in front of him like wilted celery, and he had no choice.

"My name is Ellen Hamden. I'm the social worker at Mercyville Nursing Home."

"I'm sorry," Leon said. "That must be a hell of a depressing job."

"Oh—no, not really." Her hand snapped back, a disempowered claw curling against her chest. "I love working with the elderly. They're very dear to my heart."

The five others took their chairs at a rectangular table. Glancing around into their weary, defeated faces, Leon estimated them to be as old as his parents. He felt the back of his neck getting sweaty. Tugging at his collar, he reached for the cigarette package in his jacket pocket until Ricky leaned toward him. "No smoking in here," he whispered.

How did he expect him to get through this torture without even a puff of nicotine? Before he'd agreed to come, he'd made it crystal-clear to Ricky that he wasn't planning to say a word, and Ricky had assured him that his silence would be A-Okay, but, holy shit, he'd expected a much larger group where he could get lost in the shuffle. How was he supposed to get lost at a table of seven people?

"Let's go ahead and get started, shall we?" Ellen, our lady of sorrows, took her rightful place at the head, while the chair on the opposite end remained vacant. "And please remember that everything shared here is confidential. We'll just go around the table, clockwise."

Go around the table? Leon braced himself.

"Jake, why don't we start with you? How has your month been going?"

"Just terrible." The old man's eyes collected with tears. It was hell enough to watch a woman cry, but a man's tears were anathema to Leon; the ultimate frontier of self-preservation shattered. He turned away as he listened. "Viola doesn't know when she has to go the bathroom anymore until it's too late. I have to get special underwear for her now."

"I'm so sorry, Jake. That must be so hard for you." Leon watched Ellen put a reassuring hand over the man's tremoring fingers. He yearned to make a mad dash for the car while he still had the chance, but something held him back—the same something that brought him here in the first place—and that something was Ricky. He owed it to him to stay put, but geez-o-Pete, how could Ricky *want* to come here?

"She fights me—punches and hits me when I try to put the Depends on her," the old man continued. "She tells me she wants her husband, and I tell her that's who I am, but she doesn't believe me. Last night, she threatened to call the police on me. The only good thing is that she can't dial a phone anymore."

"People with Alzheimer's live entirely in the present moment, even though their orientation is to the past," Ellen said. "Your wife is fighting you because she's probably not sure who you are anymore or what you're trying to do." She glanced around at the others, her watery eyes honing in on Leon, the apparent "newbie" of the group, as if he required the most remedial instruction. "Alzheimer's is a long, slow process that causes something called *retrogenesis*, where people start going backward in time, losing memories of their lives and how to do things—like bathing and how to take care of themselves—layer by layer, in reverse order of how they learned them. They fade more and more into their past." She returned her focus to the old man. "And maybe your wife is sundowning too."

"What's sundowning?" Ricky asked her.

Leon turned to look at his kid brother who was gazing at Ellen like she was the Dalai Lama—his vulnerability in that moment tore Leon's heart like it did when they were kids. At nearly fifty-two, Ricky's nose and cheeks were still dotted with fading freckles, a flicker of something youthful—was it *hope?*—still lighting up his eyes; the last vestiges of childhood on his vodka-ravished face. Ricky had been clean now for years, thank God for that, but the alcohol had wreaked its havoc. It occurred to Leon that this support group must be what Ricky's A.A. meetings were like; that's why he felt so comfortable spilling out their private woes to a roomful of strangers.

"… so did that answer your question, Ricky?" Ellen answered. *Shit.* Leon's musings had caused him to miss out on her explanation. "Sundowning is a very common symptom for people with dementia," she concluded.

"Why does it happen when the sun is going down?" Ricky asked.

"Because that's when—"

"It happens to my husband *all* the time."

Leon turned to face the speaker who'd interrupted Ellen, a small, plucky woman wearing a tight pink t-shirt with *World's Best Grandma* glittering across her boobs. Her small, almond-sliver eyes resembled their own mother's, but Mom wouldn't be caught dead wearing a t-shirt. Or coming to a group like this. (She said it nearly every time Leon came over, and he wholeheartedly agreed: "Your father's problems are *our* business; no one else's.")

"It doesn't matter if it's day or night," the World's Best Grandma was saying. "We live in the same house we've lived in for the last fifty years, but he keeps asking me to take him home. When I tell him he's already home, he calls me a liar."

"I see you all bobbing your heads in agreement with Gertrude," Ellen said. "It's another common symptom of this disease. Those with dementia live in their emotions; the logical part of their brains has been damaged. Home isn't so much an actual place anymore, but a feeling. Home means safety, well-being, familiarity—the people and things we love the most. Unfortunately, they're expecting home and family to look the same way they did a long time ago, and they can't recognize the way they look now."

"So what am I supposed to tell him?"

"Tell him you'll go home later." The old man chimed in, his eyes refilling with tears.

"You mean *lie* to him? I've never lied to my husband in my life."

Just go ahead and shoot me now. Leon's head was starting to spin, their faces blurring, a feeling of nausea enveloping him. His turn to speak was coming up next. His eyes darted toward the exit.

The God's-honest truth was that Leon felt sorry as hell for these people—they were living with intolerable problems, problems with no solutions, and he couldn't imagine how they were able to cope even one day when they should be enjoying the golden years they'd worked so hard to earn. But Ricky or not, he couldn't take it anymore. This was no place for them. Their father didn't have this awful disease—he was just a little forgetful now and then, that's all. "I'm suffocating," he whispered in Ricky's ear, before pushing away from the table to go and wait for him outside.

△△△

The following Tuesday, Walt was getting ready to take his afternoon nap in his easy chair when Doc Podemski called with the final test results. Mary picked up the kitchen phone, while Walt listened on the living room extension. His diagnosis was *mixed dementia,* Doc told them.

"What's that?" Walt heard his wife ask.

Doc went on to explain that it was a combination of Alzheimer's disease and vascular dementia, meaning little TIAs—mini-strokes—were happening in his brain that would likely accelerate his decline faster than Alzheimer's alone. Before Doc could finish his spiel, Mary started sniveling.

"Holy geez," Walt said. "Did I get this thing from working in the mills all those years? Is it catchy? Will my boys get it too?"

Doc reassured him that old age and his uncontrolled high blood pressure, or a host of other vascular issues, were the major risk factors for this type of dementia, not the mills, not genetics. And it wasn't like the measles where his sons could catch it from him, particularly if their vascular health remained good as they aged.

After he hung up the phone, Walt plopped himself down in his La-Z-Boy. He yanked the lever to hoist up his legs, and just lay there flat, mulling over his fate while he listened to Mary rattling pots and pans in the kitchen. She was probably getting ready to start baking everything under the sun—*chrusciki, babka,* you name it—bad news always turned her into Betty Crocker.

Walt let his thoughts drift over him like puffy clouds. Somewhere in the back of everyone's mind lingered the question of how they were going to die. Way back when, Walt had felt certain he was going to be killed in the war. When that didn't happen, he assumed he'd die of lung cancer, like his best friend, Stanley Bartkowiak, and a ton of other guys in the neighborhood who'd retired from the mills. But he never thought he would die like this, slowly losing his marbles one by one. What a helluva way to go.

Mary wasn't baking after all. He could hear her voice in the other room, a low drone, a flurry of words, though Ricky wasn't home and there was no one else around. Who the hell was she talking to? He lifted his head from the cushion to make out her words.

"Hail Mary, full of grace, the Lord is with thee," she recited in monotone. "Blessed art thou among women, and blessed is the fruit of thy womb, Jesus. Holy Mary, Mother of God, pray for us sinners, now and at the hour of our death ..."

She was praying the rosary in there. *Holy crap*. This must really be bad.

Walt put his head back down. The rosary used to give him the creeps when he was just a runt. It still did. The men at the Mazurka Inn told him he wasn't acting like a full-blooded Catholic when he said things like that, and sometimes he wondered if they were right. What difference did it make? He loved God with his whole heart and soul, and that was all that mattered. People were always chopping God into tiny little pieces—Catholic pieces, Protestant pieces, Hindu pieces, Muslim pieces, Jewish pieces, you name it—trying to make God as small as we were. What was the point of that? It was all the same God wearing a different suit.

A few minutes later, he couldn't remember what he was thinking about, though he knew it was something bad. He tried and tried to recall, but his lids were getting heavy. Must not have been that important.

FIVE

JUNE 1997:
THE INVISIBLE GIRL

Listen closely now, my little Willow—you and I are heading toward a newer world. In your case, it's beautiful California, where the sun shines so bright that everything appears to be dipped in gold. In my case, it's somewhere beyond, where I promise I'll find a way to stay close to you. Your father, too, has started a new life—I tried to find him, but he's unable to be found. Here's our secret: his name is Leon Ziemny. You are the result of a rare love, and you should know his name.

HER mother's tattered diary tucked into her carry-on baggage, Willow Trudeau was soon to board a bus heading away from San Diego, the only home she'd ever known, bound for Chicago. Once there, she planned to visit her brother, who pitched for the Chicago White Sox, and after that she would rent a car and make the drive to Willow, the town for which she was named, so small that it barely had a dot on the Ohio map. Not exactly an upwardly mobile move for a girl not quite twenty-four, but she needed somewhere new to figure out her life.

Inside the bus station, the ticket-taker gestured toward them, her and the others too poor to fly or take a train (mostly old people, Latinos, blacks, and whites down on their luck), signaling that it was time to begin the short trek outside in anticipation of boarding. With the indifference of a man who'd done this too long, he asked them to lay down their bags in front of the open belly of the bus, where he loaded them in, one by one.

Willow stood in the center of the single-file line. By the time it came her turn to climb the three steep steps into the bus and head down the narrow aisle, the front seats were already taken, their occupants giving her half-a-second of scrutiny before glancing the same way at the next entering face, as if making silent notes of who to avoid during the long trip eastward.

She found a vacant spot a little more than halfway near the back, relieved that she wouldn't be stuck in the very last row beside the toilet all the way to Chicago. This window seat would work out fine, obscure enough, cozy in its own right, with unstained cushions and straight, tall back. An overweight woman in a flowery sleeveless dress plunked down beside her, rattling Willow's seat.

If Willow leaned forward slightly, the only other faces visible to her were a middle-aged Latino couple across the aisle, and the profile of a grungy white male in the seat ahead of the couple, thirty-ish or so, who'd reeked of alcohol in the station. Though she couldn't see him now, as she boarded she'd noticed another solitary passenger sitting in the window seat beside the liquored guy, the one she'd been hoping to sit beside, a silver-haired, distinguished man, by far the most well-dressed and safest-looking among them all.

Once the bus kicked into heavy gear and rumbled onto the highway, she watched the familiar landmarks pass by through her large window—the Laguna mountain range, lush palm trees, pastel stucco buildings, the pink bougainvillea—all of them awash in the golden sheen of the California morning sunrays, just as her mother had described in her diary. Though its promise of paradise had eluded her, Willow would probably miss California. Mostly, she would miss the mountain ranges; something about being bordered by nature's majestic walls gave her a feeling of security.

Willow had managed nearly two years at San Diego State in pursuit of an associate's nursing degree but she flat-out quit a semester shy of graduation, and she wasn't sure why. After that, she'd gotten distracted with cocktail waitressing at night and painting during the day. That was what she really wanted to do, become the next Jean-Michel Basquiat, who created raw and real paintings with oil stick, spray paint, or wax crayon. When she painted, she felt most like herself, but Aunt Betsy told her she was foolish for thinking that way. "Get real, Willow. How many artists can really earn a living?" Willow was drifting through life, her aunt said, and she needed to grow up and get a grip.

Grow up. What did that mean? She was born grown-up.

After the bus hit the open road and there was nothing much to look at, she snuck a peek at the other passengers, including the woman beside her, lost in their own worlds. Traveling on a bus made everyone feel invisible. Sinking back against the cushion, she felt a rush of well-being. She was among compadres.

The truth of the matter was that Willow had always felt invisible, fading into every classroom, every landscape, including her home, like a telephone pole. There, yet not there. Seen, yet not heard. Parents saw their own kids, but not an uncle and his wife who were saddled with two orphans. Uncle Steve had tried; he was a gentle man, good to them, but he avoided conflict at all costs, and he'd make some silly joke or retreat to his hideaway in the basement during the rough patches, leaving Aunt Betsy all alone to rule the roost.

Being invisible was a double-edged sword—Willow had no real friends, yet attracted fields-full of acquaintances that drifted near enough to pour out their deepest sorrows to her on a regular basis. Tell it to Willow and it goes nowhere, like stuffing a note inside a bottle and sending it out to sea. Afterwards, they felt better, lighter, leaving Willow as heavy as a soaked sponge.

She reached inside her bag, fingering the raggedy spiral notebook filled from beginning to end with her dead mother's thoughts, written in her distinctive, flourishy penmanship as beautiful as she must've been. The diary had been Willow's lodestar ever since Uncle Steve gifted it to her on her tenth birthday.

Uncle Steve had taken them in and raised them, both her and her brother, Adam, nine years older; same mother, different father. Though Uncle Steve did all the right things to keep them nourished and housed, he was sparing in his affection because of Aunt Betsy's growing resentment of the situation. She had their *real* daughter to consider, a little over a year older than Willow, and taking her and Adam into their home had put the financial kibosh on the prospect of future children, so who could blame her? She made it a point that cousin Amy got better toys, the best clothes, most of her attention, all of her love.

Sometimes, before she knew her mother's diary existed, Willow and Adam would sit out in the backyard and muse about what their fathers were like, subject to all their imaginings, good and bad. Adam was a Ketchfield, his last name the only remnant of his father's fleeting existence in his life, while Willow remained a Trudeau, her mother's surname and the same as Uncle Steve's, of course, so she had no idea who her father might have been.

During those backyard talks, Adam shared his memories of their mother sparingly—they seemed an Achilles' heel in a heart forged strong to survive—so Willow learned to be cautious about probing too deeply, gathering each new tidbit like a mined gemstone to be stored away in the recesses of her heart. Their mother was beautiful, he'd said, with raven hair like Willow's and eyes that shimmered with flecks of blue and green. Of course, Willow had seen the lovely photographs, but Adam swore they didn't do her justice. Willow used to wonder why she couldn't have turned out beautiful too. The same features, roughly, were all there—the coal-black hair, only hers was not so thick; the cobalt eyes, only hers were dimmer—but they came out all wrong on her oblong, not heart-shaped, face. Willow's pale skin easily broke out into rashes.

After she was given the diary, she better understood Adam's reticence. Surely he must have known the catastrophic truth: she was the one who had killed their mother. She'd died as a direct result of Willow's birth. Yet Adam had never shown even a hint of resentment and was, in fact, fiercely protective of her. Constantly butting heads with Aunt Betsy while Uncle Steve hid in the basement, Adam bore scars enough of his own. As soon as he turned eighteen, when Willow was only nine, he left home. She'd understood why, of course, but she didn't understand why he'd left her behind, why she couldn't go along with him.

A year later, Uncle Steve had given her the diary, and a whole new vista had opened up. She'd phoned Adam to reveal her father's last name. Had he known him?

Yes, he'd known him; sort of, anyway. "I was really small when they separated," he'd said. "I had no idea she ever saw him again after that." And then he shared his most vivid memory, of sitting on top of a double Ferris wheel in between him and their mother. "She was happier than I'd ever seen her," he'd said. "I remember that part the most."

The only time Willow didn't feel invisible was when she read the diary. *"I wasn't supposed to be able to conceive a child, but here you are,"* her mother wrote. *"So you see, Willow, you are a miracle. You were destined to be."* Her mother's diary made Willow feel as if she had something important to do that she wasn't doing, her destiny vague and shadowy, beyond her ability to achieve or even comprehend.

Outside, a Royal King semi-truck was passing the bus. With increasing trepidation, Willow watched the trucking company's regal, colorful crest roll by in slow motion, nearly close enough to reach out and touch if her window could be opened. When she was learning how to drive and taking her driver's ed test on the open road, she'd seen that same logo overtaking her on the left and she'd swerved too close to it. Grabbing the wheel from the passenger side, her instructor had twisted it toward himself, sworn at her, and flunked her. Ever since then, seeing Royal King's logo looming on her flank seemed a bad omen—one of those silly, superstitious things that got into her head like stepping on a sidewalk crack and breaking her mother's back. She held her breath until the truck went by.

Relieved, she gazed around again at the inside of the bus. The man who stank of alcohol was asleep, mouth gaping open as he fell slowly toward the other man, the older, well-dressed one. Willow made-believe that the older one was her grandfather. (Her mother's father had died before she was born.) She often played the "Who's My Grandfather?" game. Leaning forward, she tried to glimpse his face, but all she could see was his shoulder twisting toward the window, his only barrier against the boozy sleeper. She sensed her pretend grandfather's growing desperation over the uncomfortable arrangement. He wanted to be miles away, she could tell, already arrived at his destination and back with the person to whom he was headed toward, his lovely gray-haired wife with kind eyes, and their faithful golden retriever. Willow could read his thoughts as if he was screaming them.

That was the biggest advantage of being invisible, the ability to observe people and to absorb their worlds. That quality would make her a good nurse if she ever got back to finishing her degree. Maybe nursing really was her destiny. *Feel their pain, but keep a cool head; try not to come apart at the seams.* Someone had to be able to bind the wounds and sop up the blood. Someone had to sacrifice their own energy so that others could live. Or would her artwork become her destiny? Willow was a thinker; an over-thinker. She loved escaping into the world of philosophy and trying to figure out the big picture—why were any of us here? where did we come from? where did we go afterward? She knew we must go someplace afterward because she could vividly sense her mother's presence in certain moments. Or maybe it was only wishful thinking.

She often wondered if she was depressed, but how would she know? If she was, this was the way she'd felt her whole life, isolated and alone, different from the kids at school, but at least then she was on a designated track. Now that school was out and this was it—adulthood—she was at a complete loss as to what to do next.

She reached into her bag with some difficulty because the elbow of the woman beside her was too close, the flesh on the woman's upper arm spilling into her space as she turned the pages of the *National Enquirer*. She thought about introducing herself but that didn't seem good etiquette on a cross-country bus where people relished their anonymity.

Willow managed to tug her current book out of her bag, *A Kierkegaard Anthology*, into which she'd tucked a folded newspaper. She pulled it out and opened it up. There in black and white was the other reason she was heading off to the Midwest.

The paper had an article from last summer about a new art gallery opening in Laguna Beach and featured photographs of some of the paintings they were selling. One of them—an open field of marigolds that somehow looked sad against a gray-blue sky—was created by an artist by the name of Ricky Ziemny. When she came across his name, her heart jerked. She'd called up the gallery, and they told her his studio was in Langston, Indiana.

Up until that time, the name *Ziemny* had been her and her mother's secret, a written word on a lined page, a bookmark inside her imagination. Her mother hadn't been able to find her father, but maybe she could. She slid the newspaper back into the book, back into her bag.

∆∆∆

She immediately hated the town for which she was named. Willow was obviously not her destiny either; it was a dying little speck of nothing. Connected, mostly brick, storefronts lined three small blocks on the main street before the blink of a town spread out into a smattering of non-descript churches, homes, and open, rolling pastures. The only reason she'd come here, despite needing a place to think, was to find the house her family still owned, an old white-shingled structure that her mother and brothers had grown up in. After her mother had died, Uncle Steve decided to rent it out rather than sell it, and it had been inhabited by the same family for the last twenty-four years—the Richards, Jerry and Dotty and their three daughters. Now that their girls were gone, the Richards had opted for a condo in a new city. They'd been tidy, reliable tenants, and the ugly house was left spic and span.

Uncle Steve had used the monthly rental income to help with the costs of raising her and Adam, and after she came of age, he'd told her the house was hers to do with as she pleased. Adam didn't want anything to do with it—he and his new wife lived in a Chicago hi-rise—and Willow was considering moving into it. She wandered the small rooms that first day, up to the spooky, half-finished attic, down to the antique Maytag washer and dryer in the basement, trying to imagine what life had been like for her mother growing up. The house had zilch character; it was big and dark and badly dated, especially the kitchen, with chipped cabinets and linoleum counters.

Adam had told her that Willow was a picturesque place, filled with graceful, flowing weeping willow trees, but she hadn't seen even one. Another disappointment. Everything appeared shabby to her, not just this house but the other homes too, and the cracked streets, the overgrown, neglected landscape, even the downtown stores smelled funny when she walked inside, like old basements, and their wares seemed like rummage sale items. The people looked the same—used up, tired faces with no life in them. Most of the young people in Willow left town the moment they could, and the ones still hanging around wore the same expression as their elders, except that they chewed gum and moved anxiously, not in slow-motion. The whole town made her skin crawl.

The second thing she did the first day she arrived was drive out to the Garden of Resurrection cemetery out in the middle of nowhere where her mother was buried, the first time she would see her grave. In her diary, her mother had written how much she'd loved this cemetery, the comfort it brought her, how she felt God's presence there, especially among the huge grove of weeping willows where she'd planned to be buried.

But there were no trees here either, except a large nest of dead and decaying, gnarled limbs and trunks collapsing against one another on the far end of the cemetery. Without the flourishing landmark, it took forever to find her mother's grave, but eventually she did, and she halted in front of it. Despite the fact that she'd imagined this moment since she was old enough to imagine, she felt nothing as she stared at her mother's name in granite. Not one flicker of her presence.

SIX

JANUARY 1998: NO SUDDEN DEATH

GUS was drunker than a skunk that Saturday night, hanging there on the bar stool, going on and on about Dorothy Kilgallen like some kind of fanatic. Luckily, the earlier crowd was long gone, the hour late enough for only the three of them to be left there to listen: Walt, Ricky and Bennie Niezgodski. Any other patron and Walt would've cut off the booze an hour ago, but all Gus had to do was totter upstairs to his apartment, not walk home alone in the dark, or, God forbid, get into a car and drive home. Walt would make certain that Ricky helped him up the steps before he left.

As for Dorothy Kilgallen, Walt didn't even remember that she had died, let alone under mysterious circumstances the way Gus was describing. The only thing Walt recalled about her was that she was that skinny panelist on *What's My Line,* a long neck like an ostrich, and Mary always thought she resembled the Queen of England's sister. All night long, Gus had been blabbering about how Dorothy Kilgallen's 1965 death from booze and drugs, possibly along with a heart attack, was all a line of baloney, a big, fat cover-up.

When her body was found, he explained, she was propped up in bed on the third floor of her townhouse (she always slept on the fifth floor), wearing a fancy negligee (instead of her usual pajamas), reading a book (that she'd finished two weeks earlier), without her glasses nearby (which she needed in order to read). "Doesn't all that spell fishy to you?" he asked them.

Sure it did, but what was the point?

The point was, Gus said, Dorothy Kilgallen didn't kill herself at all; she was popped off to keep her mouth shut. She was one of the first mainstream news people to question the findings of the Warren Report and was doing her own journalistic investigation into the Kennedy assassination. She was the only reporter ever granted a private interview with Jack Ruby. And shortly before she died, she confided to friends that she was about to—and Gus said this was a direct quote—"blow the JFK case sky-high." Afterwards, her complete file of information about Kennedy went missing, never to be found.

"She was just one of many, my friends," Gus said, slinging back his latest shot of Seagram's. "One in a long line of witnesses permanently muzzled. Just like I could've been; could still be. Dead people can't talk."

△△△

Walt was just about to pour himself a glass of orange juice that next Monday morning when he heard Mary call out to him from the living room. "Hurry up and come in here! President Clinton is on TV."

Big hairy deal. He got there in time to see Clinton wagging his finger. "I want you to listen to me. I'm going to say this again." Clinton wasn't looking directly at the camera but off to the side. "I did not have sexual relations with that woman, Miss Lewinsky."

"The hell you didn't, buddy," Walt said to the TV. "If you're not lying, how come you're not looking us square in the eye?"

Mary was riveted to the television, pretending to be outraged, but Walt knew better. This whole juicy scandal was more exciting for her than her soap operas, and CNN was covering the tittle-tattle nonstop. "For gosh sakes, this isn't news," he said.

"Of course, it is. We have a right to know the truth, and what he did wasn't very presidential."

"Presidential, smesidential." Walt stood there staring at the TV. He thought about saying what he was thinking out loud but Mary was too absorbed in the television to listen. It wasn't as if he condoned what Clinton had done, not by a long shot; dishonoring his marriage vows with some little tootsie was shameful. But Walt didn't like the way we disrespected our presidents nowadays. Some things should be off-limits, and what the president did when he pulled down his pants was one of them.

"Oh, this is just awful!" Mary said. "I'm going to call Helen and see if she's got her TV set on."

Walt shook his head. He was trying to remember what the hell he was doing in the kitchen before she'd interrupted him.

"What's the matter?" she asked.

"Nothin'. Why?"

"Because you're standing there in the middle of the room like you're lost or something."

"I'm not lost! I'm just trying to figure out what I was doing before that bullshit came on TV."

"I wish you wouldn't use such foul language all the time. You and Leon both. He got it from you, you know." Mary patted the cushion beside her on the sofa. "Come sit down here, Dad. Let's watch this together. This is history."

"History, my ass." He sank down beside her, digging a couple of Werther's candies out of his pants pocket and offering her one of them.

"Thanks, honey." She patted his knee.

Walt unwrapped the candy and slipped it into his mouth. Then he stretched back in his seat and closed his eyes to blot out the television screen. Nowadays being in his own head was more relaxing than TV, the pictures didn't move around so quick. It wasn't just the TV. Everything was changing faster than he could absorb. People cared too much about themselves and their own opinions and didn't respect one another anymore. Like his boss used to tell him, "opinions are like assholes; everybody has one." Yessiree; the good old days were kaput. Television was trashier, and the music was louder. Hell, he barely knew how to make a simple phone call nowadays because you couldn't talk to a human being—press one for this and two for that. Holy geez. Friends were dying off like dominoes. Hardly a day went by when he and Mary weren't getting dressed up in their Sunday best to skedaddle off to the funeral parlor.

But that was how it was supposed to be, he guessed. If a person was lucky enough to have a long life, there came a time when you started losing your place in this world. It was all part of the good Lord's plan to belong here less and less.

When the commercial came on, he opened his eyes. Some guy was reclining in an airplane, as if it was comfortable as a La-Z-Boy. Another stupid notion that Madison Avenue was trying to peddle down our throats. He and Mary took a trip to Poland a few months ago and sitting in that airplane for nine hours straight was about as comfortable as a toilet seat.

Another commercial came on. Then another. And another. Pictures jumping all around from one thing to the next. Nowadays they had so many goddamned commercials that Walt forgot what he was watching in the first place.

"Let's see what Fox has on," Mary suggested.

"Not that Nazi channel."

"Oh, come on. Bill O'Reilly's kind of cute."

"You mean that Twilight Zone guy?"

"Not the 'twilight zone', Walt. It's the 'no-spin zone'". She kept the dial on CNN. "Would you like to go out to lunch today, or should I cook?"

"Doesn't matter to me. If you want to keep watching this crap, I can make something for us."

"Don't you dare touch the stove!"

"For the love of Pete, you treat me like I'm some kind of an invalid."

As he tried to get up, Mary reached out for his hand and held on to it. "Your birthday's coming up pretty soon. I think we should have a big party this year."

"Why? You think this will be the last birthday before I forget who the hell I am?"

"Of course not." She made a balled-up face as if it was the furthest thing from her mind, but Walt knew this woman better than he knew his own mind, and that's what she was thinking alright. He'd bet his last Indian nickel on it.

"It's a big milestone birthday," she said. "You're going to be eighty years old."

Eighty years! Walt was stunned, but he dared not say it. He thought he was closer to sixty. The commercial break over, Mary's eyes returned to the screen, hanging on every word that the bearded newscaster was saying. "That Bear Blitzer has been doing the news since I was a kid."

"Not that long." Mary said. "We didn't even have TV when we were kids. And it's Wolf."

"What?"

"It's Wolf, not Bear."

"What are you talking about?"

"Never mind."

He sensed that he was annoying her. Rising from the sofa, he settled into his favorite chair, his good, old plaid La-Z-Boy. Other than the swing on the front porch when the weather was good, this chair helped him do his best thinking. He ran his hand along the fabric. It didn't feel as coarse as it used to. He looked down. Why the hell wasn't it plaid anymore? He wondered when Mary had the chance to re-cover the cushions without him knowing about it, but, oh well, it was only fabric, and this one felt good too, softer than the plaid. Yanking up the foot rest, he stretched out until he was almost horizontal, closed his eyes again and slipped another Werther's into his mouth, letting it melt against his tongue, buttery and smooth.

He was in his own zone now, the spot where his mind could start sparking like frying pan drippings under a sizzling steak. This was Shangri-La—appreciating the little things in life, the big ones too, and mulling them over just before a nap. Being thankful for a warm cup of coffee first thing in the morning and a big front porch to stare up at the moon at night. The Ziemnys still had the biggest porch in the neighborhood. The neighbors used to sit there with them on Sunday nights, just shooting the breeze. Shangri-La, that's what it was.

When Walt was high-school age or thereabouts, *Lost Horizon* was one of his favorite movies; he'd never forget the sight of that paradise nestled inside the Himalayas where everyone stayed young and beautiful. But you didn't have to be young to be in Shangri-La, that's what he was realizing. Whoever said, "God gave us memory so that we might have roses in December" was right. Hell, it probably wasn't even a bed of roses back when they were young—more likely it was dandelions. But he recalled it now like it was roses. Remembering what it was like to be young was better than being young.

Alzheimer's or not, Walt was grateful for this time of life. No alarm clocks. No hustle-bustle. No more cramming his head full of useless baloney. This was the time to get rid of the scum that collected on the soul, day by day. Like dusting off the furniture. You had to keep up with soul cleansing; otherwise, it got out of hand. That's what the Catholic mass tried to do, skim off the gunk every Sunday before it got to be too goddamned big of a job. Confess it, forgive it, let it go. Those Catholics were pretty darn clever to invent the mass—not to mention all the money it brought into the coffers.

The story Gus told them about Dorothy Kilgallen kept running through the back of his mind. A sudden death like that was the worst kind Walt could imagine. When his Maker finally came for him—the one who thought Walt was worth making—he wanted to be ready to look him in the eye, like a soldier returning home, not caught off guard. He remembered the old Polish prayer, "*Od powietrza, glodu, ognia, wojny i naglej, niespodziewana smierci—zachowaj nas Panie!*" ("From pestilence, famine, fire, war, and sudden, unexpected death, preserve us, O Lord.") Preparing for death was his full-time job now. When his time came, he wanted to receive the holy sacraments and die peacefully in his own bed, not in some shady way like Dorothy Kilgallen, propped up in fancy pajamas with a phony book stuck in his hands.

Walt opened his eyes, and President Kennedy was back on TV, wagging his finger while declaring he didn't have sexual relations with that woman. Kennedy was lying through his teeth; otherwise he'd be looking them in the eye. Walt shut his lids again. He knew he was a lucky man. He had his Mary, still as pretty as the day he made her his bride—of course, his eyeballs were covered over with cataracts now, but that was part of the good Lord's plan too. Everything was supposed to go fuzzy, softer, less fine-tuned, as you aged, so you could savor the best about life—like the difference between bright fluorescent bulbs and candle light. Who the hell would choose fluorescent bulbs?

He had two great sons—different as night and day, but he loved each of them beyond compare. Ricky was a comfort, kind and decent. And a damned good painter too, better than Mozart. Ricky had grown up with a bad nervous condition that made him break out in terrible welts like a leper, and somewhere along the way, he'd discovered that booze helped calm him down. The next thing he knew, he was hooked on the booze. But a few years back, he went to the A & P and got himself cleaned up real nice.

Leon was Walt's rock, but closed up, his hatches battened down tight enough for a hurricane. He'd been hitched to the same gal for a long time now. Walt couldn't think of her name just then, but it'd come to him in a few minutes; it always did. Leon used to be married to a sweet girl named Noël—pretty as a picture with a smile that reminded Walt of his dear mother, like the sun coming up. As long as he lived, he'd never figure out why they got divorced. She was Leon's one shot, the only time in his life when he wasn't hiding from himself.

Walt was just about asleep when the sudden sound of Mary's voice jarred him awake. "So what do you think?" she concluded.

"What do I think about what?"

"The birthday party."

"What birthday party?"

"*Your* birthday party. For your eightieth birthday?"

"I'm going to be eighty?"

"I just told you that! Don't you remember?"

Sure enough, she was pissed off. Every time he made her repeat something—and he did that a lot lately—she got pissed off all over again. Frankly, he'd never married the woman for her patience. But seeing her pissed off was better than seeing her sad. Nothing was worse than that. He hated that his mind was slipping; his memories were his treasures. "Let me tell you," he muttered to himself, "getting old is no walk on the beach."

"Did you say something, Dad?"

"I said getting old is no walk on the beach."

"That's for sure."

As grateful as he was for his life, Walt also had memories he wished to God he could forget. Like the fact that he never knew what happened to his father, but that he likely died of TB back in Poland when Walt was still a kid. Like the fact that his mother died in a concentration camp. Like the fact that she'd put him on a steamer for America when he was six years old so that he could grow up in America, the land of the free and the home of the brave. His ache for his parents was a wound that had never healed.

No one knew this part, not even Mary; it was something he couldn't say out loud to anyone. But he'd spent his whole life worrying that he'd let his parents down. It was the biggest burden, the heaviest baggage that he carried. They'd sacrificed their only son just so that he could grow up in a better world, and here he was—nothing more than a common retired steel mill worker. A bartender. And now he was losing his marbles.

He and Mary had taken a trip to Poland a year ago, in the wintertime. Or was it just a few months ago? Who the hell could remember exactly when it was? The point was, he found his mother's grave and put flowers on it—yellow tulips, her favorites—and then he'd knelt down to say a prayer and ended up bawling like a newborn baby. Two complete strangers had to help him stand up on his feet. Maybe he just thought about putting flowers on his mother's grave. Hell, where would he have found fresh tulips in the dead of winter? "Did we go to Poland last year?" he asked Mary.

"No—but we went five years ago."

Walt nodded. How come time was getting so muddled lately? Yesterday seemed like five years ago, and five years ago seemed like yesterday.

"Why do you ask?"

"No reason." His eyes were still closed. "Did I put fresh tulips on my mother's grave?"

"You sure did."

A few seconds later, maybe longer than that, he was nearly asleep again, but he asked Mary if she remembered his mother's beautiful smile. Like the sun coming up.

"Walt, I never met your mother." Her voice was stiff and prissy. He knew how much it scared her that he was losing his marbles, but he also couldn't mistake that condescending tone. Sometimes he was afraid to open up his trap for fear of saying something stupid. But right at this moment, he didn't give a rat's ass because he was seeing his mother's face so vividly in his mind that it seemed like she was sitting down beside him. She collected porcelain roosters, and their hutch was stacked with them. "Roosters are a sign of good fortune," she always told him. And her favorite color was yellow, like the tulips lining the curving walkway to their front door. His mama sang like an angel. She sang to him at night after they'd said their prayers. Over his bed hung a picture of the Black Madonna of Częstochowa.

Right before his mama put him on the steamer for America— his last memory of her—she pressed a small lacquered image of the Black Madonna into his palm and kissed his fingers closed over it. "She'll watch over you when I'm not there to do it," she'd said. He carried that same icon in his pocket every single day of his life.

He was curling his fingers around it now—or was it a piece of candy?

△△△

That night at the Mazurka Inn was another quiet one. Just him and Gus. Gus was still too hungover from Saturday night to want a drink or to talk too much, so the two of them just sat there watching the old television on the overhead shelf. More nonstop Monica Lewinsky bullshit. Walt switched the station to that *Friends* show and turned off the sound, those kids yapped way too fast for him to catch the punchlines. He poured himself a drink, a double shot of Glenlivit. It wasn't really drinking alone since Gus was sitting right there watching him.

"Business isn't so good anymore," Walt said.

"Well, the neighborhood isn't the same. The old Polacks are pretty much gone, and the Mexicans are too young to hang around in an old joint like this."

Walt looked at his wall of memories. "Yeah, I guess you're right. Things are changing."

"Yup."

Gus' heavy black eyebrows knitted together forming one big bushy line over his eyes, the wrinkles furrowing his forehead like a plow had run through it. Gus was a force of nature, durable as the wilderness, and the deepest thinker Walt knew. They could make a statue out of him when he got that way. "Yup." Walt echoed.

Gus stretched out his arms over his head, yawned. "I think I'm gonna turn in for the night. Careful walking home, my friend."

"Oh, yeah. I'm always careful."

He watched Gus climb the long staircase, his steel-toed cowboy boots clacking against each step. He wondered if Gus ever got lonely up there. Maybe he could give him some company, rent out the other studio for a little more cash since business was down. Walt would have to think about that too, but his brain was unwired now. Alzheimer's sometimes closed in around him so deep that he needed a foghorn just to think his way home.

He finished his drink, gave the counter a final scrub for the night. After putting on his jacket, he headed for the door to lock up when it suddenly opened, and she walked in, her long black hair draped over the furry collar of her winter coat.

He gasped. "Noël! Is that you?"

SEVEN

JANUARY 1998: THE HALO

ALL the way home in the shadowy night, Walt was sweating; ambling down the sidewalk between mounds of snow on either side and sweating like a stuck elephant, which made no sense. *Get a hold of yourself; it's probably just this Alzheimer's thing.* Or maybe he'd had too much to drink, though he didn't feel drunk.

He took a deep breath. In the cold it came out of his mouth like a puff of white smoke in the darkness, just like she had been. Okay, so was she just a … halo? a hologram? or whatever the hell you called it … or was she real? All he knew for sure was that when he'd opened up the door, there Noël had been, and when he called her by name, her eyes got big, and she ran away.

He reached deep inside his pants pocket, fumbling for the Madonna of Częstochowa icon—it always calmed him down. *Damn it*, he'd lost it again. Mary was always taking his dirty pants away to wash them when he wasn't looking, and he couldn't keep track of it anymore.

△△△

A little before nine p.m., Ricky was relaxing in the living room watching TV. He heard the back kitchen door open and close, then the sound of his father's footsteps coming into the room. Without moving, Ricky asked him how his night had been, but when he didn't answer, he jerked his head around to find him standing in the doorway in a daze. "What's a matter, Dad? Are you okay?"

"What?"

"Why don't you sit down?" Ricky got up and helped his father over to the sofa.

"I saw her tonight."

"You saw who?"

"I saw Noël."

"Noël?" Ricky's pulse accelerated. "Where did you see her?"

"She came into the bar."

"Was she looking for Leon?" It felt physically painful for Ricky to even ask the question, triggering a shower of long-lidded emotions. After all these years, Noël Trudeau remained the only woman Ricky had ever loved. Even after she'd become his brother's wife. Even after their divorce. Even now.

"Huh?"

"I said, was she looking for Leon?"

"Hell, I don't know what she was looking for. When I said hello, she ran away."

Ricky exhaled slowly. Staring into his father's confused face, he was having the first inklings of suspicion that none of this actually happened, especially now that he was close enough to smell the scotch on his father's breath. That Ellen Hamden was a genius. She'd warned Ricky that something like this might happen, that hallucinations were common with Alzheimer's disease, especially hallucinations of people from the past. "How did she look?"

"What do you mean? She looked the same, that's how she looked."

"But she must have looked a little different. She's nearly my age now."

"*Your* age?" His father eyed him in disbelief as if trying to assess the passing of time and where he was in it. "Hell, no, she's nowhere near your age. She's a young girl."

He was tremoring now, his ungloved hands cold as ice cubes, so Ricky put his arm around his shoulders to warm him. "I don't think she was real, Dad. I mean, she was real to you, but I think your mind might have been playing tricks on you."

"Tricks?" His father looked away. "You mean the Alzheimer's?"

"I think so."

"Hmp. She seemed so real."

Ricky saw what appeared to be mounting fear in his eyes. "It's okay, Dad. It's no big deal. Having hallucinations, I mean seeing things, is just something that might happen to you from time to time, that's all. Don't worry about it."

"Maybe it's that drug I'm taking. I should stop it."

"No, it's not the drug. Aricept is helping you."

"Helping me do what?" His father put his frigid hands out in front of him, palms up, staring at them like he wasn't certain they belonged to him. "What'd you call that thing that made me see her—a halo?"

"Hallucination."

"Yeah, that's it. Hallucination. Geez. Only crazy people have those, don't they?"

"You're not crazy, Dad. You have Alzheimer's. It's totally different."

"Maybe to you, it is. But to me it's all the same. Just a different shade of crazy."

In the dimness of the room, Ricky noticed tears forming in his father's eyes, blurring them; his pupils seemed as if they were fading away into bubbles.

"I read some of that book you left out on the table this morning for your mother. It said I would probably forget my own family if I have this thing long enough." More tears accumulated, dripping down his cheeks. "I don't want to forget you! My family, my memories, are my whole goddamned life!"

Ricky enfolded him into his arms.

△△△

The next night around closing, while Walt was busy cleaning up and Bennie Niezgodski and Gus were sitting in the back of the room playing a game of Ms. Pac Man, she came in again. This time, she walked over to the bar and sat down in front of him, wearing the same dark coat with the white fur around the collar, her long black hair shiny under the lights. Walt blinked half a dozen times or more, but each time he opened his eyes, she was still there.

"Aren't you gonna serve your guest, Walt?" Gus asked.

"You mean, you can see her too?"

"Of course, I see her! What the hell are you talking about?"

Walt wasn't sure what he was feeling at the moment, but relief was somewhere pretty damned near the top of the list. Now that he knew she was real, he studied her face closer. She didn't look as spooked as she did last night. Come to think of it, she didn't look all that much like Noël. Same hair. Same kind of build. Nice eyes, but different, not sparkly bright the way Noël's were. No smile like the sun coming up. This girl had an untrusting look about her. She was staring at him as if *he* were the halo.

"Why did you call me Noël last night?" she asked.

"No reason. You just reminded me of someone, that's all. ... You want a drink? Are you old enough?"

"Of course, I'm old enough! I'm twenty-four."

Her eyes were definitely not the same as Noël's; they were darker, doubting. "I'll take your word for it. But I'll only serve you one drink this late at night, so don't even think about asking for a refill."

"Late?" She glanced at the watch on her slender little wrist, rolled her eyes. "It's not even nine."

This wasn't Noël for sure. Noël wasn't lippy like this one. "So what do you wanna drink?"

"How about a Sloe gin fizz?"

"A Sloe gin fizz? This isn't Bennigan's. I don't know how to make that fancy stuff." He took down a glass from the rack. "How about a gin and tonic with a slice of tomato?"

She watched him hook the green slice to the lip of the glass. "You mean lime?"

"Yeah, yeah, I mean lime." He slid the drink in front of her, watched her as she took a gulp. "That's not water, you know."

She seemed irritated. "What's your name?"

His name? What the hell did that matter? Walt didn't like making small talk with strangers, especially female strangers, and especially young lippy ones. It didn't feel right. But he decided to answer her question anyway because she came in alone late at night and that didn't seem right either. "My name is Walt. I own this joint. Me and my boy, Ricky."

"Ricky?" Her eyes got big again, same as last night. "What's your last name?"

"You're a nosy little gal, aren't you?" Under the spotlight of the track lighting overhead, lousy as it was, he saw her blush, reminding him of Noël again.

"It's just that, I've heard of Ricky Ziemny, the artist, and his studio is listed at this address. Do you mean *that* Ricky?"

"Yup, that's the one I mean. His studio is upstairs." Walt nodded upward in its direction.

By now Bennie and Gus had joined them at the bar, distracting

Walt as he prepared two more of the same—another brewski for
Bennie and the usual Seagram's for Gus. "Never saw you in this
neighborhood before," Bennie said to her.

The girl turned her back on him. Walt noticed the way her
hands were shaky as she lifted the glass for another sip, and he
wondered if she was an alcoholic or something to be so jittery at
her age. "Leave her alone," he said. "It's a free country. She can go
anywhere she wants."

"True enough, but this place ain't exactly on the stop to
anywhere," Bennie said.

She glanced over her shoulder at him, narrowing her eyes, then
refocused on Walt as he wiped some more glasses and hung them
upside down on the long wooden rack behind the bar. "Look," she
said, "I think I know who you meant—when you thought I was
someone named Noël."

"Oh, yeah?"

"Yeah. I knew a Noël Trudeau. She was my … aunt."

"Your *aunt?*" Walt threw the wet rag against the back counter,
his mood enlivening. "Well, for gosh sakes, why didn't you say that
right off the bat? How is Noël?"

"She's dead." She took another sip.

"Dead?" It hit him like a ton of bricks. "Noël's dead?" His feet
felt kind of wobbly; he gripped the edge of the bar. "Since when?"

"I didn't mean to blurt it out like that." The girl's manner
changed; suddenly there was some politeness, some human
warmth in her face. "I'm sorry if I upset you."

Bennie glanced from one to the other. "You okay, Walt? You're
white as a sheet. And who's Noël?"

Gus gave Bennie a nudge in the ribs with his elbow. "Let's take
our drinks and go have another game. Let these two talk."

"Fine with me." Bennie grabbed his beer and headed back toward the brick wall where the Ms. Pac Man machine awaited. They sat down at either side, inserted their quarters for the next round.

Within seconds, the tinny music and pitchy sounds of the game, along with the TV set playing softly overhead, along with that girl who looked like Noël sitting in front of him who wasn't, who'd just told him that Noël was dead—all of that coming together at the same time began to clang inside Walt's head in a dizzying maze that made him unable to focus. Alzheimer's had a way of kicking his eyes and ears into overdrive like that. Colors looked brighter, like a thousand new shades had been invented, and normal, everyday sounds sometimes reverberated as if he was in the middle of Grand Central Station. In quieter moments, the sensory over-sharpness worked out pretty good, better than good, like a movie camera shining out of his own eyeballs. The other day when he was shoveling snow, he happened to glance up at the sky, and it looked as if Michael the Angel had painted it into life, the cotton candy clouds changing into all kinds of beautiful shapes. But when too many things were happening at the same time, like right now, it was enough to drive him bonkers.

"Walt," the girl was saying, "are you okay?"

He got asked that a lot now. She seemed even more miserable than he was feeling. After moving around the bar, he sat down on the stool beside her. "Yeah, I'm okay. There's just too much goddamn noise in here, that's all. It's hard to concentrate."

She tugged on one of the strands of her hair, glanced up at the television playing some cop show. "Do you want me to turn off the TV?"

"Yeah, turn it off."

She grabbed the remote off the bar, clicked it.

"Now go turn off those two noisy clowns over there." He pointed to Gus and Bennie playing Ms. Pac Man, and the girl smiled. No sun was coming up, but it was still a pretty smile. He knew she could do it. "By the way, my name's Walt Ziemny." He stuck out his hand.

"You already told me that; don't you remember?"

"You hit the nail on the head, little girl. I don't remember a goddamned thing anymore. I've got Alzheimer's disease." It was the first time he'd said that sentence aloud to anyone outside the family, at least he thought it was; maybe he'd never said it out loud to them either. Though Gus and Bennie, and a handful of others, already knew his diagnosis, Ricky was the one who had blabbed it, not him. Time and time again, he told Mary to zip her lip about his condition, and now here he was blurting it out to some stranger he didn't even remember. Who the hell was she anyway?

△△△

This man was her grandfather. Her very own, flesh-and-blood grandfather. No more pretending. Willow gazed at Walt with a strange mixture of melancholy and amazement.

He had Alzheimer's disease. Until this minute, she wouldn't have guessed it. She knew a thing or two about Alzheimer's. One of her internships in preparation for her degree was to spend time at a nursing home in a dementia special care unit. The residents there were in late stages of the disease, and most of them talked gibberish, if they talked at all. She remembered how they sat clustered together in wheelchairs around the nurse's station, alone in their own orbits, staring at nothing at all with haunted, glassy eyes or hollering out the same thing over and over until the nurses couldn't stand it and hauled them off to their dark rooms, closing the door to shut out their wailing cries. When Willow offered them her hand, they had clasped her fingers like a vice and wouldn't let go. "I'm sorry," she said to Walt.

"Geez, don't look so sad! It's not that bad. Not yet, anyway … so that's my story. That's why I'm sitting here like a bump on a rump. But you're a pretty, young girl. You should be out there dancing. Not sitting here talking to some demented old fart so late at night."

The word *pretty* stuck in her head over all the other significant words, warming her in a place she didn't know existed. No one ever called her pretty before. She knew she wasn't, yet somehow, this old man, her grandfather, thought she was. Somehow, she reminded him of her beautiful mother.

"Who did you say you were again?" he asked.

Dumbstruck, she was uncertain how to reply. "I'm Noël Trudeau's niece." Now she felt guilty for the lie. Why was she lying to him anyway? To hide, of course. To stay safe, invisible.

"Noël! Boy, oh, boy, how I love that girl. How is she?"

This time, Willow was more cautious with her answer, gentler in the way she delivered the news a second time. Afterwards, she watched his eyes grow heavy with a new round of grief. "That's terrible." He shook his head. "Just terrible. My boy was married to her, you know."

His boy. *Her* father. She didn't know what to say next. Everything about this old man was honest, unpretentious. In California, people tried on personalities like clothing in a dressing room. She smiled at him.

"See there?" he said. "You're even prettier when you smile. All young people should smile. Hell, if you don't have anything to smile about when you're young, you never will. What did you say your name was?"

"Willow."

"Willow? That's a tree, not a girl. What kind of name is that?"
Her grin broadened.

"You look like her when you smile. The very picture of her. ...
So where did you come from?"

She picked up her glass to take another sip and found it empty.
She thought of asking for more, but he'd already told her it was out
of the question. "I'm kind of in between places right now."

"I know what you mean. That's how I feel too ... with this
Alzheimer's thing." He beamed at her, the wrinkles deepening
around his eyes like sunbursts, making his face appear almost
whimsical. Already, instinctively, she loved him, though it was
totally bogus, and she knew it—no one could love anyone that
fast, especially her. Loving meant you let people in, that you
trusted them enough to let them in, that you believed they'd still
care about you after you did. She wasn't certain she loved even
Uncle Steve or Aunt Betsy, or anyone at all, except her brother
when he had time for her. And she loved the dead mother in her
diary. "I just moved from California."

"California?" Walt whistled, impressed. "Beautiful state. We
took the boys on vacation there one year when they were small.
That's pretty far away from here."

"Like night and day."

"So are you a college girl?

She looked down, fingered her empty glass. "I'm kind of in
between that too. I was training to be a nurse, but—"

"But what?"

"I guess I got sidetracked."

"Well, get yourself back on the track," he said, but it didn't
come out bossy like when Aunt Betsy harped on her for the same
thing. "You'd make a good nurse. And old people like me need
good nurses."

Her mixed-up emotions surfaced in another bewildered smile. "Did you fly here on an airplane?"

"No, I came on a bus."

"A bus? That's how I made the last leg to boot camp." He scratched the top of his almost-bald head. "I made some good buddies on that bus. And in boot camp too. So did you have a good trip, Noël?"

"I'm Willow."

"Oh yeah, you're the tree."

△△△

Walt couldn't remember when he'd had such a good time talking to anyone, and when he looked up, David Letterman was already on TV. Gus had gone up to bed a while ago, and Bennie had left too, and here they were, him and this little girl, still yakking away. He sensed something lost about her, and a little lonely too, and the two of them seemed to be on two ends of the same wavelength. He was surprised when Ricky came flying through the door, nervous as a cat.

"Dad, thank God! Where the hell have you been?" Walt watched his son's face go ashen when he spotted the girl's long black hair from the back.

"See there?" Walt laughed. "She isn't a halo after all."

EIGHT

JANUARY 1998:
THE BROWN PERIOD

RICKY'S heart felt as if it would thump out of his chest. But the second she turned around, he could plainly see it wasn't Noël Trudeau who was talking to his father, just a vaguely reminiscent substitute in the shadowy lighting of the bar. His exhilaration vanishing, suspicion set in.

"Come over here," his father said. "I want you to meet … Maple."

"Willow," she corrected softly, staring at Ricky with what appeared to be apprehension. Was it because she was up to no good; trying to roll his old man? Approaching quickly, he sat down on the stool beside his dad.

"Willow here is gonna work for us," his father announced.

"What?" Ricky looked at the girl, her eyes still locked on him.

"Yup," his father said. "I hired her to help me out."

"We don't have money for that. You know that, Dad."

"I know no such thing." He crossed his arms. "You boys are hardly around here, that's for sure, and this place is getting too damned much for me to handle full time."

Now the guilt was Ricky's. This wasn't the first time since his father's diagnosis that the same thought had crossed his mind—was it safe for him to be walking home alone late at night? Managing money? Mixing drinks?—but he also knew the Mazurka Inn was what was keeping his father going, a cherished routine, his purpose in life. "We'll help out more from now on," he said. "I promise."

"Hell, I don't want your help. You boys have lives of your own, and that's the way it should be. Maple—I mean, Willow here—is gonna do it for nothin', except for free room and board upstairs. And she can keep her tips."

Now Ricky was really suspicious. He sized-up the scrawny thing, drowning in her bulky winter coat, her cheeks sunken, her eyes dull. Who was she, and what did she want? Money, most likely, but anyone with a brain could figure out that this bar was a dying operation, a labor of love more than a viable business. Maybe she'd hoped to rob the register when his father turned his back; maybe she already had. "This is a bad idea," he said to her. "We're not hiring."

"The hell we aren't!" His father's face was turning red. Ricky hated to take the upper hand in front of her, treat him like a child who wasn't capable of making his own decisions, but the fact was he *wasn't* capable. Ricky would deal with the consequences later, when she was gone. "This girl is almost family," his father said.

"*Family*? What do you mean?"

"I'm Noël Trudeau's niece."

She spaced out the words, defiantly, or so Ricky thought. "Noël?" His mouth went dry. "How is she?"

"Not so good … she's dead." His father delivered the blow.

The blood rushed from Ricky's extremities in a surge that left his arms and fingers tingling. The girl was still staring at him. "How did she die?"

She broke eye contact, lowered her head. "I don't really know much. It was a long time ago. I was just an infant."

He figured her to be twenty or so, give or take, meaning Noël had died awfully young. He didn't even have to stop to calculate; this year would mark thirty years since he'd last laid eyes on Noël. *She was dead!* The mere thought of her existence somewhere on this earth had given him perpetual comfort, more than he'd realized now that that comfort was gone. The world, even this bar, felt emptier. "Phew." He blew out a deep breath. "That's quite a shock."

The three of them fell silent. Most of the lights were already shut off for the night. "Are you … Leon?" The girl's voice sounded suddenly meek.

"No, I'm Ricky."

"Oh, you're Ricky." She repeated, her posture relaxing. "I'm Steve's daughter."

Steve was the middle brother, Ricky recalled, the one that was in the Navy during the Vietnam War, but that's all he remembered Noël saying about him. He tried again to take in the news, every piece of it overwhelming. Noël had been dead for years and years, and he hadn't even sensed it, not once, not one iota. "Was it cancer?"

"I said I don't know."

Her icy change in tone refocused him on the situation at hand. "So why are you here?" he asked. "What did you come here for?"

"For you, I guess."

"For *me*?"

"Show him," his father coaxed her, and she opened up her purse and pulled out a newspaper article about Ricky's artwork being featured in a gallery in Laguna Beach.

"Well, I'll be damned." Ricky wiped his forehead. Perspiring profusely, he was hoping the welts weren't planning on making another appearance—he'd gone over two years, the longest stretch without an attack. "Dad, can I have some water?"

His father rose from his chair quickly, despite his bent back and bad knees, rounding the bar and filling a glass from the tap, then sliding it in front of him. "You okay?"

Ricky nodded, took a long sip.

"She wants to be an artist just like you," his father said. "Isn't that something?"

△△△

The next morning, Ricky awoke with a jolt. Noël was dead!

He sat up in bed. Her name had gone unmentioned for years, the wound she'd left unhealed, a thin scab, unable to scar, and the arrival of her niece had torn it open. He could only imagine what it would do to Leon when he found out. To stir all that up again . . .

He lay back down, stretched out his long legs, gazed up at the ceiling. As of last week, Leon and Stella were back home from Florida, sooner than usual because they'd left a month earlier, just after Thanksgiving, something about some goof-up in the time-share schedule with one of the other couples. Pulling on a pair of jeans, Ricky swiped his fingers through his unruly hair. He met his father coming out of the bathroom in his stocking feet, and the two of them headed downstairs. Ricky wondered how much of last night he would recall. If he didn't remember, so be it; they'd deal with the fallout whenever it came. Ma was not likely to take the news well.

She was in her purple-flowered apron cooking up scrambled eggs when they entered the kitchen. Taking their usual seats, they reached for their glasses of orange juice. "Strings!" His father said, wiping his mouth. "I hate those damned things."

"What are you talking about?" Ma turned around. "Oh, you mean the pulp."

"The pope?"

"I said the *pulp*! I didn't have time to strain the juice today. I overslept."

Dad sat there drumming his fingertips on the table as Ma doled out the eggs. He must have forgotten, Ricky thought, relieved. He watched as his father picked up his coffee mug, took a sip, and then, out of the blue, he casually announced that Noël was dead and that he'd hired her niece—some crazy tree name he couldn't remember—to help out for a while in the bar.

Ricky awaited his mother's reaction. She put down her frying pan and sat down at the table, her face going pale, her penciled eyebrows rising like exclamation points. "Please tell me this is some kind of delusion you're having. Some hidden memory from the past coming out of nowhere, the kind Doc Podemski warned us about."

"Ma," Ricky leaned over, touched her hand. "It's real. Noël's niece came to the bar last night. I saw her myself."

"What does she want from us?"

Ma could be a real piece of work sometimes; she seemed more taken aback by the appearance of Noël's niece in Langston than she was by the news of Noël's death, yet it was typical of her—she was practical to the core. "She's an artist, like me," Ricky said. "She just moved from California, but she'd seen something about my art in a newspaper there, and she came to see my stuff. I'm taking her to my studio this morning."

"You're *what*?"

"She's just here for a little while, Ma. She seems kind of down on her luck."

"Down on her luck? Well, I'll tell you something; her luck just ran out!" Ma got up from the table and went to the stove, turning the burner on, then off, then on again, off again. "People don't just show up out of thin air! California is a long way to come just to see someone's art, don't you think? What's the real reason she's here?" She started flapping the spatula like a fly swatter. "Noël ripped you and your brother apart—ripped us all apart—and I won't sit back and allow some, some *relative*, of hers to do it all over again! She wants something from us, and you're playing right into her hands!" Now she was waving the spatula as if a thousand flies had infested the kitchen. An extreme reaction, even for her. "You send her packing—today! If your father won't do it, you do it, Ricky."

"Wait one cotton-pickin' minute!" Dad said. "You treat me like I don't have one piece of brain left in my goddamned head! I know exactly what I'm doing. I made an arrangement with that girl—a promise. And Walt Ziemny doesn't go back on his word."

Leon suddenly waltzed through the back door, and they all froze.

"What's a matter?" He slipped off his coat and hung it on one of the brass wall hooks. "Looks like I walked into a minefield."

"No minefield." Ma glared over her shoulder with a look that warned Ricky and his dad not to open their mouths. "We were just talking about bacon, that's all."

"Bacon?" Leon crinkled his nose. "Only in this house could bacon be a controversial topic."

"Nothing controversial. Your father likes it too crispy. It's not good for him to eat it that way. That's all." She dumped a platter of half-raw strips onto the table.

"This batch isn't too crispy, that's for sure," Leon mumbled under his breath, scraping some eggs onto his plate.

"Look, he's gotta find out some time." Dad's voice was gentle.

Leon, the only one who was managing to stuff his face amid the turmoil, stopped chewing and swallowed hard. "Find out what?"

"No, Dad!" Ma cried.

"Yes, Mary." He looked into her eyes. "We can't hide the truth." Turning his gaze toward Leon, he put a heavy hand on his shoulder. "We had a visitor in the bar last night. Noël's niece is in town."

Ricky watched Leon get up from the table, his eyes flashing like a bronco.

"Noël is dead, son."

Leon's head bobbed backward as if struck, his face wrenching in agony.

"She died a long time ago." Ricky tried to answer all the questions he'd had himself in one big rush to get it over with. "She died over twenty years ago. Her niece—Steve's daughter from California—said she wasn't sure what took her. She was just a baby when Noël died."

Leon didn't move an inch on the tile floor, except for the twitching muscle in his cheek.

"Okay, so you told him." Ma said. "She's dead. She's gone. Not even Houdini can bring her back, and that's it. She's been out of our lives for a long time now, and we've all moved on. And as for this girl, she's moving on too. First thing today."

"What's she here for?" Leon asked.

"She's a real nice girl," Dad replied. "She's hoping to head to Chicago to finish up nursing school, but she likes art and wants to learn something from Ricky first. So while she's at it, I offered her a room upstairs at the bar while she helps me out."

"Which you're going to un-offer today," Ma said.

"The hell I am! It's not her fault Noël is dead."

She turned toward Ricky. "Then you do it. Your father's obviously not up to the task."

"Stop treating me like a nincompoop!"

Ricky stared at his brother, still standing on the far side of the room, his face hardening to stone, the same way Ma's did when overwhelmed by emotions. That's what the two of them did; they short-circuited like an old TV set—one puff of fire and smoke, then nothing at all. He watched Leon pull his coat off the hook, not bothering to put it back on as he balled it up in his arms and exited the back door.

"You see what the truth has done?" Ma said. "And for what?"

ΔΔΔ

Feeling uneasy about the night before, Willow waited for Ricky outside the locked doors of the Mazurka Inn. Coming to Langston had been a big mistake. They were kind to her, both Walt and Ricky, and she was bald-faced lying to them. What good could possibly come from that? Her plan was loosely formulated in her mind, like one of her artworks when it was still a germ of an idea, too hazy to be sketched out. She hadn't counted on getting a job here until Walt had offered it, and she hadn't intended on living right under their noses where one lie after the next would have to be told to conceal her true identity.

When Ricky finally rounded the corner, he smiled when he saw her, rattling a ring of keys in his hand. "I'll show you your apartment upstairs so that you can get settled in as soon as possible," he said. Turning the largest key, a long gold one, in the lock of the old wooden door of the Mazurka Inn, he swung it open. "Shh." He put his finger to his lips as they mounted the staircase inside. "Gus is still sleeping. Besides you, he's our only other tenant."

Willow followed silently. Once they reached the top, they walked down a long dark hallway. Ricky pulled a string to turn on the single lightbulb shining overhead, casting an eerie light on the ceiling and walls. He selected another key from the wire ring and opened the door at the far end of the hallway, allowing her to enter before him. "This is my studio."

She thought the room would smell musty and old, like the hallway, but it had a pleasant, clean scent. The room was rectangular, one bricked wall, with a high ceiling, fifteen-foot or so, and two long, narrow windows that overlooked what she now knew was Pulaski Street. Ricky's paintings hung all over the walls, piles of completed canvases stacked against one another on the floor. Through one open door sat a toilet, sink, and tub, crammed together like a storage room more than a bathroom.

Enchanted by the artwork, Willow walked from piece to piece, concentrating on each one. His style had evolved from the marigold painting she'd memorized to a more abstract, impressionistic pattern, with short, intense brushstrokes conveying a variety of emotions. One predominant color characterized each work. She was drawn to the purple paintings, vibrant and lovely like French landscapes. Standing by his easel, Ricky unveiled his latest creation. Apparently, he was in his brown period now. "You're a great artist," she said.

"Not great. Just so-so."

"No, you're great. Your style is unpredictable. It keeps changing, doesn't it?"

"I guess." He shrugged. "We change. So our art changes too."

"You think you can give me some lessons?"

"Sure. But in the end, it's all about you and what you're trying to say through your art."

△△△

After he settled her into the adjoining apartment next to the art studio—a similar, yet slightly smaller, furnished room with the same claustrophobic bathroom—he offered to treat her to lunch at Busia's Bakery, a block down from the Mazurka Inn, where Busia Kowalski offered special homemade dishes. Willow tried not to seem too eager, but the truth was, she was starving. She hadn't taken the time to eat in over a day, maybe two, partly because she didn't have much money left and partly because food never held much interest. Sometimes she'd wait so long to eat that she'd over-binge and force herself to throw it up. Luckily, she'd been able to rent out the house in Willow before she left and was living on the security deposit and first month's rent.

As they walked toward the diner, she took in the neighbor-hood. Pulaski Street was narrow with parked cars lining each side, leaving barely enough room for a vehicle to pass through. The old homes, in various stages of decay or disrepair, were built closely together, tiny or no front yards, some enclosed with chain-link fences. A few interspersed houses were vacant and boarded shut, graffiti sprayed over the brick. Other homes stood neat and tidy despite the sagging of age. As for the people, the majority they passed along the way were Hispanic, with a smattering of old white women in babushkas and old men who resembled Walt—thin hair, big noses, wrinkled, well-worn skin—brushing the melting snow off their porches with broomsticks.

Busia's Bakery reeked of fried foods, baked goods, and scents she couldn't identify. The oval-shaped room was filled with small wooden tables. The paper placemats advertised neighborhood businesses, including St. Stan's parish with a schedule of its masses. "Looks like this place was built around the turn of the century," she said as Busia Kowalski approached their table.

"Yup," Ricky replied. "About the same time as the Mazurka Inn."

"'allo, Reeky." Busia had a thick Polish accent. "Vat you and your friend vant to eat?"

"What are the specials today?"

"*Kotlet schabowy*, or *gołąbki*."

'Breaded pork loin or cabbage rolls." He translated for Willow.

"Sounds fattening," she said. Even worse, it sounded repulsive.

"You could stand to have a little fat on your bones," said Ricky.

"So could you." She scanned the menu. "I think I'll just have a salad."

"A salad? Apparently, you never heard the expression, 'when in Rome' ... If you don't want Polish, at least order yourself a good meal."

"Well, maybe a hamburger, then." She looked up at Busia. "Do you have those?" If it was too king-sized, she could purge it later. She didn't have a real problem with food, no bulimia or anything that extreme. She just hated to feel fat, that's all it was.

"Yeah, yeah, vee can make for you." Busia nodded. "I put Vegeta in it."

"Okay." Ricky shrugged. "Make it one *kotlet schabowy* and one hamburger."

Ricky was easy to talk to; a good listener, non-judgmental, and Willow ended up telling him way more than she should have. She told him about studying to be a nurse, about her art, about her favorite artists, and even a little about Uncle Steve and Aunt Betsy, though she had to keep catching herself to make sure she referred to them as *Mom* or *Dad*. It was even harder to try not to talk about her brother, and she nearly slipped a couple times.

He was a nice man, more than nice, too nice to lie to, the same way Walt was. Though she surmised that it must have been the Ziemny side of the family that had mucked up her gene pool to make her unattractive, she nevertheless thought that Ricky had the kind of face that got handsomer the more she got used to it, with eyes that flashed warmth and suffering in equal measure. She wanted to ask him about his brother, her father, but she held herself back; there'd come a time for that. She assumed he'd be just like them, like Ricky and Walt, caring and down-to-earth.

Ricky told her that he'd retired from the steel mill a few years ago; he was able to retire at forty-eight, and besides that, his art was selling well enough to earn a living. Now he had the best of both worlds, a pension and an independent source of income. He asked her what she wanted to do with her own life.

She hated the lecture that always followed that question. "I'm not sure." As she twisted a strand of her hair around her index finger, she saw him do a double-take, so she put her hands down on her lap. Had she done something wrong? Said something wrong? She was keenly aware that he could catch her in a lie at any second without her even realizing it.

"I've got to ask you something." He shifted in his chair as if uncertain how to phrase it. Her adrenaline spiked. "How did you make the connection with us? I mean, how did you know that your aunt had anything to do with the Ziemnys?"

A trick question. "I don't know." Stalling for time, she strained to seem blasé. "I guess my—dad—told me that she was married to a Ziemny. I don't really remember. But I grew up knowing the name, so I guess that's the way it must've happened."

Busia set their plates down, walloping portions that extended beyond the edges of the plates. Her hamburger dripped with grease, but it didn't matter because she was hungry as a bear, and she bit into it, gulping it and washing it down with a glass of water that tasted rusty or something. Busia had put some strange spices in the meat and maybe a little horseradish mixed in with the mayonnaise. Her cheeks were getting itchy. She tried not to scratch the tiny red bumps that were popping out; it happened whenever she ate something weird or felt really nervous, and she was plenty of both right now. The bumps would pass soon, in a minute or two.

Ricky stopped eating, staring at her as if she'd sprouted another head. His rudeness surprised her.

"It's no big deal," she said. "Just a little rash I get."

NINE

MARCH 1998:
ASHES

THE minute Leon walked into the Mazurka Inn that Saturday afternoon, he knew he'd waited too long to check out the newcomer. His family's opinion of Willow was already well set. Ricky and his dad seemed bewitched by her, extolling her rough-around-the-edges virtues every chance they got. And from the looks of things now, so was Gus Sultanski.

She was leaning over the bar—Gus perched on a stool on the other side—following his heavy finger as he pointed out something here and there on the papers he'd spread out in front of her, likely more crap about the Kennedy conspiracy. As Gus rambled on, she stood there listening, asking a question of him here and there, encouraging his kooky obsession.

Leon hadn't come to meet her earlier than today because, frankly, he couldn't bring himself to do it—unlike his mother and Stella who'd rushed to check her out as soon as they'd learned she existed. They'd come back relieved to discover she was plain, unattractive, nondescript; looking at her now with his own eyes, he saw they were right. For whatever reason, her dowdy appearance seemed to make her less of a threat to them.

But not to him. To him, she was the kick in the gut that confirmed Noël's death, even though he'd sensed Noël was dead for years now. Once, after Stella's miscarriage, he attempted to track her down. He'd gone to the library, done some research, tried to sniff out any trace of Noël in California, Willow, or anywhere in between, but he came up dry. He thought about driving to Willow to see if she was underground, laid to rest beneath the grove of weeping willows where she'd once told him she wanted to be buried, but he knew he'd never do it. There was no point.

"Yeah, sure," Gus was saying to the girl now. "You mean you never heard that the House Select Committee came to the conclusion that Kennedy's murder was a probable conspiracy?"

"Never. No way that happened."

"Way. It happened back in 1989."

"Based on what?" she asked.

"Based on scientific evidence that more than one weapon was fired."

"Then how come they're all still saying Oswald was the only one who did it?"

"You tell me." Gus stroked his long gray braid. "The truth was getting uncovered for a while, now they're covering it back up, all over again. For your generation. America likes to whitewash its ugly history rather than owning up to it and learning something. Just ask the blacks. Or ask my people, the Native Americans."

"You sound like a communist." Leon slapped him on the back as he took a seat beside him.

"See what I mean? A classic example." Gus nodded at her before turning toward Leon. "Love it or leave it mentality will keep you stuck every time, my brother. You can run from the truth, but you can't hide from it."

"I'll keep that in mind," Leon said, observing her up close. She might be Steve's kid, but she had no resemblance to the fiery Trudeaus that he could detect. And, like his father said, she might be a good listener too—the old Polacks who came here lapped up the attention—but how much talent did it take to stand there bobbing her head up and down while some silly old fool droned on?

"So what're you drinking, Leon?" Gus asked.

"Leon?" Her eyes intensified, Noël-like for half a second. Leon's heart lurched.

"Yeah, Leon—Walt's boy, Ricky's brother," said Gus. "The one who never shows his pretty face around here. To what do we owe the honor?"

"I got thirsty." Leon couldn't help but notice her intent gaze.

"He got thirsty." Gus repeated to Willow, chuckling. "Get this man a cold one, girl! We can't let him go around parched, can we?"

She stood there motionless.

" … Earth to Willow." Gus waved his fingers in front of her face, and she blinked finally. After pouring a foamy beer from the tap, she slid a coaster in front of Leon, resting the mug on top. "Willow here has been a godsend to your old man," Gus said.

"So I hear. Where is he anyway?"

"Upstairs doing who knows what. Walt gets an idea in his head about something up there and he straps on his tool belt and disappears for hours. Yesterday Willow found him trying to fix a loose leg on that wobbly old chair at the end of the hallway, every tool spread out around him, and there he sat, staring at them like they were foreign objects. When she showed him how the screwdriver worked, he was totally amazed, happier than a little kid who just discovered a new toy. That Alzheimer's is strange, isn't it? The brain gets dimmer, but the spirit gets brighter."

"What the hell does that mean?" Leon took a sip.

"Just what I said. As the brain diminishes, the soul rises to the surface. Your father is on a journey now."

"A journey, huh. Is that some old Indian legend?" Leon wiped the lather from his lips. "You know what, Sultanski? You're full of shit."

"Not shit, my friend; spirit. You, me, your father, Willow here, all of us—we're all full of the same Great Spirit."

Across the bar from them, Willow was leaning on her elbows, listening.

"So what ever happened to your cousin?" Leon asked her.

"My cousin?"

"Yeah, your cousin. You only have one of them on your dad's side, don't you? I'm talking about Adam."

"Oh, Adam." She diverted her eyes. "He pitches for the White Sox."

"No shit." Leon smiled. "Good for him." He took another swallow of beer. "Wow, the White Sox. Imagine that. ... So who raised him?"

"Who raised him?" She rifled through her hair. "My dad and mom."

Vague, disconcerting emotions floated through Leon as he digested the news. Adam was brought up in the same household as she was and she didn't immediately know which cousin he meant? The thought of Adam being raised by anyone except Noël distressed him—how she loved that kid—that kid who used to be his too, sort of. That kid who would've still been his, if they'd stayed married. Picking up his mug, he headed for the staircase. Though he had plenty of other questions, why ask them? The past was done, over, and there were no good answers.

TEN

MAY 1998:
THE YELLOW BOAT

RICKY could hear commotion in the upstairs hallway as he dressed for Sunday mass. "Walt! Hurry up!" Ma was hammering her balled-up fist against the locked bathroom door. "What on earth are you doing in there?"

"What do you think I'm doing?" Dad hollered. "Keep your shirt on!"

The same scenario played out every Sunday morning—Dad's dawdling was one of the Alzheimer's changes that exasperated his mother the most. Last Sunday they arrived at mass over a half-hour late, the congregation outraged by their grand entrance as Dad marched up and down the center aisle searching for the right pew, waving and shouting hello to friends all along the way. And it wasn't just on Sundays anymore. Whenever they had to be anywhere at a specific time, it took him forever to get ready. The more they rushed him, the slower he moved.

"Hurry up, Walt—for God's sake!"

"God doesn't care how long I stay in the crapper."

"God wants you in church, not dilly-dallying in the bathroom all day. We're going to be late!"

Giving his unruly reddish-brown hair a final pat down, Ricky laughed inwardly at the irony. All her married life, Ma was the one who had fussed and primped in the bathroom while Dad yelled at her to get going. With only one bathroom in the house, it was a ritual to which he and Leon had become frustratingly accustomed. The only difference was, when she finally came out, his father would whistle and tell her that she looked like a million bucks.

"Walt, can you hear me?" She pounded with two fists that time. "Are you deaf or something?"

"I hear you alright—the man on the moon could hear you. Just hold your horses!"

Ricky came down the hallway. "Settle down, Ma. We've got plenty of time."

"No, we most certainly do not!" His calmness seemed to rile her all the more. "You're always making excuses for him."

"Alzheimer's is his excuse. He can't help it."

"I know he's got Alzheimer's! But losing his memory doesn't mean he has to be so selfish!"

"Yes it does. It's all a part of it. Be patient with him."

She threw her arms in the air. "Yes, yes, you've told me that 'til I'm blue in the face. Be patient. Be kind. I'm terrible, I know."

"You're not terrible. You're just tired, that's all."

"I *am* tired." Her eyes changed, her anger softening. "I'm so tired, Ricky. It's like I have a child again, and I'm too old for children." She patted his cheek. "Just get him out of there, okay?"

He leaned into the door. "Hey, Dad, I gotta pee. Open up."

The glass knob jiggling from the other side, his father emerged, dressed in his pajama top and the same smelly bottoms that Ma had pitched into the hamper the night before.

"Son of a bitch!" she cried out at the sight of him, then covered her mouth. "*O mój Boże!* I'm used to those filthy words coming from him, but now I'm saying them too." Crossing herself, she burst into sobs that shook her shoulders, smearing mascara around her eyes and down her cheeks.

"You look like a goddamned raccoon," Dad said.

She wailed louder.

Hugging her, Ricky handed her a Kleenex from his pocket. "I'll take it from here and get him ready. Go wash your face." As Ma retreated into the bathroom, he tried to remember the tricks Willow used at the bar, the ones she'd picked up from her nursing training. She seemed to know exactly when to treat his dad like his normal self and when to let things slide. *It's all in the body language, make it positive*, she told him—both her and Ellen Hamden—but with Willow, it wasn't just support group theory; she was a live model he could emulate—a fair trade-off, and then some, for art lessons. Forcing a smile, he pointed down the hallway toward his parents' bedroom. "C'mon, Dad, let's get you into that new shirt Ma bought for you."

"What's wrong with this one?"

Ricky stepped back to examine it, then shrugged. "Nothing's wrong with that one. I just think that a shirt without orange and red stripes might look a lot better with your brown suit, that's all. Whataya say? Let's give it a try."

"Okay, then." His father nodded sweetly. "Let's give it the old Yankee try."

△△△

The next morning, Ricky could barely get out of bed. After vomiting in the toilet three times in a row, he hugged it like a long-lost friend, his head throbbing. The prolonged nerve attack last night had ravaged his body. One more time, his insides backed up before he felt some relief. Mustering the energy to hoist himself up from the bathroom floor, he proceeded down the stairs for breakfast.

When he reached the bottom step, he was overcome by an odd feeling, an inkling, enough to make him stop in his tracks and look around; the house seemed like a stranger's house, as if he was seeing the old, familiar furniture and wallpaper through the prism of a camera lens. Today felt like a turning point, and not a good one. For the first time in years, he was craving a drink.

He hadn't slept a wink last night—it was one of those tossing-and-turning marathons when worries and fears about the future and the past came flying out at the same time and colliding, escalating to a brutal attack of welts that lingered on his skin for hours. He lay there helplessly counting the bitter truths about his life, among them, the fact that Dad was getting worse quickly and Ma wasn't up to the challenge. Maybe he wasn't either. Or Leon, who still had his head stuck in the sand. And then there was Willow, whose appearance in Langston had reopened the traumas of their past, not to mention his growing suspicions about her. And then there was yesterday. Oh, God, church had been a disaster! When his father had gone up for communion, he'd grabbed the chalice from Father Burton's hands and downed the whole thing. Afterward Father Burton called to tell Ma that coming to mass wasn't such a good idea anymore. And he kicked them out of church! In between sobs, Ma had screamed at Dad all evening long.

As he entered the kitchen, Ricky heard his dad whistling "In the Mood", keeping time by tapping his fork on the table.

"How can you be so happy after yesterday?" Ma snapped at him.

Here we go again. Ricky's head pulsated; he put his fingers to his temples, pressed hard. No matter what he told her, she still believed that yelling at Dad, reasoning with him, reminding him about his screw-ups, could somehow whip him back into the man he used to be. Ricky kept telling her to read that book he'd left on the kitchen table, *The 36-Hour Day*, but she'd say that she didn't need some book to tell her how to handle her husband of nearly sixty years.

"What happened yesterday?" His father gazed up at her, clueless.

"Don't play dumb," she said. "You know perfectly well what I'm talking about! You humiliated us in front of the whole church yesterday."

He turned to Ricky blankly. "Who the hell tied a knot in her knickers?"

As she turned toward the counter in aggravation, the glass bowl of pancake batter crashed to the floor. Ricky leapt from his chair to help her sop it up, which wasn't easy with all that thick, gooey batter mixed in with tiny shards of broken glass, and he sliced his finger. Ma headed to the upstairs bathroom for the Band-Aids and patched him up.

Afterward, they both sat down at the table, already exhausted at seven in the morning. Ricky glanced at her. Her hair was a tangled mess. He couldn't recall a day when she hadn't brushed her hair before breakfast. It had miraculously stayed brown until just last year, but it was nearly all gray now with bald spots, another casualty of stress. "So that's it for the pancakes," she said softly.

"Not to worry." He poured his father a heaping bowl of cereal. "Look, Dad, your favorite."

"Are those my—what-you-call-its—my Happy-Os?"

"They're called *Cheerios*," she grunted.

"Huh?" Dad glanced at her.

"For gosh sakes, Ma, leave it alone," Ricky mumbled. "Yup." He grinned at his father. "These are your Happy-Os."

"The honey-flavored ones?"

"The honey-flavored ones. Your favorites." Ricky took a taste. "Yum! They're delicious."

His mother frowned. "You're always taking his side, aren't you?"

"Ma, there are no sides to be taken. Unless you're trying to pit yourself up against Mr. Alzheimer's." His stomach was churning again—he felt like he might throw up the spoonful he just swallowed. "You're just going to have to learn to stop yelling at him all the time."

"I know." She blew her nose into her napkin. "You're right. It's just that … church now too? I don't think I can live without St. Stan's."

"I know, Ma. It'll be okay."

△△△

An hour later, Ricky was resting in his room on top of the bedspread. His head felt as if a car had backed over it. After puking a few more times and watching the little Cheerios float around in the toilet bowl completely intact, he was feeling faint, so he returned to bed.

A knock at the door roused him, the sound of his brother's voice. "Ricky? Are you okay?"

"Yup." He sat up against the headboard.

"Can I come in?"

"The door's open."

Leon stepped into the room, his face apprehensive. "You look like hell. Are you sure you're okay?"

"I just had another nerve attack last night, that's all." Not only was he feeling like shit physically, but he was flat-out depressed. According to Doc Podemski, their father could live as long as another eight years with this condition, and Ricky had a hunch that it was going to kill Ma long before that.

Leon sat down beside him on the bed, holding his palm flat against Ricky's forehead. "You don't feel warm. I don't think you have a fever."

"Nah, no fever. Just tired."

"Why don't you call Doc Podemski?"

"There's no reason to—I told you, it's just my nerve thing. I've been through this routine enough times to know."

"But not lately. You haven't had an attack for a while. How long has it been?"

"I don't know." Ricky shook his head. "Long enough to delude me into thinking I finally licked it. Doc thought I'd licked it too. But surprise, surprise."

"Can I get you anything?"

"Nope, I'm good." He glanced at Leon. "But I'm glad you're here. There's something I've been meaning to talk to you about."

"You mean, Dad?" He sighed.

"No, not Dad this time. Though he's getting worse really fast. Haven't you noticed?"

Leon was silent.

"What I wanted to talk to you about is Willow."

Leon got up from the bed, walked toward the window, and looked out at the backyard. Ricky knew exactly the scene he was surveying: the dried backyard grass from a harsh winter, the badly faded Mother Mary statue with a broken-off nose—though you couldn't see the tiny hole in her face from way up here. They'd forgotten to put it the garage last fall to protect it from the long winter, and Ma had been harping on them to fix it.

"I don't think Noël was Willow's aunt."

"You don't?" Leon said. "You might be right. I didn't think she looked like a Trudeau."

"That's not what I mean. I mean …" There was no good way

for Ricky to say it, so he might as well just blurt it out. "I think Noël was her—*mother*. ... And I think *you're* her father."

Leon wheeled around. "That's impossible!"

"Is it? Just hear me out."

That crazy muscle pulsed in his cheek. "Noël couldn't have kids—after Adam. It's absolutely impossible."

"She couldn't have any more kids? Really?" Ricky tried to absorb the information; he'd been so certain about his hunch. "How come?"

"Long before I met her, her doctor told her it was impossible because of an injury."

"An injury? Hmp." Way back when, before Leon stole her away, Ricky had asked Noël to marry him. He wondered if it would've made a difference had he known she was infertile; he had always wanted a gaggle of kids. "Well ... then I guess I'm way off base. ... It's just that she has mannerisms like Noël's."

"So what? She was her aunt. Things like that run in families."

"But she breaks out in rashes too. Not anywhere near as bad as my welt attacks, but, still, don't you find that strange?"

"She gets rashes?" Leon's eyes were fastened outside the window again. "Just a coincidence, that's all. Like I told you, it's impossible."

Ricky watched him fumble in his pocket for a cigarette. Surely he had to know by now that Ma would go ape if he dared light it in the house. "Yeah, from what you're telling me, I guess it is. Guess I let my imagination run away with me."

"You're just hanging around with Gus too much, that's all." Holding the unlighted cigarette, Leon walked over to him. "Don't worry so much. Willow will be gone soon, and Dad will be okay."

Ricky raised a shoulder in a half-shrug.

"Sure you don't want me to call the doc?"

"Yup, I'm sure. I'm feeling a little better now."

"Good." Leon gave him a quick peck on the top of his head, then tousled his hair like he used to do when they were kids. "Rest, then. Okay?"

Warmed by the brotherly gesture, Ricky grinned.

△△△

Later that night, Ricky's skull continued to pound. The sound of one of Dad's old Lawrence Welk videos playing in the den told him that his father was in there. His mom always sat beside him when he played them, one of their sweetest times together—sometimes they even danced around the small room—but she was keeping her distance today. Ricky heard her running the Mixmaster as he entered the kitchen.

"What're you making now?" On the counter sat a fresh batch of oatmeal cookies.

"Polish coffee cake." She didn't look up. When she revved up the Mixmaster to its highest speed, he seized his chance to grab the full bottle of vodka from the kitchen cabinet behind her, the one they saved for company. Before she could turn around, he was already descending the basement stairs.

△△△

The unfinished side of the basement, with its old cement floor, was Ricky's favorite place in the whole house—not the big paneled room on the other side, the one with the bar, left liquorless and abandoned since the day he went dry. He'd spent a lot of time down here over the years, especially after he'd moved his art studio into that corner by the washing machines. It had a great smell about it, a mixture of laundry soap, turpentine, and must. Part of it was still sectioned off for his art, where he created some of his newest ideas before hauling the canvas off to the Mazurka Inn to finish or to store. For some reason, he was back into traditional landscapes. A few days ago, he'd completed his first oil painting of a weeping willow tree.

He stared at it on the easel, turning his head this way and that to scrutinize the painting from all angles before transferring his gaze to the full bottle in his hand. His faithful comrade, Mr. Stolichnaya—or just plain Stoli—had been calling his name all day long: *Let me help you escape, Ricky. A couple of swigs will make you feel good as new.*

Before he could talk himself out of it or dig his sponsor's info out of his pocket, Ricky unscrewed the cap, guzzled a sizeable amount. Holy shit, it tasted good. Like ambrosia.

Ten years of sobriety down the tube, just like that.

The relief, a few minutes later, felt blissful—enough to erase his shame. He settled down in the big plaid chair that used to be upstairs in the living room, his father's pride and joy before his mother had gifted him with the fancy new state-of-the-art La-Z-Boy that he never quite cherished as much. This was a great old chair, soft as a cloud. Getting off his feet made Ricky realize how utterly exhausted he was.

As he took another swallow, his eyes were set on his painting— a solitary willow tree sitting at the edge of a riverbank, its graceful, drooping branches hanging over the water like a defeated ballet dancer. The sky was a misty shade. Next to the tree on the river-bank was an empty yellow rowboat, the one splash of color in the otherwise muted setting. Was it a hopeful or hopeless scene? He could see it both ways.

He knew why he had painted a willow tree after all this time— because of the girl with the name like a tree who brought all those old memories along with her. But after he got the idea for the painting in his head, he did a search for willow images on the Internet and stumbled across the legends associated with weeping willows. Hailed by prophets and poets alike, they were a symbol for a variety of things—among them, fertility, lost love, death.

It's just a tree, he thought; a breathtakingly beautiful tree. He took another gulp.

Ricky was bone-weary. After living so long without a nerve attack, it was harder than he remembered to rebound. Especially at his age. Holding up the half-empty bottle of Stoli, he smiled at his old buddy. Giving up his sobriety wasn't such a big deal; the blast of exhilaration was already wearing off. Getting old was a bitch— even getting drunk was harder. He swigged down a little more before pulling up the handle for the footrest, tilting his head back into the cushions. No wonder his father loved this old chair. It was a chunk of heaven. The stabbing pain in his head had vanished— Stoli had knocked it out—and the relief from its absence was stoking a growing euphoria, warming him from his toes right up to his cheeks. For the first time all day, not one twitch of an ache or pain racked his body. Or anxiety. Gone were his worries about his dad. It would be okay; just take it one day at a time, like the people in the support group kept telling him. Stop borrowing tomorrow's worries or reviving yesterday's. He could handle things that way, one day at a time.

He closed his eyes, let his mind roam. So Willow wasn't the child of Noël and Leon after all; Leon had squelched that theory. Well, if it was impossible, it was impossible, Ricky guessed, but a part of him still believed it. He felt it in his bones. Did bones lie? After that night of tossing and turning, he was starting to see things differently. Gone was his hurt over losing Noël. As the years had passed, Ricky had come to believe that their unspoken memories of Noël had actually woven him and Leon closer—she was their shared wound, their secret light; somehow she was both. But the truth was that she had always fit more with Leon than she had with him, and somehow Willow had cinched that in his mind. Having a kid changed everything, didn't it?, and being an uncle was starting to be enough. Stubborn butthead that Leon was, he was an honest man, a good brother, a blood brother in every way. The best brother. And Ricky loved him, pure and simple.

He opened his eyes. Things worked out the way they were meant to, he supposed. Even falling off the wagon wasn't the end of the world. Tomorrow, he'd just climb back up on it.

Or not.

The Stoli was gripped in his hand. Tomorrow, he'd have to go to the liquor store to sneak a new bottle into the cupboard, and he'd figure it out then.

Right now, everything was starting to spin, sweetly and gently, like a merry-go-round—the memories, the faces, the feelings, the old washing machine, the yellow boat waiting on the shore. Rocked by the motion, yet safe and grounded in the soft cushions, he sat back and watched them circle round and round and round.

ELEVEN

May 1998:
Of Things in the Night

THE whistle of a train blowing far off in the distance like the wail of a restless spirit roused Willow from her agitated dreams. It was three a.m. on the dot; she could set her watch by that old, faithful train, chugging down the tracks on the edge of Langston to some city on the East Coast, or so Ricky had told her. Her eyes still closed, she listened to the low rattle of its wheels on the track. She imagined it traveling through slumbering city after city in the darkness under the engineer's watchful eye. When she first arrived in Langston, she found the nightly train sounds a nuisance, but now they soothed her; a sign of life during these loneliest of hours.

She got out of her warm bed and squatted on the floor, pulling out her mother's diary from the drawer of the nightstand and opening it to her favorite page:

The night your father proposed to me, we were stopped on the very top of a double Ferris wheel, Adam in between us, our seat rocking back and forth. I was terrified that we'd tip out, until I focused on the night sky, a black ocean of stars surrounding us, and when I turned to look at Leon, he was holding out a little velvet box with a diamond inside.

Let me tell you about your father. He's a complicated man, very much a man who—

The sudden sound of a ringing telephone made her jump to her feet. Walt kept a phone on a tiny stand at the end of the outside hallway so that he could grab it quickly when he was doing chores upstairs, but it never rang when he wasn't here. Pulling on her robe, she rushed to answer it.

"He's dead!" A distraught woman screamed from the other end of the line.

"Who's dead?"

"Ricky!"

Willlow's heart dropped to her knees. "It can't be!" she shouted, still uncertain of the caller's identity. "What happened to him?"

"Stella?" The voice asked.

"No, this is Willow."

"Willow? Who? … oh … oh dear, this stupid speed dial …" The woman's voice trailed off. "I must've dialed the Mazurka Inn by mistake …" The phone went dead.

△△△

Within minutes, Willow arrived at the Ziemnys' house. Since she walked Walt home every night from the bar to assure he got there safely, she knew the home well—from the outside, anyway—a brown brick, two story, with a big, railed front porch.

When her knock went unanswered, she opened the unlatched door and stepped inside. In a room without light, Walt sat alone on the sofa, his face buried in his hands. "Oh, God. Not my Ricky," he sobbed

Willow had been hoping it was all a nightmare, but obviously it wasn't. Stunned all over again, she became aware of a bitter chill in the room. The windows were wide open, the cool spring air filling the house, the lace curtains fluttering like ghosts. Walt didn't seem to notice her; he wept into his bent fingertips, groaning as if in physical pain.

Spotting an afghan on the La-Z-Boy, she nestled it around his heaving shoulders before sitting on the floor beside him. His cries came out in thick spasms that sounded as if he was choking on them. Unsure what to do next, she remained in that position for what seemed like hours, when it must have been only minutes. Where was Mrs. Ziemny? Where was Ricky? How had he died?

Gingerly, she rose from the floor, searching through the rooms of the cold, dark house, lit only by a little overhead light over the kitchen sink, but her eyes had already adjusted. An old organ, covered with magazines and boxes, sat in the corner of the den, backlit by the garage light shining through the window. Eventually, she climbed the staircase which opened to a long hallway. Spotting one of the doors ajar with a light streaming through, she pushed it open. Mary Ziemny was splashing her face with water from the bathroom basin.

"Willow!" Her voice sounded relieved when she spotted her image behind her own in the mirror of the medicine chest. "I'm glad you're here. Father Burton and Doc Podemski are on the way. Leon and Stella too. I thought we might need the coroner, but Doc says he can take care of things."

Willow was confused by the scene, by Mrs. Ziemny's odd actions—washing up at a time like this, her warmth toward her, her seeming detachment from her own son's death—until it dawned on her that she was probably in a state of shock.

"Where is Ricky?" Willow asked.

Mrs. Ziemny flinched. She started brushing her hair. "You didn't close the windows, did you?"

"No."

"Good. His soul needs to get out, you know. We can't trap him in here."

Willow nodded. She'd heard about cracking a window so that the soul could fly to heaven, but she didn't realize people actually did it. "Where is he?" she asked again. "How did he die?"

For a moment, Mrs. Ziemny didn't seem to comprehend. "My precious boy, my life," she said, "is dead in the basement. But I think his soul is already gone, don't you?"

Willow didn't know how to respond. "Do you want me to leave? I know this is a horrible time for you, and I—"

"No, dear. Stay." She turned around, smiling at her. "I'm afraid to be here alone." After heaving one violent sob, Mrs. Ziemny took immediate control of herself. Picking up her brush again, she swiped through the thinning strands of gray, staring at her own reflection in the mirror. "They'll all be here soon, Doc Podemski, our priest, Leon and Stella." The sound of another wave of Walt's sobs came through the floorboards. "And then there's him. Go make sure he's okay."

Returning to the living room, Willow put her arms around Walt.

"You'reagoodgirl." He slurred his words together. She noticed that his eyes were glazing over, and she was afraid he was having another mini-stroke. But when Leon and his wife bolted through the front door, he seemed to snap out of it.

Mrs. Ziemny came down the stairs dressed in a clean pink-flowered house dress and rhinestone earrings that sparkled incongruously from her anguished face. She headed straight for Stella's arms. Leon stood in the doorway, glaring at Willow as if annoyed by her presence. "Where is he?" he asked.

"In the basement," his mother said.

As Leon tried to exit to the kitchen, Walt stood up, grinning and blocking his way. "Hiya, son. You here for breakfast?"

"Breakfast?" Mrs. Ziemny said, her face aghast. "How can you talk about breakfast at a time like this? How could you forget that your son is gone?"

"Gone where? And why the hell are the windows open? It's freezing in here!"

"For Christ's sake." Leon shoved past his bewildered father. "Get out of my way, you crazy old man."

Willow jumped up from her seat. "I'll have breakfast with you, Walt." She flashed him the biggest grin she could manage. As Leon bolted from the room, Walt clasped her hand as tightly as those people in the nursing home.

△△△

Leon found his brother lying in the old, plaid chair, a shadowy smile on his lips, his eyes wide-open, a broken bottle of vodka resting beside him on the floor, apparently crashing to the cement at the moment of his death. A pool of alcohol surrounded him.

Anyone else would've broken down and cried at the scene. Crying was mercy; crying released the torrent of toxins inside. But Leon was unable to cry and that sharpened his punishment all the more.

Stepping into the alcohol to reach him, he flipped through a thousand images at once, memories racing through his mind, good and bad, of Ricky at all ages. In every scene, there was one common thread: Ricky's tenderheartedness, the light inside of him. Ricky was the soul of their dreamless family, the part of them that lived beyond the emptiness, the part that loved in art.

Even in death, he smiled.

Taking each of Ricky's cold, hard cheeks into his own palms, he kissed his brother on the forehead, the same way he'd kissed the top of his head the day before. He stared into his open eyes. Already, the light was gone; he was unrecognizable. Dead eyes had a film over them, a cloudiness that reduced them to a mannequin's gaze. His sorrow rising, he kicked away a broken piece of the bottle. "Damn it, Ricky! Why did you start drinking again?"

His brother, the best person he knew, had been a lifelong addict, yet his addiction was never about being a derelict, a drunk. His brother was a dreamer, trying to steal some peace in a savage world, and drinking had been the quickest way, the only way, he'd found to keep himself sane in spite of it.

Leon's thoughts raced incongruently. What would become of them without him? They were already falling apart. He should've listened to Ricky about their father's dementia—he was a clueless old fool now, an idiot too overcome by senility to remember his own son's death. And Mom had always been clueless in her own severe way. Stella was a stranger, performing her part on some make-believe stage while Leon sat in the back row, unmoved and unapplauding. And now there was this girl—why the hell was she here at a time like this?—hanging around them like Poe's black raven. In the midst of his chaotic thoughts, he turned around, and there it was: Ricky's good-bye note, of sorts, his last painting on the easel.

Now he understood. Now he grasped why Ricky had started drinking again.

Leon punched his fist into the sharpness of a tool bench by the washing machine, the blood trickling from his hand, and he wiped it on his pants. He hated the booze, and he hated Alzheimer's, and he hated his life, and he hated Willow, no doubt the inspiration for that final scene on Ricky's mind. Most of all, he hated Noël Trudeau, the only one who had made life better for both of them and the one who had come between them.

"I'm sorry, Ricky." He gazed dry-eyed at his dead brother. "I'm so sorry."

The sad fact of the matter was the booze had protected Ricky far better than he, his big brother, had been able to do. The booze could make Ricky's welts disappear. The booze could calm him down. The booze could relieve his broken heart. And now it had taken him away, away from this, away from them, in a yellow boat.

TWELVE

MAY 1998:
CELLULOID EYEBALLS

IT was a Monday night, Walt's eightieth birthday, the same day that Ricky had been buried, and Willow was sitting with Gus and Walt in the Mazurka Inn in gloomy silence, ruminating over the day's events. Ricky had been buried in an old Polish cemetery enclosed on all sides by a black, wrought-iron fence. Willow had been astounded by the sea of elaborate tombstones and graveside statues, including angels in full human height with magnificent wingspans of five feet or more—stunning works of art, now perches to the crows, just chipping away.

She and Gus had been sitting there for hours, Gus sipping his whiskey while she drank gin, and Walt had joined them later on, after tucking Mary safely into bed under the influence of a sleeping pill the doctor had prescribed. Willow watched as Walt polished the same spot of the mahogany bar over and over again with his trusty wet dishcloth. "There's only one picture of Ricky up there," she mused.

"What?" Walt looked up, befuddled. "Where?"

"Over there, on your wall," she replied.

"There is?" She noticed the concerted way he redirected his glance, as if with great effort, to focus on the brick wall covered in photographs, his cherished wall of fame, until he finally spotted

Ricky's high school graduation picture back when Ricky was still a fresh-faced, freckled boy. "I guess you're right. But he'll be here soon. We'll take a picture of him when he comes."

Willow eyed him sadly; he'd forgotten again. Alzheimer's was a cruel disease, to be sure, though it had its redeeming side. Profound sorrows could be disregarded in an instant; the heaviest burden wiped from the brain like a computer without a "save" key. The bad part came later, when the memory resurfaced, and the horrific news was brand-new again. She glanced at Gus.

"Our photographs are our history," he said, not challenging Walt on his forgetfulness. Gus was wise enough to pick up on the right things to do and say instinctively. He never argued with Walt, never confronted him when he slipped from one time period to the next without rhyme or reason. He rode his changes like a surfer rode the waves. She watched Gus get up from the stool and move behind the bar, tipping another splash of Seagram's into his shot glass. "But they also keep us tied to the past." He slugged the liquor down in one gulp, poured another. "The past can shackle you in chains sturdier than a steel cell."

"Hey, fix me one of those, would you?" Walt said.

Gus took out another shot glass from the overhead rack, and then one more, pouring them straight up and leaving the uncapped bottle on top of the counter. "When Abraham Zapruder was loading film into his 8 mm Bell & Howell movie camera that day, he never dreamed he'd become the key eyewitness to the murder of the twentieth century. Did you know he never used or owned another camera after that?"

Here comes the Kennedy onslaught again, Willow thought. Even now, on a day like this …

Raising his shot glass high in the air, Gus proposed a toast. "To

Ricky. May you have smooth sailing on your journey." As Willow eyed Walt for his reaction, they drank to that.

"Yeah," Walt said, bowing his head. He seemed to be re-remembering the earlier events of the day. Throughout the funeral and right now too, he looked older than eighty to Willow, and eighty was plenty old enough. His walk was more unsteady, the battered skin on his face etched with deeper lines, overstretched by a lifetime of painful emotions, including the past several days of vigils and burying his son.

"I hope my boy isn't traveling to the Great Beyond in steerage," Walt said. "That's the way I came over here, to this New World, or so we called it, and it felt to me like dying. Let me tell you, steerage is the worst torture you could imagine. It was dark, cold, cramped, and it stunk like hell. Everyone was seasick, crapping and puking, day after day. And there weren't any windows, no ventilation." Walt's eyes were stuck on his shot glass; Willow could sense the traumatic pictures playing out in his mind's eye.

"Some people, mostly the older ones and the little kids, got sick and died from diseases they picked up in that hell hole," he continued. "Then someone from the ship would come down and haul their bodies away, just throw them overboard like garbage. I'll never forget the sound of those wailing mothers when that happened. Oh Jesus, how they carried on! Most kids had mamas to comfort them, but not me. All I had were the Rudinskis and the Bartkowiaks who had their own kids to worry about."

Willow knew the sting of being a parentless child.

"I never felt so scared and alone in my whole life," Walt said. "I bawled all the way. I bawled so hard they thought I had an eye infection when we finally got to Ellis Island."

"And was it worth it?" Gus asked.

"Coming here you mean?" Walt slugged down his shot. "Hell,

yes, it was worth it." He turned around to look at the wall of photos again. "We need more pictures of Ricky up there. I don't want to forget his face."

△△△

They drank for the next couple hours. They drank until the old photographs on the wall seemed like living beings to Willow, scrutinizing their every move—the array of unknown immigrants stared with their judgmental, black and white, celluloid eyeballs as the three of them drank to everything under the sun. They drank to Walt's eightieth birthday. They drank to life. To the bar. To Ricky, again and again. The last toast, Gus' toast, was to truth.

Willow put her glass down. She was a liar; she couldn't bring herself, even drunk, to drink to that, especially after Gus started his latest diatribe.

"Muffling the truth is like trying to contain a flood," he said. "You can bolt the door, bar the windows, but the truth seeps in, sometimes slowly, sometimes in a mighty rush."

As expected, he climbed back onto his conspiracy soapbox. Walt's eyes were glazing over, Willow was too tired to sit upright, but Gus was on a hot streak, revving himself up to fever pitch to the point that he trotted up the stairs to his room and brought down a small steel box with a lock on it, along with an overstuffed folder. "Don't ever tell anyone that you saw what I'm about to show you," he said.

Now he'd piqued her interest, enough to remain downstairs anyway, for a little while longer.

Retrieving three or four square photographs from inside a manila envelope, he held them carefully in his palm. From the distance of two stools away, she saw that they resembled the old photos that Uncle Steve used to show them—small, square Kodak photographs with a tiny rim of white on all sides—the kind used to capture ordinary moments back in the 1960s. The photos in Uncle Steve's album were of family members and others she never met, but there were a few shots of her mother from around the time she went to high school and a couple from her wedding to Adam's father. He'd given her that photo album when she left San Diego; it was stuffed into one of her bags upstairs.

"You ready?" Gus passed the first photo to Walt, and she leaned over to see it. Two men appeared to be standing in front of a tall, wooden stockade fence, one of them attired in a dark suit and sunglasses, the other a construction worker, hardhat and all, dressed in a light-blue work shirt with rolled-up sleeves. "What the hell are we looking at?" Walt asked.

"You're looking at the truth, my friend."

"Huh?"

"I took these pictures myself."

"What are you talking about?" Walt said.

"These photographs were taken on the grassy knoll in downtown Dallas on November 22, 1963." Gus handed him the next photo. The man in the immaculate suit seemed to be assembling something while the construction worker peered over the fence. "I was off duty that day, but I noticed these guys because they made an odd pair. I thought the well-dressed one was secret service, and maybe the other one too since they were together, though he didn't look the part. Anyway, they intrigued me, so I kept watching them, keeping myself out of view. I was good at that kind of surveillance stuff; that was my specialty."

He handed Walt the last picture. "This one's the bombshell."

Willow tilted further toward Walt's shoulders to get a closer look. In that photograph, the man in the suit was firing a rifle, the construction worker facing the direction of the camera. You could see his face clear as day.

"While I was taking that picture, a loud pop exploded from that rifle, and I just about jumped out of my skin. The next thing I knew, everything was pandemonium. Kennedy had been hit."

Willow caught herself before falling off the backless stool. "You never showed these to anyone?"

"Just once, like a fool. After that, I ran. Who was I gonna show them to, little Ahyoka?" It was a Cherokee name he'd been calling her lately; he said it was because she brought happiness and that's what the name meant. "Even in that chaotic crowd after Kennedy was shot, I knew something was off right away. I saw plenty of suits taking away people's cameras, confiscating or exposing their film, playing the role of secret service when their real job was to cover up the truth before Kennedy was even cold. I saw first-hand that there was a hell of a lot of people out there who had no interest in the truth. I was trained to see those things. I was a Dallas cop, remember?" He turned to Walt. "You talk about there being lots of shit in steerage. But there's never been a bigger load of shit than that Warren Report."

Willow's head was spinning. Gus had two faces. Her body felt drunk and wasted while her addled brain processed the informa-tion like a sieve trying to filter out the gunk from substance. Gus was wound up like a toy sprung into over-animation.

"Dorothy Kilgallen was only one of many," he continued. "See this file here?" He plopped the bulging folder onto the bar. "These are newspaper clippings about other witnesses connected with the assassination that ended up dying under mysterious circumstances. Names like Rose Cheramie, Jack Zangretti, Mary Pinchot, George DeMohrenschildt—and on and on."

The names whizzed past her. She didn't recognize a single one of them.

"Not to mention the most famous ones—Oswald and Ruby.

Look at this." He pulled out an article dated in 1967. "It says that this group of dead witnesses, as many as 103 people, was alleged to have been killed by a conspiracy 'clean-up squad'." He turned to Willow. "So why didn't I show my photos to anyone? There was no way I was gonna let myself be 104."

△△△

Willow was unable to fall asleep that night. Images of Ricky's funeral kept her wide awake, despite the alcohol she'd consumed. Closing his casket. The dour funeral mass. Leaving him all alone in the dark grave. What an unbelievably tragic way for Walt to have spent his eightieth birthday.

Two loud knocks on her locked door startled her. "Remember, I never told you any of that tonight, and you never saw those pictures," Gus said from the hallway. "Walt—he won't remember a thing—and even if he does, he's senile and unreliable. But you, little Ahyoka, you're a different story."

"Don't worry, I won't say a thing," she called back to him. She heard him walk away, down the hall to his own room and shut the door. In truth, she'd forgotten half of it already.

She lay on her back, staring up at the ceiling. Gus was over-the-top obsessed, no doubt about it, one of those conspiracy nuts people made fun of. Though she couldn't account for the photographs he'd shown them—maybe he'd taken them out of context somehow—she knew a bald-faced lie, especially a whopper like that, would be out of character for him. When he wasn't going on and on about Kennedy, he was one of the soundest, most rational and grounded people she'd ever known, and that was the weird part. Sometimes you thought you knew somebody, but you really didn't.

Rolling onto her side, she wondered why the truth mattered so much to him. President Kennedy had died long before she was born, and a whole new generation—her generation—had their own, more relevant concerns to occupy them. No matter how the assassination had happened, Kennedy would still be dead, and hashing it over was like dissecting the Battle of Waterloo. She preferred the wisdom of the Serenity Prayer over history, and as that prayer said, accept what you can't change, change what you can. The future was what mattered.

THIRTEEN

DECEMBER 1998: NEW YEAR'S EVE

SEVEN long months had passed since Ricky's death, but to Stella it felt more like seven years. As she packed their bags for Tampa Bay, she hoped that tonight, New Year's Eve, they could finally put the horrible year behind them. A rattling sound in the garage snagged her attention—already, Leon was home from visiting his parents. At breakfast, Stella had insisted that he clean up the garage, enough at least to fit one car into the space before they left for Tampa, and rather than come inside, he must've decided to start cleaning.

Leon had been at loose ends since Ricky died. A few weeks after his death, he'd enrolled in a woodworking class, of all things, graduating from building paper towel racks to creating hideous, unusable pieces of furniture until their garage became so cluttered with his useless creations that there wasn't room for either of their cars.

When he wasn't woodworking, Leon was lethargic, doing nothing at all for hours at a time—conversation included—just staring into space with unfocused, distracted eyes. Doc Podemski had since diagnosed him with high blood pressure, an ulcer, and acid reflux. He was drinking more than usual too, exacerbating the other ailments. Stella was at a loss as to how to help him.

Though he would slaughter her for saying so, Leon was exactly like his mother. Mary didn't anesthetize herself with woodworking and alcohol, though a glass of wine at night might do her some good. Instead she busied herself with housework, church work, any kind of busy work a woman her age could manage. She'd joined all the church committees, baked the majority of goodies for the church bazaars, cleaned out every closet in the house from basement to attic, singlehandedly keeping Goodwill in business. Her extracurricular activities agitated both Stella and Leon; keeping an eye on Walt should have been full-time job enough for her, but Mary let him flounder on his own. Last week he'd burnt a pan on the stove, nearly setting off a fire in the kitchen. Luckily, Mary came up from the basement just in time.

Stella heard a crash in the garage, so loud that she stopped packing and went to investigate. She found Leon standing amid a pile of boards, searching for something on the floor. "Looking for this?" Stella picked up a thingamajig that had broken off one of his masterpieces and handed it to him. "What's this supposed to be anyway?"

"It's a *finial*." He shot her a look that warned her to drop the subject.

"I thought you were at your mom's house."

"I was." He stuck the finial on top of an unrecognizable piece of furniture—was it supposed to be a bed frame?—and stood back to admire it.

"You didn't stay too long."

"I couldn't stand it anymore, so I left."

She couldn't fault him, really, for fleeing after such a short time; she hated being there too. Walt was unraveling at a startling pace, getting into everything and making a mess of it; not to mention his constant angry outbursts and mood shifts. He argued with them all the time, insisting his wild notions were facts. His parents' battles had become an ongoing saga that prompted one or the other to summon Leon over to their place at least three times a day to referee. Unfortunately, Leon was even worse at handling his father than Mary—he and Walt would quarrel until it turned into a screaming match. Doctor Podemski attributed Walt's rapid decline to the trauma of Ricky's death accelerating another cascade of otherwise undetectable mini-strokes.

"What happened this time?" Stella asked.

"He keeps looking for Ricky."

"Just remind him that he died. He doesn't remember."

"I did remind him—over and over again. The more I remind him, the more he yells at me, or calls me a goddamned liar. Or cries like a baby, as if it just happened. There's no good answer."

"Maybe you should go back to that support group."

"I don't need a support group. I need a cure for this thing."

"Well, the group seemed to help Ricky."

"Not enough to keep him from going back to the bottle."

"That's not fair. You know it really helped him understand how to deal with your dad."

Resuming his cleaning with a vengeance, Leon clattered around on purpose to drown her out. Trying to give him advice was as pointless as trying to reorient Walt. She sighed, looked around. Cleaning up this mess should keep him busy for hours. "Leave yourself enough time to get ready for the party tonight," she said.

△△△

The Mazurka Inn was hosting a big celebration to ring in 1999, mostly Willow's idea to help cheer up Walt and to help attract more, and younger, clientele to the bar. Since she'd arrived, business was slowly picking up. As Stella walked in with Leon a little past eight p.m., she was surprised by how festive the place felt—decorated with streamers and disco balls and filled with thirty people or so, mostly older, familiar faces, but some young Latinos too, and a couple of black families. A buffet of food from the local market was spread out on a long, paper-clothed table—fried chicken, little meatballs, chips and dips, munchies of all shapes and kinds.

Bennie Niezgodski had pulled together some of his cronies, a five-piece band, to perform for the evening, and they were playing "Moonlight Serenade," or at least that's what Stella guessed the tune might be. With all of them being over eighty and not having played much since high school, the sound was pretty rusty.

She and Leon sat down at a table in the far corner by the brick wall of Walt's pictures where Mary was waiting for them. Walt remained contented behind the bar, 'helping'—which meant mostly watching—Willow and Gus make drinks and do all the work. "You look beautiful tonight," Mary said to her.

"Thanks." Stella beamed, glancing down at her sparkly white dress, a bargain she'd picked up for the occasion at the downtown Ayres that fit her like seamstress-made. When she'd tried it on in the dressing room, she couldn't help but beam at her own reflection in the mirror, certain it was flattering enough for even Leon to notice, but oh well, at least his mother did. "Looks like we've got a—*mixed*—crowd tonight," Stella said, frowning slightly as she glanced around the room at the ethnic faces. Willow had been putting up advertisements for the Mazurka Inn on bulletin boards all over the area, opening her arms to the entire neighborhood, and Stella had been hearing disgruntled rumbles from some of the regulars.

Leon eyed the table of black patrons sitting beside them. "You sound like an old Polack," he said to her. "This is a neighborhood bar. And this is the neighborhood now."

Shrugging, Stella turned her attention to Willow—mixing and serving drinks, running from table to table until her cheeks were red. She wasn't even dressed up; she wore blue jeans covered by a full apron tied behind her back. Why she'd remained here in Langston nearly a year—even after Ricky's death—was anyone's guess, except for the fact that she and Walt had forged some kind of bond. Oddly, Mary was glad for it, encouraged it even, and Stella had once asked her why that was. "She's the only one who can handle him now," Mary had said ruefully.

After Willow made a whirlwind appearance at their table to take their order, Stella watched her behind the counter, wiping the lips of the discarded glasses she'd collected and guzzling the leftover liquor before tossing them in soapy water and taking down fresh glasses to mix the new drinks. Stella recalled that Ricky used to do that when he tended bar at their home parties, a disgusting habit, as if wasting one drop of liquor, even from a used glass, was a sin. Walt stood beside Willow, his head keeping time with the music.

"I was worried about your father tonight," Mary said to Leon. "All this commotion. I thought it might upset him. But as long as Willow is around, he's happy as a clam. Look at him over there enjoying himself. She's even better with him than Ricky was."

Stella noticed the way Leon shifted in his seat. The mention of Willow's name always prickled him, probably because the girl knew exactly what to say and do for his own father while he didn't have a clue. Whatever the reason, Stella was glad for it. She'd been afraid that having a relative of Noël's hanging around in their lives would ignite his old torch or even stir up an attraction between them, but Willow seemed to have had the opposite effect on both of them. Leon resented Willow, while her presence emboldened Stella: Willow was a living, breathing reminder that Noël Trudeau was dead.

Returning with their drinks on a tray, Willow set them down in front of them.

"The place looks great." Stella smiled. "Doesn't it, Leon?"

He semi-nodded before twisting in his seat to watch the band. She saw the way Willow looked at him, always interested in his reactions and seemingly disappointed by their ongoing negativity. Quickly, she left to take care of another table.

"I wonder when she's going back to school." Stella took a sip of wine.

"Not in the near future," Mary said. "Ricky's death broke her heart, you know. She told Walt she wanted to push school off another semester or two. Which reminds me ..." she turned to her son. "When are we going to start cleaning out that studio of his upstairs?"

"*We?*" Leon laughed without smiling. "*We'll* get to it when I get back." He tasted the vodka, dabbed the corners of his mustache with the cocktail napkin. "It's not hurting anyone up there, is it?"

"I suppose not." His mother's lips pursed.

"Maybe it's good that Willow waits to go back to school," Stella said softly, more to herself than to either of them. How differently life might have turned out had she taken more time for soul-searching back when she was Willow's age. "She needs to find herself before plunging into life."

Leon knotted his eyebrows. "If she wants to find herself, why doesn't she just look in the mirror?"

After the three of them had their fill of junk food, with a couple more rounds of liquor in-between, Willow returned to the table to take their latest drink order. "I've got to ask you something, dear." Mary patted her arm. "Walt's been asking for Ricky all day long."

"Again?" Leon stirred in his chair.

"… and every time I—*we*—explain to him that Ricky died, he gets upset all over again. What should we tell him?"

"We tell him he's dead," Leon said. "We can't lie to him."

"Yeah, that's a great idea." Willow gave him a dirty look. "How's that been working out for you?"

"Then what's your brilliant idea? Tell him Ricky's hiding in the attic?"

"He forgets! He can't remember things short-term!" Willow seemed livid; the first time Stella had ever seen her tangle with Leon, though his lack of surprise indicated it wasn't the only time they'd tussled. She eyed both of them, awaiting the outcome. Willow turned to Mary. "Try telling him he's at the steel mills. That usually works pretty well."

"Lying to him like that will only make him more loopy," Leon said.

"It's not lying!" Willow's face flattened into the same patronizing expression that Leon had mastered years ago. "It's called *therapeutic fibbing*. It's what all the books say to do."

"And Doc Podemski too." Mary nodded.

"Well, Doc Podemski can shove his books up his rear end. He's my father! I owe it to him to be straight with him. And I'm not going to start lying to him, no matter what the books—or Willow the wise—say."

Stella sat up straighter, honed her focus. Was that a rash breaking out on Willow's cheeks? Turning around in a huff before Stella could be certain, Willow stormed back to the bar.

"Why do you have to be so rude to her?" his mother asked. "She's trying to help us. She's almost a nurse, and she knows the tricks of how to handle people with this—problem. Better than the two of us do anyway."

"She's a smart ass. We don't need her help."

"Yes, we do!" Stella noticed the way Mary clenched her fists as she said it. After ten minutes or so of non-conversation, she turned to Stella with a stiff, unnatural smile. "Are you all packed for Florida, dear?"

"Just about." Stella struggled to think of something to add.

The three of them listened to the awful music, the junk food churning inside Stella's stomach. Never before had she so looked forward to leaving Langston behind for two whole months, back to the sand and surf, far away from death and Alzheimer's disease. Gene had sent them a postcard a few weeks ago with a picture of Busch Gardens on it. On the back, he drew a little smiley face with rays of sunshine sticking out from its head like the Statue of Liberty. When Stella had shown it to Leon, he said, "Your boyfriend draws real cute."

"I'm beginning to think that going to Florida this year is a bad idea," Leon said. "Frankly, I'm having second thoughts."

"What?" Stella's mouth flapped open. "And when did you come to that conclusion?"

"I don't know." His fingers tore at the cocktail napkin. "All this stuff with Dad is getting to me, I guess. I just don't think Mom's going to be able to handle it by herself."

Mary lifted her chin with skittish eyes. "That's very sweet of you, dear," she said. "But I don't expect you to stay here to babysit us. Your father and I will manage somehow. And I don't have to handle him by myself. I've got Willow." Reaching for her purse on the floor, she stood up. "Time to make a trip to the little girl's room."

Once his mother had thoughtfully excused herself from the table so that they could talk things out, Stella tried her best to restrain herself. "And when exactly were you planning on telling me that you didn't want to go to Florida?"

He shrugged. "Yesterday Dad started fighting with Mom when she tried to get him into the shower, and he almost took a swing at her. This thing's getting too big."

She bristled.

"Ladies and gentlemen, the moment we've been waiting for is upon us." Bennie Niezgodski had taken the microphone, requesting all heads to turn to the side of the room, where he and the other members of the band were getting ready to hoist champagne flutes into the air. "Let's all count down together to a brand-new year. Ready? Ten ... nine ..."

Surprisingly, Leon took Stella's hand, holding it loosely between his fingers. Mary joined Walt behind the bar.

"Eight ... seven ..."

Leaning across the table, Leon gave her a quick peck on the lips. "Happy New Year."

"Six ... five ..."

"Please, honey." Stella gazed into his eyes, desperate more than angry. "We've *got* to go to Florida and get away for a while. For both our sakes."

"... four ... three ..."

"Maybe you should just go by yourself this time."

" ... two ... one ... Happy New Year!"

The room exploded in paper horns and other joyous noises, as the band eked out "Auld Lang Syne." The couples around them, even Walt and Mary, were kissing. Others high-fived or shook hands. Even perfect strangers were embracing. And there they sat, the two of them, cold as marble as they silently sipped their drinks.

FOURTEEN

January 1999:
Sack of Potatoes

WILLOW made it a habit to stay with Walt on Sunday mornings so that Mrs. Ziemny could go to mass at St. Stan's, that massive, architecturally-ornate structure with double steeples that towered over the neighborhood; it had left Willow nearly breathless the first time she saw it. Gus gushed over her selfless offer to spend half of her free day with Walt, but the truth was, Willow enjoyed his company—not just enjoyed it, she relished it. She felt both protected by, and protective of, her grandfather. They *saw* each other when no one else bothered to look.

They sat watching "The Hour of Power" on television, Walt in his Laz-Z-Boy and Willow cross-legged on the sofa, as Reverend Robert Schuller delivered his sermon from the Crystal Cathedral in California. "What frustrations are you facing today?" Schuller smiled as he asked the question. He always smiled, that's why Walt liked him so much, or so he told her, because he was a happy preacher who never screamed or got angry. "I offer you four simple words," said Schuller. "Don't tape, scrape, escape, or drape your frustrations."

"That guy's a real poet, isn't he?" Walt said.

"Some people try to drape them," Schuller continued, peering at his congregation over his bifocals. "But you can't bury or repress live emotions; they'll eventually rise to the surface."

"He's right about that." Walt nodded.

Somewhat surprised that Walt was able to follow the sermon, Willow remained silent.

"Don't you think he's right, Mishka?"

Walt always called her that now because he didn't remember her name anymore. Though she couldn't figure out how he managed to remember *Mishka*, she didn't mind. No one, except Gus, had cared enough to give her a nickname before. "Probably."

"Probably?" Walt said. "There's no probably about it. You gotta unload your baggage. Otherwise, it weighs you down like a sack of potatoes. You don't wanna die with a sack of potatoes on top of you, do you?"

Willow tried to imagine it, both figuratively and literally. "I guess not."

"No guessin' about it. You gotta get rid of it while you have the chance."

"Some people tape them," Reverend Schuller said. "They record their sorrows and frustrations and play them over and over again."

"Do you believe in reincarnation?" Willow asked.

"In what?"

"Do you think we come back to earth again after we die?"

"Nah, I don't believe in ghosts."

"Not as ghosts. I meant coming back again as another person."

Walt thought for a minute. "Like George Washington, you mean? Nah, that doesn't happen. We stay us."

"But if we die with a sack of potatoes weighing us down, don't you think we have to come back to earth until we learn how to get rid of it?"

"Get rid of what?"

"The sack of potatoes."

"What sack of potatoes?" He looked around the room.

"Some people scrape their frustrations," said Schuller. "They scratch them like a mosquito bite and end up making them much worse."

"We don't come back here again." Walt shook his head. "Once we're done here, it's *dobranoc*. We go straight to heaven."

"Do you believe there's a hell?"

"Hell, no."

She smiled. "I thought you were a Catholic."

"I am." He looked confused. "So what?"

"So why don't you believe in hell? Most Catholics do, don't they?"

"I don't know what most believe. I just know what I believe. And hell doesn't fit." He pointed to his head. "I may not have much of a noggin left anymore, but I still know what I know."

"How come you think it doesn't fit?"

"What doesn't fit?"

She tried again. "How come you don't believe in hell?"

"'Cause that would be like sticking a thumb in God's eye. He tells us to forgive our brother for seven years, or until we're seventy—I can't remember exactly how he said it—but the point is, God tells us, over and over again, that we're forgiven and that we have to forgive each other. So after all that forgiveness here in this mixed-up place, why would he pitch us into hell after we leave it? Think it about it, Mishka. I thought you were smarter than that."

She *was* thinking about it. Long and hard. She uncrossed her legs and sat back against the sofa cushions. Back in California, Uncle Steve didn't take them to church except for one Sunday morning when they went to a shopping mall to listen to some woman preacher from Palm Springs piped into closed-circuit TV. A lei of fresh flowers around her neck, she had a bright yellow, bubble-cut head of hair, and she sat against a white wicker fan chair, explaining how each person was a sparkling dewdrop in the vast ocean of mankind. She made religion seem light and airy and, frankly, vacuous. A religion that ignored suffering was kind of like living with Uncle Steve.

"And finally—" Schuller beamed over his thick glasses, "—some people try to escape their feelings and frustrations. They just check out."

"Are you afraid of anything, Walt?"

"Nah, nothin'. There's nothin' to be afraid of." He paused. "Are you?"

"I guess I'm kind of afraid of the future. That I won't do the things I'm supposed to do."

"I guess I'm the same way," he said. "Only backwards. I'm afraid of the past. That I didn't do the things I was supposed to do. … That's the hardest part, Mishka—to forgive yourself."

Even though she wasn't sure she believed what either he or Rev. Schuller was saying about these matters, she was amazed how philosophical Walt could be when no one else was around. He still pondered things deeply, if you took the time to listen. The problem was that everyone else gave up too soon. True enough, it was tricky to converse with someone with Alzheimer's—you had to be able to figure out when they were in there and when they were somewhere else.

"And I'm afraid of ships," he said. "I sure as hell hope I don't have go to heaven on a ship."

"And I hope I don't have to go in a King Royal truck."

"What?"

"Nothing."

Schuller was raising both arms high into the air, but Willow had stopped listening. She was thinking about the book she'd been reading about the Buddhist concept of Bardo—a place in-between life and death—and she wondered if that was what Alzheimer's felt like. She was also mulling over her own sack of potatoes, the way she'd scraped, draped, taped, and escaped her way through life, and she was suddenly overcome with the urge to disclose her real identity before it was too late. "Hey, Walt. Can I tell you something?"

"Sure, Mishka. You can tell me anything."

Her heart sped up; her moment of truth. "Noël Trudeau was my mother, not my aunt. And your son, Leon?—" Her voice trembled. "—He's my father. Walt, I'm your granddaughter."

"I knew that." He smiled at her before turning back to the TV. And that was that.

Did he really know it, she wondered, or was he somewhere else?

△△△

After Mrs. Ziemny got home, Willow stuck around for a while. As usual, Mrs. Ziemny floated past Walt without paying much attention to him. Before too long, he fell asleep reclined in the La-Z-Boy while she helped Mrs. Ziemny fold a load of laundry.

"This is the way it happened, you know," Mary was telling her. "Stella gave Leon an ultimatum—Florida or the highway—so off he goes. I hoped he would stay, of course, but I know his place is with his wife."

"Do they have a good marriage?"

"Oh, you know." Mary picked up a large bath towel, unfurling it, as she prepared to fold it. "Marriage is a lot of work. Some people work harder at it than others, that's all."

Willow didn't say anything. She doubted Stella was the slacker in the situation. Biological father or not, Leon bugged her, and she was tired of waiting for another side of him, a redeemable side, to show up. No wonder her mother hadn't tried harder to find him when she was pregnant. Now Willow knew that his "new life", the one her mother had referred to in her diary, had been the one he'd started with Stella, meaning, he wouldn't have cared one iota about his pregnant ex-wife or her unborn child. He was too self-centered, with ice water in his veins. Even if he hadn't gone to Florida, she doubted he'd be here on a Sunday afternoon.

"I'll bet you miss California, don't you, Willow?"

The thoughtfulness of Mary's question surprised her. As far as Willow was concerned, Mary had already revealed her redeemable side. At first, she wasn't so nice to Willow, but lately she treated her like a member of the family without knowing she really was. Sure, it was because she needed her help with Walt, Willow knew that, but she also saw Mrs. Ziemny's sorrow in certain moments when she thought no one was looking, just like the people on the bus. She still yelled at Walt more times than not, and it used to really get to Willow until she realized that fighting with him was Mary's way of hanging on to the husband she was losing—it was really the Alzheimer's Mary was fighting with, not Walt. But this Walt was the only one Willow had ever known. No wonder it was so easy for her to accept him the way he was.

Willow considered Mary's question. In California, her peers had been young, beautiful, filled with vitality; expectations were super high. In Langston, there were no expectations. Being here was like hiding away in a towel drawer. A warm towel drawer. She brushed one of the washcloths, fresh from the dryer, against her cheek. "Not really," she said.

"Well, I would miss California if I were you." Mary smiled. "All that sunshine. It must have been just beautiful."

"It was."

"You know, Willow? Sometimes it feels to me like the sun will never shine again."

△△△

After Willow left and Walt awoke from his nap, Mary's day deteriorated quickly. He'd been wanting to leave for work at the steel mills for the last two hours. Though telling him he'd been retired for more than thirty years made him madder, she kept repeating it anyway, for lack of a better answer. Now he was staring at her as if she was some sort of demon, and she looked back at him the same way.

He was itching to leave the house. At Willow's suggestion, she'd resorted to hiding the car keys. "I'm going to be late for work," he said again. She watched him roam around the room, opening drawers. "Where the hell are my keys?"

She decided to try another tack. "Walt, for God's sake, there's no work today. It's Sunday."

"Sunday?" He stopped in place. "Well, why didn't you tell me that?" He went back to the La-Z-Boy, sat down, and she breathed a sigh of relief. "Where are the boys?"

Mary hated to lie to him. What did Willow call it?—*therapeutic fibbing*—but whatever fancy name you called it, it was still lying. "Ricky's painting in his studio, and Leon's in Florida with Stella." At least it was half-true.

"What the hell is he doing in Florida?"

"He has a condo there."

"A what?"

"An apartment."

"Why does he have an apartment in Florida? What's wrong with his room upstairs?"

"For heaven's sakes, he hasn't a room upstairs for years."

"Huh?" He scratched at his forehead anxiously, a repetitious gesture whenever he felt uncomfortable; he did it so often it was beginning to leave permanent red marks.

"Nothing's wrong with his room upstairs. He just wanted to get away for a while."

"That's a pretty highfalutin' way to get away, if you ask me. Why didn't he just go out for a drive?"

The mention of taking a drive jarred her; she was afraid he would start asking for the keys all over again. Now she had to— what did the "do's and don'ts" paper hanging on the refrigerator call it?—redirect? distract? *Just change the subject*, Willow had clarified. "Would you like a bowl of ice cream? I'm having some."

"Ice cream? Yeah, that sounds good. Make it chocolate."

Leaving the room felt like a vacation. Mary opened the upright freezer beside the fridge where twenty gallons of chocolate ice cream stared back at her. Pulling out one of them, she scooped a generous portion into two dishes. On Saturdays, she and Walt still got out and did things together—errands like grocery shopping— but that was becoming next to impossible too. He kept tossing things into the cart whenever she turned her back. Last week she wasn't paying close enough attention, and the next thing she knew, the clerk at the checkout was ringing up three more gallons of chocolate ice cream. When Mary told her that she didn't want them, Walt raised such a ruckus that she ended up buying them; the same way she'd ended up buying the other seventeen gallons. He lived in his emotions now, said Willow, not in logic, and it was all about keeping Walt happy.

On weekdays, he spent the whole day at the Mazurka Inn where Willow and Gus kept a watchful eye on him as he 'ran' things, though Mary guessed he was in the way there too. Sunday was the worst day of all. After church, there was just the two of them, all day and all night long. If she could make a wish, she'd wish that Willow never moved on to nursing school in Chicago until Walt was dead and gone. She swallowed a big spoonful of ice cream to drown the guilt over such a terrible wish. She was feeling a lot of guilt lately over too many things to count, and she was drowning her woes in this warehouse full of chocolate ice cream. Even her baggy clothes were getting tight.

"I'm tired of this place," he called out from the living room. "I want to go home now."

Mary took another gulp, closed her eyes. That was the first time he'd said something like that, the first time he didn't recognize his own house. Now what was she supposed to do? She stood in the kitchen, paralyzed, until she collected herself; she had to stay strong. Returning to the living room, she set the bowl of ice cream down on the coffee table in front of him, praying it'd be enough of a distraction. "Here's your dessert, honey. Doesn't it look yummy?"

"Dessert?" He looked down at it. "I don't want to eat now. I'm ready to go home."

"Walt, you *are* home."

"The hell I am!"

Every morning, she pulled that damned "dos and don'ts" sheet off the refrigerator, the one that Ricky had picked up from the support group, and she tried to memorize it. By the time evening fell, or even the late afternoon shadows, she was so worn-out that she went right back to doing the don'ts all over again. What was she supposed to say now—agree with him that he wasn't at home?

She was an old woman, who'd never felt older, and she didn't have the energy to keep doing this day after day. Doc Podemski said her heart wasn't so good anymore. "Of course, it's not," she told him. "It's broken." Then, Doc went into a harangue about her needing to get some ... what was that word he used? *Respite*. All these new words. She didn't know what he was talking about until he explained that it meant to take a break. "Call a home health agency to come watch him," Doc had said. So she'd looked into it. A home health agency cost sixteen dollars an hour, even more on the weekends. Multiply that by three or four hours a day for the next eight years. *Respite.* She laughed out loud now whenever Doc mentioned the word. "Who's going to pay for this respite?" she'd ask him. "Santa Claus?"

"I want to go home!" Walt was getting more insistent.

"This *is* your home. See?" Mary moved over to the orange lamp, a birthday present from years ago. "Remember when you gave this to me, honey? I always loved this lamp."

"I never saw that ugly thing before." He struggled to get up from his chair. "Get me out of this goddamned place!"

"Walter Casimir Ziemny!" she shouted. "Stop using that foul language all the time! I already told you that this *is* your house, so sit back down and mind your manners." He was no longer her husband; he was a bratty child who deserved a swift kick in the behind. Forget those do's and don'ts! Forbidding his bad behavior was *her* strategy—good enough for Leon when he was a boy, and good enough for Walt now too.

"Who the hell made *you* boss?" Weak knees and all, he finally managed to get up from the chair. "Where's Mary? Where the hell is Mary?"

Her heart plunged. They told her this day might come, and here it was. Just when she thought they'd hit bottom, the bottom dropped lower. She wiped the tears away as they fell, but they kept pouring like a broken faucet. Walt was climbing up the stairs, calling out her name with a little more volume after each step. "Mary? Mary? Where are you?" She heard him moving from room to room. Unable to bear it, she raced for the phone. With shaky fingers, she punched the speed dial button for the Mazurka Inn. Thank God, Willow picked up.

"Honey, please come over right away." Mary pleaded. "Walt doesn't recognize me anymore." Just saying the words out loud was unthinkable, and she broke into sobs. She hadn't wept since Ricky's funeral, and now the floodgates had broken open. Willow assured her that she'd be right over.

Within minutes, she entered through the kitchen. By that time, Walt was downstairs again, heading for the front door. Willow sauntered over to him, giving him a big smile as she approached. *Move toward him slowly.* Another one of the "do's", Mary noted, as she studied Willow's actions in hopes of copying them. "Hiya, Walt. Where're you going?" Willow held out her hand. "Stay here and visit with me. It's good to see you!"

"It's good to see you too, Mishka."

"Looks like your favorite snack." She pointed to the dish of melting ice cream on the coffee table. "Can I have a bowl too?"

"Yeah, have yourself a bowl." Like magic, a slow grin spread on his craggy face, revealing those horribly discolored teeth that repelled Mary now that he wasn't brushing. He could no longer grasp the sequence of steps and trying to coax him into cleaning his teeth spiraled into World War III, so she'd given up trying.

"Whatsa matter?" He walked over to Mary, slipping a sympathetic arm across her shoulders and pointing at her. "You see this? This here is one sad woman."

"She loves you very much," Willow said. Her sympathetic words brought fresh tears to Mary's eyes; she was so hungry and grateful for solace.

"She does? That's nice of her." He patted Mary on the head with his palm, flattening down her hair as if it was full of cowlicks. "She's a good old mom."

"I'm not your mother!" Mary snapped, pulling away from him, wiping her eyes.

"I know that!" he snapped back. His mood had switched like a light. "I know my own mother when I see her! My mama has a beautiful smile. She's not a crabby old apple like you are. ... I'm going home." He started heading for the front door again.

Mary froze.

"Your mother's not home," Willow said sweetly. "She told me she's shopping for roosters today at the market." Apparently, Walt had told Willow enough about his parents for her to create such a believable lie. "A pretty yellow porcelain one that she's had her eye on. For the hutch in the kitchen."

"Mama and her roosters." Shaking his head, he smiled wide enough to reveal his brown teeth again. "She gave me a real one, you know. Or was that a hen? Let me show you something else she gave me." He reached into his pocket, then panicked. "Where's my blessed mother—the Madonna of Czes—Chess—Chins? Where is it?" He reached so deep that he pulled out the lining of the empty pocket. "It's missing!"

How's Willow going to fix this one?, Mary wondered.

As Willow approached him, too fast that time, Walt almost took a punch at her. "It's—well—it's—not missing." Willow stammered for an answer, pasting on a smile. "It's—upstairs—in your jewelry box. Where you keep your watch and cufflinks."

"What's it doing up there? It's always in my pocket."

"You wanted to keep it safe. You were afraid you'd lose it, carrying it around in your pocket."

"Oh yeah, that's right." Walt's posture relaxed. "I can't remember a damn thing anymore."

It went on like that for the next several hours as Walt "*sundowned*"—another terrible new term—his way through the rest of the evening, jumping from one mood to the next, one era to the next, as if time and emotions were a game of hopscotch. He must've asked to go home more than a hundred times all totaled, but Willow somehow managed to come up with responses that kept him on an even keel. It wasn't so much what she said, but the way she'd say it—as if there wasn't a thing wrong with him. How was she able to do that?, Mary marveled.

By nine p.m., all three of them were exhausted, and Mary sent Willow back home. Finally, she was able to get him upstairs into bed, where he seemed to know her again. He called her by name, but also asked where the "other Mary" was.

"The other Mary?"

"Yeah, you know, my bride. That one's a real looker." He winked.

It was those kind of moments, rare and gentle, that gave her the strength to live another day. "Go to sleep, sweetheart." She kissed him on the forehead, shut off the light.

She tiptoed to her own bedroom down the hall, the one that used to be Leon's. Never had she dreamed a day like this would come when she and Walt would have separate bedrooms, a necessity for a few months now. That stranger in the other room had been the only man she'd ever loved, and she missed him with all her heart. It was different for Leon, and for Ricky too when he'd been alive; it was natural to lose your parent first, one way or another. But she had lost her partner, the one person who helped her make sense of this world, and she was terrified to be left alone in it.

Weeping into her pillow, she finally drifted off to sleep.

△△△

A few hours later, Mary was awakened by thumping sounds downstairs. Afraid that it was an intruder, she rushed into Walt's room.

His bed was empty. By the time she got down the staircase, it was already too late. The front door was wide open.

Racing to the end of their sidewalk, she looked in every direction on the dark street. But there was no sign of him.

FIFTEEN

January 1999:
The Curve-Ball Sidewalk

F OR the life of him, Walt couldn't figure out why he was walking to the mills today instead of driving his car there, and in the middle of the night too, no less. It was pitch-dark outside, with a great big full moon shining down on him. That new straw boss must have assigned him to the graveyard shift, or maybe Walt was doing some overtime. He couldn't remember a damn thing anymore.

He noticed a thin layer of snow on the grass. Yeah, that was it. It was nearing Christmas time, and he was pulling an extra shift so he could buy Ricky that snazzy red bike he'd been begging for, the one he'd spotted in the display window at Kresge's. The whole family went there a few Saturdays ago—they had cherry cokes at the soda fountain, and Mary told Ricky that maybe Santa would bring him the bike. She worried about spoiling them, but nobody was getting spoiled; they were good boys. Mary worried about everything. Over the years, Walt had to learn when to sit up and take notice and when to tune her out.

He looked down at his hands and saw that he wasn't carrying anything. Damn it, he must have forgotten to bring his lunch. Mary always packed his pail with something delicious, including a little sweet surprise of something or other she'd wrapped up in aluminum foil. She never told him what it was gonna be, 'cause she wanted to bowl him over when the time came to unwrap it. She stuck a little note in there too, with plenty of Xs and Os at the end.

He must have left the lunch pail on the kitchen counter. He couldn't remember a damn thing lately. Should he go back home to get it and risk being late? He looked down at his wrist; no watch either. He must have forgotten that too. What a pickle to be in. He didn't have the slightest idea what time it was. He probably shouldn't try to go back home for … for … now he couldn't remember why the hell he needed to go back home. Oh well. It'd come to him eventually.

It was awfully cold out here, he thought, quickening his pace. As he stepped into the street to cross over to the other side, some guy came out of nowhere in his fancy car, almost leveling Walt to the pavement. Now the guy was laying on the horn as if it was Walt's fault that he drove like a jack-ass. "Same to you, buddy!" Walt thumbed his nose and kept walking.

Gradually, he slowed down, step by step, until he was standing as still as a tree trunk. He wasn't so sure he was heading in the right direction. He looked this way and that down the quiet street, but he couldn't spot one recognizable landmark. For a fleeting second he felt afraid. He didn't have a clue where he was.

He started walking again. Something was bound to look familiar sooner or later. Suddenly he noticed a stone cottage down the street with a curve-ball sidewalk leading up to the front door—his own home. Thank God, he wasn't lost anymore! But where were his mother's tulips? She always had bright yellow tulips lining the front walk. Other than that, he'd know this place anywhere.

His mama loved tulips, her favorite flower. Tulips were the first sign that the long, cold winter was over, and spring was on its way.

Spring was Walt's favorite time of year; it always felt to him like life was starting up all over again. But, damn, if it wasn't cold out here. Way too cold for spring. His hands felt like a snowman's.

That was what was wrong with this picture. That's why there weren't any tulips lining the sidewalk. It was Christmastime, for gosh sakes. Reverend Schuller came to the house to see him yesterday and told him he couldn't drape or escape Christmas. Why the hell would anyone want to escape Christmas? He guessed it didn't matter. That Reverend Schuller had a heart as big as outdoors. And he was always smiling. That was the sign of a real preacher. A miserable holy man was no damned good to anyone.

Walt's pace quickened. He couldn't wait to get inside and warm himself by the limestone fireplace where his Christmas stocking with the white angel was hanging, the one his mama knitted herself. She made one for each of them, but his was the only one that had an angel sewn on it. He could almost smell the scent of fresh bread baking in their cast iron wood stove.

Pa would be sitting in the den, smoking his pipe, wearing half-glasses, a big wrinkle creasing the skin between his eyebrows as he read some big, fat book. Mama told him he was going to look old before his time if he didn't stop bunching up his face like that, but frankly Pa didn't give a damn. He'd rather read and think than look like Rhett Buttons.

Later on, Pa got sick.

The memory stung worse than the bitter night air. His pa got sick all right, coughing all the time, spitting up bloody gook that made Mama hide in the kitchen to cry. She hid his pipe too and wouldn't give it back to him, but he kept getting sicker anyway.

After reaching the front of the house, Walt stopped again because something else didn't seem quite right. The house was bigger than it should be. And why were there so many other homes surrounding it? Their cottage was off by itself, on a quiet country road. He looked for the chicken coop out back—and for his pet hen, Frajerka—but there was nothing but a pick-up truck parked on the spot where it used to be.

As he moved up the front walk, he was consumed by a wave of happiness. He loved the way their sidewalk meandered up to the front door like a picture in a fairy book; curve-ball walks were more welcoming than ordinary, straight ones. When he reached the entrance, he gave the knob a twist, but nothing moved. The door was locked. What the hell was going on? His mama never locked the door.

Walt tried to shuffle through his pockets to find the key, but he couldn't even find his goddamned pockets. For some reason, he had on flimsy pants with stripes, and his feet were soaking wet. No wonder he was so cold. The morning dew on the grass must have seeped into his shoes, which were just as soft and shabby as the pants he was wearing. His teeth chattered; he was so cold he couldn't stand it.

"Mama, I'm home!" he called out. "Come open the door."

No one answered. Cars were moving down the paved street every once in a while—sleek, shiny shapes that moved too fast—and a big white dog next door was barking from behind a wire fence. Walt kept on hollering and pounding on the door until a light finally went on inside the house.

When the door opened, a man was standing there, looking at Walt through squinting lids. "What 'chu want?" He had a funny accent.

"Who the hell are you? And what did you do with Mama and Pa?"

"Mama and Pa?" The guy scratched his head. "Man, 'chu must be over eighty years old!"

Walt tried to explain that he was just a little boy, but for some reason, he wasn't able to talk right. "I yi-yi-yi-yi-yi-yi," he said to the man, flapping his gums while the words flew away like yellow roosters.

"Are you loco?" The guy looked at him as if he was some kind of weirdo.

"You're the weirdo, not me." Walt thought he said it out loud, but maybe he was just thinking it. As Walt stared him square in the eyes, he suddenly recognized him for who he was. Why didn't he see it right off the bat? He was in cahoots with the ones who murdered his mother!

"What did you do to her, you goddamned Nazi?" Walt screamed, but it came out like gibberish. He took a swing at him, nearly toppling over in the process.

"You're loco alright! I'm calling the police." Taking a step back, the man put up his dukes, ready for the knockout if Walt came any closer. Walt was petrified. He wanted to take another whack at him, but he was just a kid who had no real chance against a grown Nazi like him. And there had to be more of them around—Hitler's Gestapo were surrounding him, listening to his every word. He spotted two of them squatting in the bushes, pointing an uzi straight at him.

He had to make a quick getaway, and he did; he turned and ran like the wind, the bitingly cold wind, even with his feet squishy wet. He made it all the way to the end of the curve-ball sidewalk … and then … he had no idea which way to go.

SIXTEEN

JANUARY 1999:
SEARCHING

B Y ten a.m. the next day, Leon was already home from Florida, able to catch a five a.m. flight out, leaving Stella behind to spend the rest of their vacation on her own, or at least until he could return.

His mother managed to fill him in on the whole story:

The police had come to the house shortly after one a.m. to file a missing-persons report. She didn't think it necessary to call them so soon, but after Willow and Gus went out searching the neighborhood and couldn't find him, they'd insisted. "Here's the problem," the police had said. "Alzheimer's patients don't realize they're lost. They keep moving and usually don't respond to people calling out their name. They're often found pretty close to home, but if we don't locate him within twenty-four hours, there's a good chance we won't find him alive." The next thing she knew, Walt's picture—taken the night of their anniversary party last year—was splashed all over the local morning newscasts. Willow had circulated flyers throughout the neighborhood, and shortly after that, neighbors and friends began forming small search teams, block by block. Only one sighting had surfaced so far. A Mexican couple with the last name of Rodriguez, who lived three streets over, had informed the police that Walt came hammering on their door in the middle of the night looking for his parents.

"His *parents?*" Leon was incredulous.

She nodded, turned her head away.

Without a shred of sleep, one bite of breakfast, or even a cup of coffee, Leon set off on foot to scour the neighborhood on his own.

△△△

Willow was sitting in the living room trying to comfort Mary when Leon returned an hour later. He looked positively beat, Willow thought, with dark circles under his eyes. "Still no sign of him?" she asked, though the answer was obvious.

The TV played in the corner of the room, the sound turned down low. For the next thirty minutes or so, none of them said much, nothing that mattered anyway. The sudden ringing of the telephone made them jump, and Mary rushed to answer it. Willow held her breath. It was just another friend calling after seeing Walt's picture on the news.

By that time, Leon had lit his second cigarette, triggering a rash of complaints from his mother—about how he couldn't seem to sit still without a cigarette, about his slouching posture, about how she couldn't imagine why he'd picked up so many horrible habits when he was a teenager—and so he stopped abruptly, squelching the butt in a coffee cup. It was the first opportunity Willow had to observe their relationship up close for an extended period of time. Had it always been this way, she wondered, or was it just the strain of the situation? She watched Leon pace around the room. Without his cigarettes, he was a like wrecked ship tossing at sea.

"I'm going out again," he said.

"Just leave it to the police," said his mother. "You look terrible, like a walking corpse. You're going to drop dead if you don't sit down and rest."

"So which one am I—already dead or soon to be?" he snapped. "Anyway, I can't rest. And I can't just sit around here doing nothing. Where are your car keys?"

"I don't want you driving when you're so tired."

"I'm not so tired, Mom. Where are the keys?"

"In the top drawer, over by the door."

"I'll go with you." Willow rose from her chair, grabbing Walt's heavy afghan from the La-Z-Boy in case they found him. "I'll drive, and you can scan the streets." She cast Mary a reassuring glance.

"Deal." He tossed her the keys.

His easy surrender surprised Willow. He must've been even more discombobulated than he looked to give in so easily. Seconds later, she was backing out of their driveway, pulling into the street. Slowly—the speedometer read less than five miles an hour—the car inched down the narrow road as they scanned between houses, behind bushes and trees, even driving through back alleys to search the tiny backyards.

"Oh, dear Jesus," he muttered, stroking his temples. "Why did I go to Florida? I knew I shouldn't have gone."

"It's not your fault." Willow's voice lacked conviction. It was expected to say that kind of thing at such a time, but deep down, she blamed him, not for the fact that Walt was missing, but for leaving his parents alone at such a vulnerable time. The same reason she was blaming herself for going back to her apartment last night.

By now, they were a couple streets away from the Ziemnys' house, passing by a posse of friends and neighbors combing the streets on foot, not just old Polish people, but plenty of Hispanic and black faces among them. Standing in their midst, Gus held out both palms flat, indicating a fruitless hunt. When Willow reached the end of the road, she took a right turn, heading toward the next street over. "He could be anywhere," Leon said. "This is like looking for a needle in a haystack."

"Someone will find him—eventually," she said. "He couldn't have disappeared into thin air."

"Yeah, but what shape will he be in?"

At the end of the block, she made a left turn. Street by street, they continued their painstaking search. They drove by St. Stan's, Busia's Bakery, by the Mazurka Inn for the umpteenth time, all the familiar landmarks. Another hour or so went by. To Willow, it felt like they'd been riding around for days.

"It's no use," he said. "Let's go back home and see if there's any news."

Once more, almost on a whim, she decided to go past St. Stan's.

"Look over there—it's Mrs. Lipinski." Leon banged his index finger against the glass, where an old lady in a crooked gray wig labored to scurry down the steps, frantically waving her arms. Willow slammed on the brakes.

"He's in the church!" Mrs. Lipinski shouted.

Bolting from the car, Leon raced up the twenty or more steep steps. By the time Willow parked and caught up with him, he had already located his father. Walt was lying splat out in the back pew near the wall of burning votive candles. "Are you okay?" Leon was asking. "We've been looking everywhere for you!"

Walt's eyes were wide with panic. "Get away from me, you Nazi!" Both arms flailing, he tried to get up from the pew, fell back down.

"Leave him alone," Willow said to Leon. "He doesn't know who you are."

Leon stepped back into the aisle as if hit by a Taser. Dressed only in his pajamas and slippers, Walt was shivering, reeking of urine and other assorted foul smells. His lips were blue. "I'm here to take you home, Dad."

Walt lifted his head, squinting to get Leon into focus, and when he did, his eyes bulged again in terror. "I'm not going anywhere with you! Get the hell away from me!" He put up his hands in front of his face. "You killed my mother, and now you came for me too!"

Willow couldn't tell which one of them looked more trauma-tized. She fought for the strength to remain calm, to somehow form her mouth into the shape of a grin, for Walt's sake. She squatted down in front of him. "Walt, it's me—it's Mishka."

His pupils shifted toward her. "Who did you say you were?"

"Mishka."

His face went blank. The name didn't register.

"Let's go home and get you warmed up, nice and cozy. How does that sound?"

"It sounds good. It's freezing in here, don't you think? I lit a fire, but that didn't help." He pointed over the pew, toward the direction of the votive lights.

She extended both arms. "Would it be okay if I tried to help you up?"

"I don't need any help!" He looked frightened again.

"I know you don't, but I do." As she tried to redirect him, Leon sat down beside him in the pew, next to his head. "Is it okay if I hold your hand, Walt?" she asked. "I'm feeling kind of weak, and I'm hoping you can steady me. Do you mind helping me?"

"No, I don't mind."

Again, Walt tried to get up on his own steam, collapsing on his back in frustration. "Soggy shoes are no damned good, you know that?" He looked upside down at Leon. "Maybe that guy up there with the mustachio can help us out."

"Maybe he can."

"What are you, fella, some kind of bandito?"

"Nope. Just a regular old guy with a mustache," Leon replied, slipping both hands beneath his father's armpits, gently raising him upright, which allowed Willow to slide Walt's legs over the edge of the pew. His pallid skin was chilled to the bone. "At the count of three, let's do this," Leon said. "One. Two. Three." Though he felt like dead weight, Walt was upright.

They allowed him time to catch his breath, get his bearings. "He'll never make it down all those stairs," Leon said. "Let's get him as close to the altar as we can, and I'll drive the car around to the side door." Doubtful that he could walk even a few feet, Willow glanced down the long aisle. This wasn't a church, it was a frigging basilica—the aisle seemed to stretch out for eternity. Apparently catching the expression on her face, Leon shrugged. "We'll just have to take it slow," he said. "Dad, do you think you can make it?"

"Make what? Pee-pee? I already did."

A stream of urine was trickling to the floor.

"Good God." Leon moaned.

Propping him up firmly between them, they inched toward the altar, Walt taking tiny, wobbly steps, resting between each one. "I sure am cold," he said. When they reached the front of the church, he faltered, nearly toppling over if Leon hadn't managed to steady him. After they sat him down in the front pew to rest, Leon drove the Toyota around the church parking lot to the side door. Finally, they were able to ease him into the back seat of the car.

If the walk down the aisle loomed forever, the ride home seemed even longer. Willow sat in back with Walt, the afghan tucked around him, while Leon glanced at his father through the rearview mirror every few seconds, his own face ashen and drained. An overwhelming stench of urine and dried feces filled the car, and she struggled to keep from throwing up.

△△△

Once they were back home, Leon called Doc Podemski, while Willow helped his mother clean up his father and get him into dry clothes. Leon's second call was to notify the police that the search was over. His hands were shaking; he was dying for a cigarette.

Doc made an immediate house call with his black bag. Even with Willow's help, Leon couldn't manage to get his father upstairs to his own bedroom, so they made a makeshift bed on the sofa in the living room. His father looked wasted and feeble lying there, vulnerable as an infant. He kept falling asleep as the doctor examined him, even when a vial of blood was drawn. "Do you know what year this is, Walt?" Doc shouted, awaking him.

"Huh?"

"Do you know what year it is?"

"Yeah … it's 1923." His eyes remained closed.

Leon was stunned; his mother gasped out loud. The recriminations inside his own head were unrelenting. Why the hell had he gone to Florida? Why hadn't he realized how out-of-control this situation had gotten?

"He's badly dehydrated, folks." Doc said. "He's got a bit of hypothermia, and he's in shock. It's lucky you found him when you did. And it's lucky for him that he found the church, instead of staying outside all night. Otherwise, there might have been a totally different ending to this story."

"Will he be okay?" Leon heard his mother ask.

"I think he'll be fine."

"Thank God." She crossed herself.

"You're a tough old Polack, aren't you Walt?" Doc said to him. "Huh?'

Raising his voice loud enough to rouse the dead, Doc repeated it.

"Yeah, I'm a tough old Polack." Walt's eyes were shut tight.

"Don't you think he should go to the hospital?" Leon asked.

"No, I think he just needs to rest, drink plenty of water, and to warm up. Going to the hospital would only be another shock for him. And that's the last thing he needs right now."

As his father rested, the remainder of the day was taken up with prevention plans so that he couldn't wander out again. Leon installed double cylinder dead bolts on both the front and back doors. His last task was to put an army of safety latches on the basement door, overkill, maybe, but he was determined to keep him protected. Doc Podemski had suggested they buy a couple packages of Depends. Maybe his father wouldn't need them forever, he said, or maybe he would; at this point, it was too early to tell whether his incontinence was part of the ordeal or a new phase of the disease. At any rate, Leon couldn't bring himself to do it, so he gave Willow the money and sent her to the store instead.

While he worked on the deadbolts, his mother was badgering him to hire Willow to help them full time. "We can manage on our own." Leon was adamant.

"Maybe you can, but I can't," she cried. "I can't do this anymore!"

Father Burton arrived around dinnertime to offer prayers of solace. The neighborhood posse had transformed into cooks and bakers, bringing endless platters of casseroles, cakes, and cookies. Among them was a pan of macaroni and cheese from the Rodriguez couple. "We're so sorry," Miguel Rodriguez said to Leon. "If we knew your papa had Alzheimer's, we would have done everything differently."

"Don't worry about it," Leon said. "I should've done everything differently too. And I *knew* he had Alzheimer's."

As evening approached, the commotion died down. His father remained on the sofa in the living room, knocked out and snoring. Just before his mother headed upstairs to bed, Leon informed her that he'd made the decision to move back home, into Ricky's old room upstairs. She smiled; the first one he'd seen all day, maybe all year. "What about Stella?"

He shrugged.

Willow kept hanging around, offering to stay downstairs with his dad and sleep in the La-Z-Boy beside him, and Leon was too tired to fight her on it. Though her constant presence—when she wasn't helping—felt like an intrusion, Leon couldn't miss the adept way she had handled his dad earlier. He'd never admit it, but he was as startled by her competence as he was by his own lack of it.

The silent recriminations kept coming. He was rattled beyond measure by the events of the last twenty-four hours. Why hadn't he listened to Ricky? His brother had tried to sound the warning bell months before his death, but he'd remained a fatheaded fool who'd kept his blinders strapped on tight. Well, they were off now. And what he'd seen today hurt like holy hell. His own father didn't recognize him. Not only that, he thought Leon was a Nazi, the enemy he'd risked his life to defeat as a young soldier, the murderers of his sacred mother. His own father had mistaken him for the most despicable aberration of humanity ever known.

Throwing Willow a blanket and pillow, Leon headed to the kitchen to pour himself a tall glass of vodka.

△△△

Willow immediately regretted coming into the kitchen and sitting down with Leon at the table—he'd looked up at her with a short, annoyed glance that made it obvious her presence was unwelcome. In her mind, she cursed him, father or no father. She was sick and tired of being used by him, then cast aside, and besides that, she was probably every bit as upset as he was about Walt, if not more. As soon as she made her request, she'd go right back into the living room and leave him alone to drown his sorrows, or whatever it was he was doing. "Can I have a drink too?" Asking was better than stealing it on the sly.

He slid the bottle toward her. "The glasses are in the cupboard by the sink."

God forbid, King Tut could get up to find them for her. She rummaged until she located another one of the goblets he was using and poured it fuller than his.

As she was walking out, he said, "This is one hell of a disease, you know that?" Taking a cigarette from the cellophane package inside his pocket, he offered one to her, an unexpected gesture; an invitation, albeit a subtle one, for her to remain.

"No, thanks. I never smoked." She stood there debating whether or not to stay.

"That's good. It's a nasty habit, expensive too. Don't ever start." When she noticed his fingers trembling as he lit the tip, she decided to take a seat again. "Look at me," he said, "I'm talking to you like you're some kind of kid." He took a puff. "How old are you anyway?"

"I'm twenty-five."

"Twenty-five." He raised his eyebrows, blew out a long stream of smoke. "Kids grow up slower nowadays, don't they? When I was your age, I was all settled in, with a family. Or so I thought." His eyes narrowed on his glass, transfixed.

He had to be referring to his marriage to her mother. Her

pulse raced; she hoped he'd say more. When he didn't, she pursued it. "You were married to Noël then, weren't you?"

The question hung there.

His prolonged silence discouraged her from probing further. They could hear Walt trying to catch his next breath in the adjacent room, a disturbing, recurring sound since he'd fallen asleep. "Too bad you had to leave Stella alone in Florida."

"She'll be okay. Her boyfriend will take care of her."

"Her *boyfriend*?"

"The old stallion next door."

Leon frequently made odd comments like that, as if he was trying to be funny, and lots of the time he was, though he never cracked a smile as he said them. She'd come to realize that it was just the way he talked, wry and caustic, the same way he looked at the world. Frankly, she kind of liked that about him, or could appreciate it anyway. It was one thing they had in common. The room lit only by the lone light over the kitchen sink, they sat there nursing their drinks and battling their private thoughts, every once in a while distracted again by the sound of Walt's labored breathing.

"So why did he think it was 1923?" he asked.

"Because he's stuck in the past!" Why couldn't Leon seem to grasp that concept?

"And we're stuck in the present," he said.

Stuck in the present? A strange way to phrase it, she thought. Wasn't the present the place where all the mystics found nirvana? She looked around the kitchen.

Some nirvana.

He emptied his glass. "For all our sakes, I hope this thing of his goes fast."

SEVENTEEN

February 1999:
Twinkling Lights

AMONG the many lessons Stella was learning during Leon's prolonged absence was the difference between loneliness and being alone. When he'd first taken off and deserted her to return to Langston, then gone ahead and moved in with his parents without so much as a discussion, she felt like a single woman, alone for the first time in her life. Much to her surprise, she felt lonelier when he was there than she did without him.

The first month she spent long hours by herself, strolling up and down Tampa Bay. She'd walk until nightfall, forgetting to eat, losing track of time, keeping her distance from the neighbors. By the time she returned to the condo in early evening, she'd be amazed at her changing reflection in the bathroom mirror. Her skin was darkened by the sun, her hair lightened by it—funny how that worked—and she was losing weight. She'd become a softer, more attractive version of herself. And then it dawned on her that what she was seeing was the bloom of self-love. Much more potent than falling in love with someone else.

Up until early February, she'd declined every single one of Gene Henke's invitations to accompany her on her strides along the shoreline. But she eventually relented because she was ready to talk to another person, and he seemed eager to listen. Gene was the diametric opposite of Leon in every way imaginable; he was a well-educated, attentive man who shared every single thought in his head.

Now it had become a daily pattern the two of them shared—each evening after twilight, they took long walks together, having intimate conversations and trying to decipher the meaning of their lives. She anticipated their walks, waiting all day for the sun to go down. Without Leon, the Great Silencer, she had transformed into a regular talking machine, surprising herself with her own strong opinions and rich ruminations.

As she readied herself for Gene's arrival that particular night (she had two more weeks before she had to be back to work at the mills), it occurred to her that it felt like she was preparing for a real date. Her mind tripped backwards. Dating Leon hadn't felt like this. Dating Leon took energy and determination; every moment spent with him, she lost a little more of herself. Being with Gene was effortless, a journey into herself. She put a fresh flower, a white lily, behind her ear, but it wasn't to entice Gene. It was to symbolize her newfound freedom.

He tapped on her patio door, his face lighting up at her approach. "You're so lovely, you take my breath away." She offered him a cocktail, and they sat on her patio and watched the sun go down.

It was dark when they started their walk. Not only was the air cooler and less humid, but this time of night felt mystical, more conducive to deep sharing. As they strolled down the shoreline, she felt his fingers brushing against hers. Then he took her hand outright, a bold, new intimacy between them, and she tightened her fingers around his. Even their footsteps—though his legs were long and his stride much wider—were in unison.

"Stella, I'm deeply in love with you."

His confession came out of nowhere. Or had it? She walked on silently, her hand still in his. No, it hadn't come out of nowhere; it had been there for a long while, unspoken. The only surprising thing about it was that he'd said it, finally, and put it out in the open. "Thank you." What a silly response, she thought, yet it seemed the right one.

"… And I'd marry you in a minute, if you were free."

As she touched her hair, the flower fell to the sand. "That's not going to happen, Gene. I'm a Catholic. Divorce is out of the question."

"But it's no marriage for you. Is it?" She didn't say anything. "You deserve more. You deserve it all."

They kept on walking, both silent. The moon was full and low, the lights of the city visible across the bay, twinkling in the distance. A warm wind moved through her hair. This was paradise. She squeezed Gene's hand. They strode for another half-hour that way, maybe longer.

"I wish I'd found you before he did."

She wasn't sure if she wished it too, but if it wasn't that she wished, it was something close. They were on the other side of the bay now, far from the scrutiny of human observation, when he stopped abruptly. She knew why he did, and she let it happen. She let him put his arms around her, let him kiss her on the lips, opening her mouth to him as his intentions grew more fervent. She let him put his large, strong fingers beneath her top and feel her like a treasure. But when he moved on top of her in the sand, she stopped him.

It wasn't because she was Catholic. And it wasn't because of her marriage vows. Or her lack of desire. It wasn't even the thought of Leon that held her back. What kept her from going further was her awareness that she didn't return his love. At least, not in the same way. And having sex with someone you didn't love only muddied the truth.

"Should I apologize?" he asked.

"No." She flattened her clothes, kissed his cheek, readjusted her hair. "But maybe I should."

They strolled back to their condos in the same way they'd left them—hand in hand.

"Other than being Catholic," he said as they parted, "what kept you with him all these years?"

Stella had to think long and hard before she answered; honesty was the only thing he expected from her. This was the most honest answer she could come up with. "I guess I didn't want to be alone."

Now that prospect didn't seem so bad.

EIGHTEEN

FEBRUARY 1999:
I Wanna Go Home!

OKAY, she'd be the first to admit it, Mary thought, as she scrubbed the dinner dishes—patience was never a virtue she'd been blessed with. But compared to Leon, she was Joan of Arc. He had the patience of a jack rabbit.

She could hear them in the other room, Walt demanding to go home every few minutes, and Leon's repetitive response, "You *are* home!" On and on it went, except that every time Walt asked the question and Leon answered it, each of them grew more agitated than the time before.

"Just tell him we'll go home tomorrow," Mary yelled from the kitchen.

"This *is* your home!" Leon repeated. Either he hadn't heard her or he was too worked up to listen. Or too stubborn, the most likely of the three.

"The hell it is!" Walt bellowed.

"For Pete's sake, you've lived here for over sixty years."

"You're a goddamned liar!"

As Mary crossed the threshold from the kitchen into the living room, the tension enveloped her like a suffocating fog. They were sitting there facing each other, red-faced and bristling, like two mad dogs. By now Walt had given up trying to open the front door because Leon had it locked up airtight with all his fancy deadbolts and sliding chains. Even she had trouble getting out the doors nowadays.

"If you're not at home, where do you think you are?" Leon asked his father.

"In jail, that's where!" Rising from his chair, Walt went back to the door, yanking on the knob. "Lemme out of here!"

"Stop that!" Leon stood up.

"Shut your pie hole!"

"Dad, you're gonna break it!"

"And I'll break your chops too!"

"Walt, honey." Mary tried to intervene. "Come sit here beside me on the couch." Though her anxiety was off the charts, she tried her best to say it as calmly as she could muster, nice and sweet, the way Willow would.

"What's a matter with your face?" Walt asked her.

"What do you mean?"

"It's pinched up like an old prune."

Leon sighed, went back to his seat, turned the TV set louder. Eventually, Walt came back to the sofa and sat down again, beside her as she'd requested, and Mary pretended to watch the screen, but it was no use—she was focused on every one of her husband's movements from the corner of her eye. He required that kind of constant vigilance, but that was nothing new. His catastrophic outbursts had become their new normal for this time of evening. During the day, he wasn't so bad; his lovable old self came shining through in certain moments. But when sundowning hours rolled around—starting around four p.m. and not letting up until eight or nine at night—he was worse than a two-year-old without a nap, fueled by Leon's impatience. It was always the same scenario: Walt wanted to go home. They told him he already was home. Walt got

more upset and tried to leave. *I wanna go home! I wanna go home!*
Even when they managed to think of a better answer that he'd
accept without becoming more agitated, (we'll go home later; your
mother is out shopping)—Walt forgot it as quickly as they'd said
it, and they were back to square one. *I wanna go home! I wanna go
home!* Doc Podemski had prescribed an antipsychotic medication,
but Mary was too afraid to give it to him.

Walt got up from his seat again. She braced herself. She
watched him walk toward the fireplace, then back over to the door,
pacing between the two.

"Just let him work off some steam," Leon said softly.

She tried to ignore it, but, really, how could she? Back and
forth, he walked. Forth and back. He could trip, or pick up something he shouldn't, or who knows what else? The next thing she
knew, he had the fireplace poker in his hand and was hurling it at
the doorknob. "Oh, good Lord, he's going to hurt himself!"

"Dad, stop that!"

The poker came down hard on the door frame, denting the
molding. Leon rushed over and tried to pull the poker from his
hand, and Walt clunked it against Leon's head. "Holy shit! I didn't
see that one coming," Leon groaned. Before he could make another
grab for it, his father bashed it against his face, the poker tumbling
from his fingers and falling to the floor. Leon pressed his hand
against his bleeding eye as he kicked the poker across the carpet.

Walt coiled his fists. "Don't you come at me again, you Nazi!"

"You came at *me*! I'm the one bleeding here!"

"In God's name," Mary wailed. "Stop this!"

"He started it!" Walt said.

"I don't care who started it—I'm stopping it!"

"The old straw boss has spoken," Walt said.

She turned toward Leon. "Go into the kitchen and put some ice on that eye."

As soon as he left, Walt's posture visibly relaxed. Mary tried to calm herself down too, inhaling a few deep breaths, in and out, like Doc Podemski had coached her, but it still felt like Buddy Rich was drumming inside her chest. "Come on, honey." She tried again, patting the cushion. "Sit down here with me, and let's watch this TV show."

"Just give him the pill, okay?" Leon was back in the living room, holding a bag of Green Giant frozen peas over his eye. "Unless you *want* him to kill me."

"Don't be ridiculous."

"Then, do it."

Walt returned to the front door, twisting the knob. "This is a prison! I'm going to call the police!"

"What do you think Doc gave you that medication for?" Leon threw up his hands. "To decorate the inside of the cupboard?"

When she'd picked up that prescription, Mary had read all the fine print, and every time she did, she ended up putting the bottle right back inside the cupboard. As bad as things were, the possible side effects were worse—things like seizures, trouble walking, stiff muscles, increased confusion, jerky movements and tremors, dizziness, trouble swallowing, on and on.

"Police! Police! They're holding me here!" Walt beat his fists against the door.

She couldn't take it anymore. After stomping into the kitchen, she reached high into the cabinet to retrieve the small vial labeled Risperidone. Leon followed her, filling a glass of water at the kitchen tap. Second-thoughts stopped her. Those side effects ... "Let's just call Willow first."

"Forget about Willow," he said. "She can't be at our beck and call whenever things get tough."

"If we pay her like we talked about, maybe she will. I don't know why you won't at least ask her." He mumbled something that Mary couldn't decipher as he reached out for the bottle she was holding behind her back. "I'm afraid it'll turn your father into a zombie."

"Better a zombie than a raving madman."

"If you ask me, I have two raving madmen. Maybe you should take one of these." She stood in the middle of the kitchen floor grasping the Risperidone for dear life.

"Come on, Mom. Give him a pill. Just try it once, at least."

Walt was still shouting for the police. If they didn't do something, one of the neighbors, or maybe even Adult Protective Services, God forbid, might come knocking on their door. "Okay, okay!" she said. "But I'll be the one to give it to him. He's not going to take a pill from *you*, that's for sure."

Leon shrugged, conceding the point.

Snatching the water glass from his hands and spilling some in the process, Mary walked into the living room. By that time, Walt had taken a crucifix off the wall and was pounding it on the doorknob. "Oh, no, honey, not that!" As she hurried toward him, Walt struck her with it, a trickle of red dripping from her right nostril.

"That's it!" Leon grabbed his father's arms from behind, wrestling him to the floor, facedown. "You're a crazy old man, you know that?"

"And you're a crazy old Nazi!" Walt's arm and legs flailed against the carpet. "Mama!"

Wiping her nose with her apron, Mary scurried to the phone, punching the speed dial for the Mazurka Inn and begging Willow to come right over, while Leon kept his father down on the floor, trying to steady him. The gash in Leon's head was starting to bleed all over his shirt, not to mention her carpet, and his eye was swelling up.

Minutes later, Willow burst through the back door, which Mary had left unlatched, her eyes widening in shock at the scene. Walt had stopped writhing under Leon's weight, but every time he tried to get up, he was provoked all over again.

"Give him the sedative," Leon said to her.

Mary watched her scoot down on the floor beside him. "Hiya, Walt," Willow said. "What are you doing down there?" Her cheerful voice made the awful pose seem almost natural.

"A Nazi is sitting on top of me."

"Him?" Willow glanced at Leon. "I don't think he's a Nazi."

"Then who the hell is he?"

"He kind of looks like your son—Leon."

"That's not my son! My son's a good boy, not a goddamned Nazi."

"You're absolutely right, Walt." Willow smiled. Mary saw Walt's fist unclench. "That other guy was the Nazi," Willow continued, "and Leon here chased him away. I saw the Nazi run out the front door."

"How the hell did he get it open?"

"I don't know, but he's gone now," said Willow. "And the police took him away."

"You mean, they finally got here?"

"Yes, they did. And they hauled him off. Thank goodness, Leon was able to get the Nazi out of here." Mary watched as her husband's breathing slowly became more even. "Now that he's gone," Willow said, "how about we go into the kitchen and get something to eat?"

"I wanna go home!"

Here we go again, Mary thought.

"Just keep me company while I have a big bowl of chocolate ice cream." Willow said. "After that, we can go home. You can't go home on an empty stomach, you know."

"I can't? Okay then, just a little ice cream. But after that, I'm going right home."

"Absolutely."

As Leon slowly moved off of his father, Willow remained squatting on the floor. "What was that song you told me you used to sing in Polish with your best friend Stanley when you were little?" she asked Walt.

"What song?"

"It started out something like … *U-marl* … "

"You mean … Umarł Maciek umarł i lezy na desce (Matty's dead, he is, and he's lying on a board)," he sang.

"Yeah, that's the one."

"Gdyby mu zagrali podskocyłby jesce (he'd jump up again if he heard a lively chord)." He busted out laughing. "That Stanley is a goofy kid."

Hearing Walt singing and laughing again brought tears to Mary's eyes, and she wiped them quickly before he noticed. She watched as Leon lifted him to his feet, the few hairs on Walt's head slightly rumpled, but otherwise, unlike the rest of them, none the worse for the wear. "Hiya, kiddo!" Walt winked at her. "What you doin' here? Just lookin', good-lookin'?"

Taking his hand, she coaxed him into the kitchen. "Let's go get that chocolate ice cream. What do you say?"

When they were seated at the kitchen table, all of them except Leon who lagged behind in the doorway, Mary slipped the Risperidone into the first spoonful. Walt made a sour face as he swallowed. "There was something bumpy in there."

"Just a chunk of ice." Willow smiled.

△△△

The pill had worked well. And fast. Willow felt good that she could help Mary get Walt upstairs to his own bedroom and between the two of them, they were able to nestle him under the sheets before he fell soundly into a snoring sleep.

"I'm turning in too—I've had it," Mary said to her. "Thank you so much, Willow. Have I told you yet how glad I am that you've become a part of our household?"

Touched, yet guilty as usual for lying to her, Willow wasn't sure how to respond. "How's your nose feeling?"

"It just bled a little and that was it." Mary said, touching her nostrils as if she'd forgotten. "But take care of Leon's eye, will you, dear?"

When Willow returned to the living room, she found him gathering up all the sharp objects and tossing them into a cardboard box. "Let me have a look at your eye," she said.

"It's fine."

As he turned around to pick up the crucifix from the carpet, she caught a glimpse. "It looks horrible! I'll put something on it."

"I already told you, it's fine. I gotta put this stuff away in the basement before Ham the Wrecker makes an encore appearance."

"Okay, then. It's fine." Heaven forbid, he should say *thank you* once in a while, instead of snapping her head off.

He headed into the kitchen and toward the basement door, the box in his arms. As he disappeared down the steps, Willow cracked open an ice tray from the fridge, creating a cold pack with several cubes tucked inside a wet dish towel, loaded and ready for him when he finally reemerged. "Don't be so bullheaded," she said. "I've had nursing training, remember? Just sit down here and let me treat that eye. It's swollen shut, you know."

He pulled out a chair, slumped into it, flinching as she put the pack against his face. Next she parted his hair, stiff from dried blood, to examine the wound on top of his head. There was a small gash—about an inch long but not too deep. Though it was still bleeding a tiny bit, the injury appeared to be mostly superficial. The eye, on the other hand, was worrisome, turning purple. "You should go to the hospital."

"The hospital? Are you crazy?" He scrunched his other eye. "No hospital. No way."

"You have a first aid kit around here?"

"There's one upstairs. In the bathroom, I think."

She trotted up the stairs. It took her a while to find it. When she came back down to the kitchen, she spread out an assortment of astringent and bandages and began tending to the gash, poking his wound a little harder than need be in the process, just enough to make him wince.

Outside, the wind was starting to pick up. A tree branch scraped against the shutters with a low, dull thud. "That's all we need," he said. "A storm to wake him up." With his one good eye, he stared at the tabletop. "Maybe we need to start looking for a home for him."

"You mean, a *nursing* home?" She was appalled by the thought. She poked at the wound again, harder.

"Ouch! Are you trying to make me pass out or something? I guess you missed the class about bedside manners."

She couldn't fathom the thought of Walt in a home, sitting in a line at the nurses' station in a wheelchair with all the others. If Ricky were still around, it wouldn't have come to this.

"All he wants to do is go home, and he's already here," Leon mused. "So where does he really want to go?"

"His memories are regressing to the past, remember?" Why was he so dense?

"Yeah, right, the past. He's lived here for over sixty years."

"He's probably looking for his house in Poland." She finished taping the wound, sat down.

"In Poland? Really?"

She nodded.

"He was six years old when he lived there! Holy shit. He really thinks that's where he lives now?" Taking the compress off of his eye, he flopped it down on the table in frustration. Or could it be, at long last, in surrender? "And I won't let him go there. If I were him, I probably would've beat the crap out of me too."

"You better put that thing back on your eye. If you still want to see out of it, that is."

He replaced the pack. "You're pissed at me, aren't you?"

"I just don't think your father's ready for a nursing home, that's all."

"You don't, huh?" The arrogance and crossness in his tone had vanished. "Not even if they're trained to do this kind of thing?"

Willow thought about what he was saying. He had a point. Walt could be a handful, and neither Leon nor his mother had the skills to do this for the long haul, that was for sure. The staff in dementia units was getting better training all the time. In a more supportive, controlled environment, Walt might fare a heck of a lot better. He might thrive, even.

"Or there's another plan we could try," he said.

"Like what?"

"Mom has been talking to me about hiring you to help. Maybe four to six hours a day. What do you think?"

She was astonished. "You mean, like a job or something?" The offer took her aback, her conflicting thoughts bashing together as she tried to sort out the implications. If she was the one who could keep Walt out of a nursing home, didn't she owe it to him to give it a try? And to Ricky too. "You wouldn't have to pay me. I'd do it for free."

"What are you—independently wealthy?"

"Not hardly." She glared at him. On the other hand, why shouldn't she accept his money? Never having had kids—well, except her, that is—Leon must be loaded by now, with his fancy cars and Florida time-share, while she was struggling to make ends meet.

Outside, thunder rolled in the distance. "I just don't seem to get it, do I?" he said.

Which thing, among so many, did he possibly mean? "Get what?"

"Alzheimer's."

"No, you don't." His expression was so defeated, she felt kind of sorry for answering that way. "But it's a lot to get."

"*You* seem to get it just fine."

"I didn't get it by osmosis, you know. I took the time to read and learn about it. So did Ricky."

"Touché."

His face sagged even further. Just when she thought she had him figured out, he slipped into another mode. In her diary, her mother had written, *he's a complicated man …* " and he seemed to be. He was a puzzle. "So you want me to try to explain what's happening in his brain?"

"Yeah. But give me the quick version. It's getting late."

"It's slowly dying. Lobe by lobe." She tried to remember the order her textbook had laid it out, the way it had first made sense to her. "Alzheimer's starts in the hippocampus, where short-term memory is stored." She touched her temples on both sides. "This part of his brain is broken. That's why he can't remember new stuff—new things go in one ear and out the other."

"Tell me about it." He pulled out a cigarette, lit it. "But don't tell Mom I'm smoking down here, okay? She'll throw me to the coyotes."

"I don't have to tell her. She'll smell it." She watched him take a long drag, his eyes closing as he entered nicotine heaven. "You know, second-hand smoke can kill too, don't you?" she said.

"What? For Christ's sake." Crushing his cigarette in a glass ashtray on the table, he took a deep breath. "Go on. Tell me more."

"Alzheimer's destroys the frontal lobe next." She put her palm across her forehead. "Right here. This is the part that makes decisions, understands logic. It's not that your dad doesn't *want* to be logical; he *can't* be. That part of his brain isn't working anymore."

"Hmp." He thought a while. "Hmp."

Could it really be soaking in this time? Maybe a clunk on the head with a poker was exactly what he needed. But she'd seen it happen before when she was working in the nursing home—the way caregivers seemingly out of the blue (yet it never really was) faced their own Damascus. Though some conversions came much slower and harder than others, it was always painful to witness their self-reproaches, their grief—accepting the *what is* of Alzheimer's meant giving up the *what was*.

"And then it gets into the left side of the brain," she said. "That's where language is stored."

"You mean he won't be able to talk?"

"Well, at first, he won't be able to understand or remember certain words. We've already been seeing that for a while. But the longer he has it, the more words he'll lose."

She watched him get up from the table to retrieve a bottle from an upper cupboard. "This just graduated into a whiskey night," he said. "I don't know if I can hear any more." Taking a couple ice cubes from his compress, he clinked them into a glass, poured generously. "You want one?"

In truth, she was dying for a drink. But this was a monumental night, her first substantive conversation with her father, and she opted to have full awareness of it. Later, when she got back to the Mazurka Inn, there'd be plenty of time for a nightcap. "No, thanks."

He sat back down. "Is there any part of the brain this disease doesn't eat away?"

"The right side of the brain stays pretty much intact: music, emotions, intuition, spirituality. And swear words too; that's where they're stored. Since he can't reason, he lives entirely in his feelings."

"Emotions and music, huh? Except for the swear words part, I guess my right brain has been dead for a long time now."

The comment threw her for a second; she'd have to mull over this new insight into his character later, maybe over her nightcap. "… And he can still form new emotional memories, which means he can either like someone or not like them."

"Like the way he hates me now?" He ran his fingers through his hair, inadvertently touching the gauze bandage, grimacing.

Lightning, still far off, flashed through the curtains. "The bottom line is, you have to go where he is, and, stop trying to force him where you are. You have a choice: You can have a relationship with your dad, or you can be right all the time."

"Ouch! But well said, Nurse Ratched."

"I'm not trying to be mean. I'm just trying to tell you the way it is."

"You might find this hard to believe," he said. "But I love that old man more than anyone else on this planet."

She nodded. Another thing they had in common.

△△△

While doing weekly inventory with Gus the next morning at the Mazurka Inn, Willow was mentally preparing to start the next phase of her life: part-time barkeeper and part-time caregiver. Leon had offered to pay her ten dollars an hour, so the money—though not plentiful—would start accumulating, along with the income from the rental house in Willow, the tips she made at the bar, and the free room and board upstairs tossed in. It was a patchwork life, but it worked for now.

Checking off the last order item on their list, Gus told her he'd make the call to Walt's liquor distributor. He knew way more about running the business than she did, and he was virtually keeping things afloat.

"By the way, I think they're closing in on me," he said to her.

"What? Who's closing on you?"

"Yeah, *who*, that's the question. Some guy in a shiny suit has been snooping around here, asking questions."

"About you?"

"About lots of things, according to Bennie." Bennie Niezgodski was another one who regularly pitched in to help. "Including Ricky."

"*Ricky*? He was asking about him?"

"Yeah, he was asking about his studio and what all—and who all—works upstairs and owns the joint, stuff like that." She could see the tension in Gus' face. "Maybe they finally found me, little Ahyoka. Maybe my jig is up. But this time, I'm not running. Walt needs me here."

NINETEEN

MARCH 1999:
THE SOUND OF MUSIC

BY the time Stella passed the "Welcome to Langston" sign, she felt a tightening sensation in her chest, the anxiety flooding back as if she'd never lost it on Tampa Bay. The farther north she drove, the grayer the country seemed, and now she was back in Langston, the dingiest place of all, back to a routine job at the steel mills, back to an empty house. Foolishly, she had assumed Leon would join her at home when she returned, but he'd informed her otherwise. Night was the worst time for his father, he'd said, and he had to be there for him.

Her first stop was the Ziemnys' old brick house on Pulaski Street. When she tried to enter the back kitchen door with her key, she found it didn't work anymore. She knocked loudly, a tad indignant to be shut out. From the other side of the screen door, she could hear someone trying to unkey the shiny new deadbolt lock, then the sliding of multiple chain locks. Good grief. Had it really come to that?

Alas, Willow opened the door. Leon had told her they hired Willow to help out, so it was no surprise to see her, but it still felt odd not to find Mary or Leon standing there instead of this dark-haired girl, still virtually a stranger. Once Stella stepped inside the kitchen, cluttered in disarray with Walt's disease paraphernalia—from diaper pails to an assortment of Ensure bottles stacked everywhere—she was uncertain what to do next. A hug seemed too intimate; a handshake too formal.

"Welcome home." Willow smiled. That girl was way too gaunt for her age, downright anemic.

"Hey, you!" Walt called to Willow from the living room. "Let's get back to this thing here."

"I'm coming, Walt," she replied

Stella followed her into the dark room, drapes drawn, where Walt was stretched back in his recliner watching *The Sound of Music* on television. He pointed to the screen; the family von Trapp was warbling together in their final Austrian concert. "Why did you get up and leave?" He chastised Willow. "Don't be so rude to these kids."

"I'm sorry, Walt." She returned to what was apparently her place on the sofa, hugging Walt's afghan against her body briefly as she sat down cross-legged.

"They sure are singing their hearts out," he said.

"They sure are." Willow agreed, tossing the afghan aside.

There was no sign of Leon or Mary, just another messy room filled with more of Walt's equipment, including a commode chair in the corner of the room. "Hello, there, Walt." Stella bent to kiss him on the forehead. "How have you been?"

"Who the hell are you?"

"It's *me*—Stella."

His face was blank.

"You know, Leon's wife? … your son's wife of twenty-six years?" She pronounced each word slowly, the painful memory of celebrating her anniversary alone this year zipping through her mind. "Don't you remember me at all?" Laughing nervously, she glanced at Willow. "I haven't been gone *that* long, have I? He used to at least recognize my face."

Leon entered the room. Like Willow, he also looked too thin, pasty, the strain showing in his face. "You got back." He came over and pecked her on the cheek. "Did you have a good trip?"

A peck was better than nothing, she supposed. "A lot of rain, but other than that, it was uneventful. Did you miss me?"

"Sure, I did." His eyes suggested otherwise. "How was Florida?"

It was a rhetorical question, considering they'd talked regularly on the phone. "Like I've been telling you, the weather was fabulous the whole time. Too bad you didn't join me. Especially now that Willow is here to take care of things." She eyed the girl briefly as she sat twirling a strand of her hair around her finger.

Balling up the afghan and hurling it at Willow, Leon plopped down beside her on the sofa. "You didn't eat your lunch," he said to her.

"I did too!"

"Then how come I found it in the garbage can?"

She rolled her eyes. "I don't eat that much. I'm not a horse, you know."

"You're starting to look like a sack of bones."

"So are you."

"That's because I can't stand my own cooking."

Stella looked from one to the other like a ping-pong match. "You're cooking now?" she asked her husband. "What's wrong with Mary?"

"She hasn't been feeling too hot lately," he said. "She's upstairs resting."

"Is she okay?"

Pointing to his father, he shrugged. "Anyway, so now I'm the chief cook and bottle washer. And Willow here, she's the big boss."

"Oh, I am not."

"The hell you aren't. I live under Willow's golden rules now. Don't argue. Don't correct. Stay calm. Slow down. Agree with him no matter what crazy-ass thing he's saying."

"Those aren't *my* golden rules. They're *the* golden rules. They're in all the books, including the Bible, which I'm sure you never read since you won't read anything thicker than a pamphlet."

"What do you mean? I'm gonna read that tome you left on the kitchen table, what is it called?, *The One-Hundred Hour Day?*"

"Yeah, right, a *tome*." Looking at Stella, she sighed. "That's what he calls anything bigger than that one sheet of paper hanging on the refrigerator that he glances at during breakfast."

"That I do." He nodded. "Every morning with my jolt of caffeine, I study Willow's do's and don'ts until the paper goes blurry. And I still fuck up."

"Hey, there, watch your mouth!" Walt shook a finger at him. "That's not nice."

"See?" Leon smiled. Willow laughed.

Listening to their perplexing, new banter, like a bossy older brother and his headstrong kid sister, Stella sat down on a wing chair, puzzled. Was it playful or adversarial? She couldn't quite tell which one it was, only that Leon had strung more sentences together in the span of the last few minutes than he did in an entire month with her. She hoped it wasn't romantic, though her own eyes and gut told her it wasn't. Still, there was an underlying affectionate tone, a familiarity and ease she herself had never experienced with him. As Stella stared at the television without seeing it, she noticed her husband looking at her from the corner of her eye. She turned to him. "What?"

"Florida agreed with you," he said. "You're looking good."

The compliment, unusual and unexpected, further bewildered

her. She felt unmasked, a tad guilty. He'd noticed the change in her.

"So how's old Gene doing?"

"Just fine. He said to tell you hello."

He wiggled his fingers in a silly wave. "Hello, Gene."

It was a childish gesture, but she held her tongue, mostly because Willow was watching. Could he really, finally, be jealous of Gene? Miraculous as that might be, he wasn't jealous enough; his reaction tepid, at best. Already, his attention was refocused on the old nuns running around to help the von Trapps, their conversation ending there. After two long months, they had nothing more to say to each other than a few sentences of small talk. Another revelation. She had spent her whole married life waiting for something to change, and it never would.

The four of them remained that way, sitting silently in the dark room with the drapes drawn, watching *The Sound of Music* in the middle of the day while the world passed them by. Willow was an anomaly, an old woman in a young girl's body, seemingly content in this dead-end arrangement. And Leon?—who knew where his head was nowadays? Stella sightlessly watched the German soldiers search the monastery, while the von Trapps hid in the shadows of a graveyard.

"The Nazis are here!" Walt tried to climb out of the La-Z-Boy. "They're coming for us!"

"That's the TV, Walt," Stella said. "It's just a movie. There're no Nazis here."

"Yes, there are! They're everywhere!" He pointed at the television. "Can't you see them?"

"They're going away now." Leon clicked the remote control; the television screen went black. "See? No more Nazis."

"Where they'd go?" Walt scrambled to his feet, hobbling

toward the picture window and jerking open the drapes, the sun streaking into the room. He tented his eyes with his hand to block out the sudden light.

"Oops. I forgot about that part of the movie," Willow said sheepishly. While she went over to calm Walt down, Leon jumped up to grab the soiled protector pad from his father's chair and replace it with a clean one, the stench of urine filling the room. The two of them worked like a well-oiled caregiving machine, Stella thought, holding her nose.

Too much had changed since she left, and too much had remained the same. She could barely wait to get back to her own house.

ΔΔΔ

Later that night, alone in their quiet home, she was chain-smoking, holding the long, slender cigarettes made for women between her fingers, a habit she'd picked up in Florida despite years of lecturing Leon about the repugnance of the act. After dinner, Gene would always lean in close to give her a light—she'd hold the cigarette between her acrylic nails, manicured and polished in some shade of pink, to accept it—and she'd felt like Audrey Hepburn in *Breakfast at Tiffany's*.

But not here. Here in Langston where all the tinsel rubbed off, smoking felt like nothing more than a filthy addiction that was yellowing her teeth and making her breath stink, though Leon's breath smelled fine whenever he got close enough for her to smell it. After squelching the butt in the ashtray, she pitched the brand-new carton into the trash.

Restless, she roamed the house, neat as a pin, the way she'd left it. Their lovely, perfect home—Henredon furniture; a thick Persian rug in the living room; leather-bound books, never read, lining the shelves. Passing the bookcase, she brushed Leon's pristine

LP-record collection with her long nails. Maybe she should pull one out, play a tune from when she was young. Would he notice if she stuck it back in the wrong place—put The Animals next to The Yardbirds? There on the end table sat the phone.

She considered calling Gene. She got as close as stroking the buttons, then recoiled. Fleeing to the dining room, she found herself standing by the patio door. Their house was on the outskirts of the neighborhood, a beautiful home, really, two-story, brown-brick with ivy up one side, moss-green slate roof, paver sidewalk leading to the front porch, and a fenced-in patio out back, lushly land-scaped come spring. The only spoilers were the black wrought-iron security front door and iron bars on the basement windows. They had bought the home three weeks after they married—at a bargain price—and slowly through the years they made one improvement after the next until they remodeled it way beyond a reasonable worth for the area. They knew they'd take a beating whenever they chose to sell it, which was mostly why they didn't consider it.

She thought about giving her parents a call in Chicago, but it was too late in the day. Her brothers and their families were scattered all over the country, consumed with their own lives and busy with their children's activities. She hardly talked to Pete, her favorite brother, anymore. Stepping outside into the cool night, she sat down at the patio table, the umbrella still tied up tight for the season, wishing she hadn't been so hasty to pitch the ciga-rettes. She supposed she could dig them out from the trash, but that would make the habit seem even more despicable.

Tomorrow at seven a.m., she'd be back at work again, the first time she dreaded returning to the mills after her vacation. The other secretaries were thirty-ish, all they talked about was their children, and she didn't fit in anymore. Though she could retire any time now, what was the point? Maybe she and Leon should have tried again to have a child. Maybe then …

Rushing back into the house to curtail the futile ruminations, she dug into the trash for her carton of cigarettes, breaking her index fingernail in the process. She didn't notice the nail had popped off until she was lighting her cigarette—Holly Golightly transformed into a dumpster diver. Now what would she do? She couldn't show up to work like that.

In Florida, she had felt like a butterfly breaking free from a tight, dark cocoon, on the verge of self-discovery. Even Leon had noticed the change in her. Now, less than nine hours after returning to Langston, she was crawling back into that same old cocoon. Only it didn't fit anymore. What in the world did she want from life now? She was lost.

∆∆∆

A week later, on her first Saturday night back home, Stella was sitting with Mary in the living room trying to have a conversation, while Walt paced the length of the room. Leon was taking the trash out from dinner. He'd been gone an awfully long time; he must be smoking out there. "I noticed the Mazurka Inn looks pretty empty," Stella said.

"Oh, you know," Mary said. "The neighborhood is so different now. The old-timers can't live forever, and that's the way these things go. Leon works there on the nights Willow doesn't, but with Walt and all—" She looked up at him, made a face. "It's getting to be too much."

"I wanna go home." Walt stopped in front of his wife. "I've been here long enough."

"Yes, dear." She smiled at him, the lines deep around her eyes. Even in the dim light of the room, Stella could see how much Mary had aged since Stella had left for Florida—her wrinkled, ashen skin hung loosely on her angular face; her eyes hollow and dull. "Leon's seriously thinking about selling the bar."

"Really?" Stella wondered why he hadn't mentioned it.

"Are you deaf or something? I said I wanna go home now!"

Stella glanced at Mary quizzically, then back at him. Why wasn't Mary saying anything to reassure him? The situation seemed easy enough to handle. "This *is* your home, Walt," Stella said pleasantly.

Mary gave her a firm nudge in the ribs with her elbow. "Don't," she whispered. "It doesn't help."

"Why not? It's the truth. It'll make him feel better."

At the front door, Walt was twisting the knob round and round, but there was a child safety protector over it, and he couldn't get any traction. "I wanna leave this place!"

"This *is* your home, Walt." This time Stella's voice was not so pleasant. She got up, approaching him slowly. "The same beautiful home you and Mary have lived in since you were married."

He erupted like a volcano. "This is not my home! Stop lying to me! I wanna go home right now!"

By that time, Leon was back inside. Strolling toward them, he grabbed the car keys from the top bookcase. "Then, come on. Let's go."

"What are you doing?" Stella asked.

"What does it look like? We're going home."

"It's about time." Walt grunted. "Where's my hat?"

Retrieving his father's trademark sports cap from the coat rack by the door, Leon plopped it on top of his father's head. "It's right there where it belongs."

"Does it look okay?"

"It looks stunning."

"Don't be a smartass."

Off they went into the night.

As soon as they left, Mary explained it to Stella—it was a strategy they learned from one of the books Willow had brought from the library. The plan was that Leon shuttled Walt around the neighborhood for a while, and when he pulled up in their own driveway again, he'd announce to Walt that they were home.

"And that works?"

"Just watch." Mary disappeared into the kitchen, returning with a bowl of chocolate ice cream along with one of Walt's pills in her palm. As soon as she heard the car drive up, she rushed to the front door. "Welcome home, sweetheart." She hugged him.

"It's good to be here." As he replaced his cap on the rack, she scooped a spoonful of ice cream into his mouth, the pill dipped inside.

"Doesn't that taste good, dear?"

"It tastes delicious." Returning to his recliner, he sat down, leaned back, while Leon took a seat on the wing chair.

Stella stared at her husband for a minute, stunned. She had to admit it, he was learning new tricks. She thought him beyond that, the proverbial old dog who had long ago closed himself off to transformations, but here he was, changing in front of her eyes.

Maybe, just maybe, there was hope for them yet.

TWENTY

APRIL 1999:
FATHERS

O N the first of April, Leon made the decision to put the Mazurka Inn on the market, and Gus chided him for being an 'April fool'. "This building will be just one more relic to add to the unsellable collection," Gus said. Leon knew he was probably right—the neighborhood was glutted with defunct businesses, 'available to buy or rent' signs nailed or spray-painted on their boarded-up exteriors.

Later that same evening after Gus had returned to his room upstairs, the man Bennie Niezgodski had warned them about reappeared in the bar, the one in the shiny suit asking too many questions. He looked to Leon to be in his forties, with mono-grammed cuffs and manicured nails, and this time he showed up with a spikey-haired, young accomplice, also impeccably-dressed. An out-of-place duo, to be sure, in this rugged, unpretentious neighborhood.

"Are you the owner?" the older one asked.

"Yup," Leon said. "What's it to you?"

The man pulled a paper from his suit pocket. "We show that this is the address for Ricky Ziemny's art studio. If it's still a good address, we're guessing it's got to be upstairs." He eyed the wooden staircase.

"Like I said, what's it to you?"

"We're interested in buying and showing his art work."

Leon soon discovered that they were art dealers from New York City. Apparently, in death, Ricky had developed quite a following in the East Coast art world, his paintings becoming hot commodities since there'd be no more of them. Leon let the men know that he was Ricky's older brother, that it was up to him and his mother to make the decisions.

Somewhere in the middle of their conversation, he eyed Gus coming down the staircase, Gus' face exploding in panic at the sight of the two strangers. "These are art dealers from New York," Leon announced quickly, before Gus had heart failure or something. Gus sagged against the bannister in obvious relief, eventually taking a stool beside them.

The men were eager to see Ricky's studio, his works from the last few years, especially his final painting, likely the most valuable of all, but Leon put them off. It wasn't a good time, he told them. He took their business cards, said he'd be in touch as soon as he could get things in order. They seemed pleased enough, relieved to have found the right contact, and they shook his hand, and Gus' hand too, still unsteady after the false scare.

After they left, Leon poured Gus a tumbler-full of their best Glenlivet over ice, on the house, as all his drinks had been of late. "You gotta get a grip, Sultanski. Nobody's running after you. If they were, they would have caught up with you by now."

"You're probably right." Gus stared straight ahead. "I guess I'm nothing but an old cat chasing his own tail."

△△△

The next morning, Leon sat with his father at the table while Willow fried up a pan of bacon. For some reason, she had offered to cook breakfast this morning. He was glad for the break; he detested cooking almost as much as eating his own creations.

"Did I tell you that I have a boy named Leon?" Dad asked.

By now, he was well used to his father no longer recognizing him, but this was a painful new slant on it. "Dad, who do you think I am? *I am* L—" He looked up at Willow, stopping himself in midsentence. "… You don't say?"

"By George, he's got it," she muttered.

"Yup," His father continued. "We named our new baby Leon. My wife is still in the hospital." Leon nodded; the two of them had just been upstairs in his mother's bedroom—she'd felt too ill to get up for breakfast. "Isn't that right?" Walt turned his head toward Willow.

"That's right." She glanced at Leon sadly.

Folding his arms against his chest, Walt leaned back. "Wait 'til you see my baby boy. Big green eyes. Black hair. He's gonna be somebody when he grows up. You watch and see."

Willow turned around again, with a sympathetic half-smile.

Leon stood up to join her at the counter. "Looks like those eggs are about done." He scooped a helping of scrambled eggs from the frying pan onto a plate as he prepared a tray for his mother. In the process, he detected a whiff of liquor on her breath. What was that all about? "I think we should skip the bacon for Mom, what do you think?"

"That's probably a good idea," she said. "Too hard on her stomach."

He looked down at the plate; Willow had prepared the eggs to perfection. She wasn't slurring her words. She seemed to be functioning at capacity, not the slightest bit drunk. Maybe she was just having a bad morning, saw the bottle there in the cupboard, and decided to take a quick snort. Hell, he had mornings when he thought about doing that himself. He picked up the tray and took it upstairs.

When he returned to the kitchen a few minutes later, he saw that she had already placed three full plates at the table and was waving her hands over Walt's portion to cool it off faster. It looked delicious. Leon took a bite of bacon before he even sat down. Finally, something edible.

As Dad clumsily shoveled his eggs with a spoon (forks were now too difficult for him to manage), Leon spread the morning newspaper out in front of him. It had been one of his father's daily habits for as long as Leon could remember, and the Alzheimer's books kept saying that keeping up his past routines was important, fruitless as it might seem. Leon knew, of course, that the paper would remain on the same page he'd opened up for him, or end up upside down, while his father stared at it. It used to drive Leon bananas—he would grab the paper out of Dad's hands to rearrange it right-side up. It still drove him bananas, but he knew better now.

His father's eyes glazed on a photograph of President Clinton on the front page. Dropping the spoon, he gathered up a bunch of eggs with his fingers, shoving it into his mouth, half of it falling on his lap, the rest to the floor.

"Not that way, Dad. Use the spoon."

"The what?"

Leon picked it up, held it in front of him. "This is a spoon. Use it."

"Use what?"

"The spoon."

"For what?"

"Aw, skip it," Leon said softly. "Fingers are fine."

The smell of liquor on Willow's breath first thing in the morning was gnawing at the back of Leon's mind. It reminded him of the early days when he used to sniff it on Ricky's. He glanced at her across the table. It occurred to him that he knew virtually nothing about her past, mostly because he never dared ask. To ask more about her past was opening a door into Noël's world that he wanted to stay shut. He watched as Willow assisted his father with the juice. "So how is your dad doing?" he asked her, in spite of himself.

"Huh?" She eyed him curiously. "Fine."

"You never mention him."

"What do you mean?"

"I mean, you never mention him. You never talk about your family." Reaching for the butter, she scraped a big chunk on her toast. He'd never seen her eat butter before, let alone a mountain of it. "I only saw Steve once," he said.

"Oh." She glanced at him sideways, over-salting her eggs. "Did you think he looked like Noël?"

Her name, so suddenly, stabbed him. "Yeah. The whole family looked the same."

"How long were you and Noël married?"

"That's enough." He raised his fingers. "That subject's off limits."

"I figured." She salted her eggs again.

"So … are you planning to go visit your parents in California any time soon?"

"Nope. Not really."

"You know what?" He set his napkin down on the table. "You remind me of someone."

"Oh, yeah? Who?"

"Me. …You're a closed book."

She looked at him, a strange expression on her face. His

father, too, glanced up from the newspaper, then burst into song. "California, here I come ..."

"Now, where did he get *that* from?" Leon shook his head.

"You said the word *California*. I guess it stuck in his head for some reason."

His father kept on singing until he finished the entire first verse. Seemingly contented, he resumed his interest in the newspaper. "How can he remember every word to some old song, but he can't remember me?" Leon wondered.

"Alzheimer's is weird," she said. "And he does remember you."

"As a baby, maybe."

"He remembers more about you than that. The other day, he was telling me about your hot rod."

"My hot rod? Did he use that word?"

She nodded. "The yellow one."

"That was my first car. Back when I was seventeen."

Willow smiled at him. "It's kind of like he stores things somewhere inside of him—sights and sounds and music and all kinds of other bits and pieces of his life, the important things to him. And they come popping out at random."

"Like a black box inside an airplane, you mean? The one that no one gives a shit about until there's a crash?"

"Yeah, like that. Maybe we all do it; Alzheimer's just makes it more obvious. Maybe that black box is his soul or something, where he holds on to the stuff he wants to take with him."

"Take with him where?"

"Wherever he's going next."

"Willow the mystic." Leon raised his eyebrows. He was a Catholic, sure, but he never was one much for philosophizing beyond that. Heaven, hell, purgatory; the next life seemed as much of a crap shoot as this one. "… Not to change the subject, but what about school?"

"School?" Her face creased in annoyance. "Talk about things popping out of nowhere. What about it?" She got up and started clearing the dishes. "How come you're asking me all these weird questions today?"

"Tax, tax, tax, tax." Walt had picked out one of the words from a headline.

"Yeah, tax, tax, tax, tax." Leon nodded at him. "Taxes are a real bitch, aren't they, Dad?" Grinning, his father mimicked his nod as Leon refocused on Willow. "You've got a life to live, that's all. Maybe we're not being fair to you, keeping you here to take care of Dad."

"I love being here with Walt." She stopped clattering around at the kitchen sink, sat down again. "He's my best buddy. Aren't you, Walt?" Leaning over, she kissed him on the cheek.

"My sweetie-pie." Dad patted her face.

"I just don't want to see you sacrificing your future for an old man who's fading into oblivion."

"Don't say it like that! If you don't want me to be here anymore, just say so!" She tried to choke back tears.

"There, there." His father stroked her hair. "It'll be okay. Don't cry, my little Mishka. The sun is clean."

"It's got nothing to do with that," Leon said. Picking up his napkin in lieu of Kleenex, he handed it to her. "You're going to make a great nurse someday. You already are. But you need to finish your training and get your degree first. I just don't think you should keep putting school off."

She sniffled into the used napkin, wiped her eyes, blew her nose. "I'll get there someday. Just not now."

"As long as you don't forget about it … and by the way, you've got egg on your face." He flicked off a piece of scrambled egg.

As she broke into a smile, more tears formed. "You sound kind of—I don't know—*fatherly* today. Too bad you and Stella never had any kids."

"I would've made a lousy father. I *was* a lousy father." He started playing with the pepper shaker, twisting it round and round between his fingers as he fought the sudden onslaught of unwelcome memories. Eventually, he stopped the motion and sat still, his lids half-closed, the sealed door in his mind ajar. "He wasn't my natural kid; he was my wife's. But that shouldn't have mattered, should it? He was still mine."

"You mean Adam?"

"Yeah, Adam." He could picture the mop-topped child in his mind, a little blonde Beatle, playing with his balsa wood airplane, tossing a baseball, in that tiny courtyard out back of their old apartment. "I was never there for that kid. I mean, I was always there physically, but sometimes even when you're there, you're not there. If only I'd …" He stopped the sentence. "Anyway, that's the worst kind of father you can be."

"He turned out all right," she said.

"Yeah, sounds like it. No thanks to me. A big ball player." He was seeing other faces in his mind now. "You know, I knew the man who first taught your cousin how to pitch. Even as an old man, that guy was good enough to be in the Major Leagues. His name was Freddie Chavis."

"Chavis?" She sat up.

"Yeah. You know the name?"

She paused, shrugged. "Adam's probably mentioned it."

"I bet he did. Freddie was something. Quiet but mighty. He had a wife named Theckla." Pictures of the past were flooding

Leon's brain. Images, places, faces snapping into focus. "I lost track of Theckla after I … married Stella. I moved, then she must've moved … the number I had for her wasn't good anymore … But those are two people I'll never forget. I learned a hell of a lot from them."

Finally came the image he'd been fighting against.

He let himself see Noël in full detail. In the candlelight of a shadowy room. In broad sunlight. He saw her smiling. Crying. God, she'd cried a lot. He saw her beside him on top of a Ferris wheel under the stars. He saw her face beneath him in bed. The door was wide open now. He let his mind drift away. Drift away with her on a rock in front of the lake in the moonlight …

When he realized Willow was staring at him, he fought to reorient himself, to anchor himself back to the present. Noël was dead. So was Ricky. This is where he lived now.

Looking around the messy kitchen, he saw it anew; it seemed suddenly dated and rundown, littered with a counter-full of clutter and crap that Mom would never have allowed back then, in the land of where he'd been. He glanced at his demented father. Was that what it felt like to be him? Lost somewhere in a bygone world, trapped in this one? Leon was still able to bring himself back to now, to this disastrously disordered kitchen, but his father could not.

And was that so bad?

TWENTY-ONE

July 1999:
John-John's Plane

M ARY didn't want to add to Leon's worries and that's why she'd kept her shooting pains to herself for more than a month. Now that she'd awoken in a bed soaked with blood, she had no other choice but to tell him. She was still hemorrhaging down there, like a period. She spent a long time in the bathroom cleaning herself up, cutting up one of Walt's Depends to make it fit like those dreadful old menstruation products. By the time she got down to the living room, she found Leon and Walt watching television, eating their cereal together on TV trays.

"You won't believe this," Leon said. "But John Kennedy Jr.'s plane is missing."

"You mean John-John?"

He nodded.

Afraid to sit down, Mary stood in front of the television screen. CNN was reporting that the private plane which John Kennedy Jr. was piloting had never made it to the airport at Martha's Vineyard. He was traveling with his wife, Carolyn, and her sister, Lauren Bessette. Apparently the plane was late in arriving for a wedding rehearsal dinner for his cousin the night before, and now dozens of aircraft and ships were out searching for the lost plane. From afar, CNN showed a shot of a huge wedding tent assembled on the Hyannis grounds. It was so unbelievable that Mary nearly forget her own calamity for a minute. "Leon, can I see you in the kitchen?"

He followed her to the kitchen table, and she blurted it out. "I need to see Doc Podemski today. I'm bleeding inside somewhere."

"How do you know that?"

"Because my bed is covered in blood, that's how." A gulf of tears overwhelmed her.

He put his arms around her loosely; her hands remained at her sides. They'd never hugged each other much, not even when he was a child, and neither one of them was quite certain how to manage it at this stage of the game. "Don't worry, Mom. It's going to be okay."

The awkwardness of the hug, her shameful display of tears, brought her to her senses. She couldn't let Walt see how upset she was. Willow was always harping on the fact that he'd mirror whatever emotion he was being shown, and things were bad enough without him getting into the act.

It was a Friday morning, and Doc Podemski told her she could come in at high noon. Though it was Willow's day off, Leon called her and asked if she could stay with his father, and of course she was right over. As she'd done with Leon, Mary took her into the kitchen and told her the news, while Leon cleaned up her soiled bedroom and Walt snored in his easy chair. "It's a feminine problem," she whispered to Willow. "I'd rather have you there with me. Not Leon."

△△△

The long wait in the reception area was unbearable. As each name was called, Mary watched them enter the inner sanctum— screaming children being led by nervous mothers and old decrepit people, probably as old as she was—who had trouble getting out of their seats. Like her, the rest of the patients sat there awaiting their turn, mindlessly flipping through dog-eared magazines. Walt was right; this place did smell like sauerkraut.

"I hope you know how grateful I am for all your help," Mary said.

"No problem." Willow smiled.

"And so is Leon, of course, though I doubt he tells you that." Mary searched her face for any sign of unusual reaction to the mention of his name, but there was none. The two of them, Willow and Leon, had been spending a lot of time together since she'd been ill, and she'd been wondering, as she lay in her upstairs bed, if anything of significance was being shared between them.

The nurse appeared, propping the door open to the hallway that led to the examining room. "Mary Ziemny?" she called out. "The doctor will see you now."

The pelvic exam was humiliating. Mary squeezed her eyes shut and tried to think of other things as Doc Podemski probed her with a long thing he called a speculum. When she opened her eyes and saw his concerned expression, she was more afraid than embarrassed. Next, he ordered all kinds of tests, including a blood test to measure levels of CA 125, whatever that meant. Mary was glad Willow was there because she didn't understand a single word he was saying. Next, he ordered surgery—a biopsy—for first thing Monday morning. The only words she understood was the diagnosis he suspected: ovarian cancer.

△△△

The long weekend passed by slowly. Selfishly, Mary was relieved to have another Kennedy tragedy unfolding on television for the distraction it offered. The gigantic tent at the Kennedy compound was being used now as a place for prayer, not a wedding celebration. Mary was glued to the coverage.

Walt watched with her. CNN kept showing scenes of the sparkling blue sea surrounding Hyannis Port because there was really nothing else to show except past footage of John-John—as a toddler saluting his father's coffin; as an awkward teenager; as the dashingly handsome prince he'd become, his lean and lovely wife on his arm. And then there was the water again. "Look at that, would you? It's so blue." Walt said the same thing every time he saw it.

The catastrophe now seemed personal to Mary. If, by some miracle, John-John was still alive, she knew she'd be okay too. If they discovered him dead, then she would get bad news. It was silly, she knew, but silly or not, she was convinced that God had his plan and that was the way it would work, the Kennedys and her suffering together, their concurrent tragedies intermingled, and she couldn't talk herself out of it.

By the middle of Saturday afternoon, there was breaking news: A piece of luggage with Lauren Bessette's tag had washed up on the shore. Mary felt a stab in her heart. She'd just come downstairs from the bathroom, and she was bleeding down there again.

"Oh, look—the water is so blue." Walt smiled.

"Yes, it is," Mary said.

On Sunday, they stopped looking for survivors, and the 'rescue' search became a 'recovery'. All her life, Mary had been watching Kennedy tragedies on TV, one after the next, each son taking up the torch where the last one had dropped it—first Jack, then Bobby, then Teddy, before that Chappaquiddick disaster— and now the heir to the throne was gone. By the time they dismantled the wedding tent, Mary had gone numb. There was no torch-bearer left. There was no future.

ΔΔΔ

It took another week before it was confirmed. Doc Podemski's initial hunch had been right on target. "Your mother has what we call epithelial tumors in both ovaries." He was talking to Leon, not to her, the same way he'd done after diagnosing Walt's dementia.

"What does that mean?" Leon asked him.

"She has stage-four ovarian cancer."

She wanted to tell Doc to look at her when he spoke, that she was still here, that it was *her* body, not Leon's. Why were younger people so patronizing, so dismissive of the old and sick? Didn't they realize their turn was coming and sooner than they'd ever imagine, that it was just around the corner?

"So what's the treatment?" Leon said. "Radiation? Chemo?"

Doc shook his head. "Radiation and chemo may shrink the tumors but won't stop the disease. I'm afraid it's already metastasized into the liver and the lungs."

The nitty-gritty of his words floated by Mary in a blur. The gist was, she was dying. For some reason, it wasn't a shock. She took the news in as if Doc had said she needed a new furnace. Bad news, to be sure, but what could you do? Even when she heard the word *hospice*, she didn't flinch.

Leon, on the other hand, looked as if he'd been thrown against the wall. She doubted she'd ever loved him more than in that moment.

TWENTY-TWO

September 1999:
Mother Mary

AS Willow approached the Ziemny's back door that morning, she noticed the hospice nurse's gray sedan in the driveway. Leon was outside in the backyard, bending over the little replica of the Virgin Mary propped against the garage. Stopping several feet behind him, she watched as he took a small bottle of glue out of his jacket pocket and gave whatever he was holding in his hand a squirt, then pressed it against the statue and held it there. She then realized what he was doing: he was repairing Mother Mary's broken nose. She wondered if it was some small act of redemption.

The lie she was holding inside seemed heavier, chewing away at her insides. Her plan had been only to see what he was like and be gone, but maybe she should have told him he was her father right off the bat when she first came to Langston. But Ricky had died, and with Walt getting worse, the time never seemed right. And now, she'd waited too long.

He looked tired and drawn bent down in the grass that way. Still, Leon was as handsome as her mother had been beautiful. So why hadn't she turned out pretty, at least? Our DNA was a convoluted thing. And why hadn't her mother put more effort into finding him and telling him about her? She knew why, and that was the weirdest thing of all. Here she was blaming her mother for not telling him the truth when she was doing the exact same thing.

She let herself in through the unlatched back door, where she found Walt sitting alone in the kitchen, dressed only in an undershirt. A kitchen towel laid over his privates.

"Hello, buddy." She kissed him on the forehead. "Where are your pants?"

He looked down at himself. "Beats me."

Leon entered the kitchen. "Oh, shit! I forgot I left him like that!" After dashing downstairs, he came back up with a large bath towel flung over one shoulder, a clean pair of trousers on the other, both warm and fresh from the dryer. "I went outside to toss the dirty Depend into the garbage before the trash pick-up today and got sidetracked," he said. "Maybe I've got Alzheimer's too."

"Just too much on your mind," Willow said, taking a seat beside Walt.

"Look who's here, Dad—our favorite nurse." Leon opened a box of disposable briefs stacked in the corner of the kitchen and pulled one out. It was a new kind, with gathered elastic around the waist and legs, an upgrade from the usual diaper-style type with tape-ups on the sides.

"Did you win the lottery or something?" she said. "Since when did you start buying the Cadillac of briefs?"

Leon grinned at his father; the rare smile made him look younger. "Since when, Dad?"

"Since the cows came home," Walt replied.

"That sounds about right."

Willow sat back in her chair as Leon soaped up a wet washcloth in the kitchen sink and came back to his father.

"What are you gonna do with that thing?" Walt pointed at it.

"I'm gonna wash you up."

"Wash me over and out?"

"Over and out. That's right."

Willow moved to the far side of the table, diverting her eyes during the scrubbing. It wasn't like she hadn't done it herself countless times, but she wanted to give Walt the dignity of not having an audience. "I saw you out back repairing the statue."

"Yeah, it was the darndest thing," Leon said. "I was looking for garbage bags, and there it was, clear as day, lying on the garage floor—the long-lost missing nose, all in one piece. Mom's been after me forever to fix it."

"Now, don't get tricky." Walt warned as Leon cleaned him.

"I'm fresh out of tricks, Dad." He threw the washcloth toward the laundry basket on the floor, making a bullseye landing, then lifted each of Walt's feet into the clean disposable underwear, followed by the warm legs of the trousers. "Now stand up so I can pull this up for you."

Willow gazed around the kitchen, at the sink of dirty dishes, at Mary's copper Jell-O molds hanging on the walls, the rust-stained backsplash. She'd grown to love this ugly room, as she'd grown to love this old house. And Walt, oh, of course, Walt. And somehow, some way, over these past long months, something else had happened that she didn't quite expect. She'd grown to love Leon too. She loved her father.

After several frustrating moments of Leon trying to yank up Walt's things before he sat down again, the job eventually got done. "There," Leon said to him. "You're fresh as a daisy."

"I like tulips better."

"Okay, then, you're fresh as a tulip."

Satisfied, Walt picked up the morning paper, starting reading it upside down.

"How's your mom feeling today?" Willow asked.

"She's in a lot of pain. None of us slept too good last night."

Yesterday, Mary had been moaning so loudly that Willow could hear the awful sound downstairs, the cadence of her deep, agonized breaths echoing through the house like a sorrowful drumbeat. "Has Walt seen her yet this morning?"

"Oh, yeah. He told her, 'get the hell out of bed, you lazybones.'"

She glanced at the kitchen window. The trees were already starting to turn colors; the bottom limbs of the silver maples bright red in the morning sunlight. "I wonder if the leaves can sense the change that's about to come."

"Huh?"

"If they realize they're about to fall off and die."

"I doubt if leaves have feelings."

"I don't … I think that's why they get so beautiful right before they die."

He continued his dogged cleaning from his father's earlier accident, running a wet mop over the tile floor beneath his chair and the surrounding area. By now, it had become a familiar, well-oiled routine. A hamper lined with a trash bag for the soiled clothes stood off to the side of the kitchen, alongside a lidded trash can for the throwaway briefs. Even though Leon had already deposited the latest bagful of wet briefs in the backyard trash, the kitchen still smelled like urine. No matter what they did, the smell never completely went away. Retrieving a can of air freshener from the cupboard beneath the sink, Willow gave it a generous spray, enough to cover the room, and the three of them, under a foggy mist.

"What a lovely scent," Leon said. "Piss and roses."

Willow started to laugh. It wasn't that funny, but for some reason she couldn't stop. Each time she inhaled, it got funnier. She laughed until tears poured out of her eyes. When she finally got a hold of herself, she leaned back in the kitchen chair, fighting the uncontrollable urge to tell him the truth, right there and then, the same way she'd confessed it to Walt. "Leon? I need to tell you something."

"Yeah?"

She paused, the words sticking in her throat. What if telling him changed everything? She didn't want it to change. Not one thing.

"Well, I'm waiting."

She couldn't bring herself to do it. "I forgot what I was going to say."

△△△

Another of Willow's assorted duties assigned to her by Leon was one she was relishing. Now that New York City was interested in Ricky's paintings, Leon had asked her to organize his art studio. Sort through them, he told her, and take an inventory so that they could make decisions about which ones to sell.

The art studio didn't match with the rest of the Mazurka Inn. Ricky had updated it to have a more modern look—with track lighting, polished hardwood floors still covered with a tarp under his easel, and a coat of bright, clean paint. It smelled different too. Like balsam and turpentine. She loved the way the sunshine streamed through the large windows in the afternoon; loved the feel of his artwork surrounding her. Ricky had given her a fair number of lessons in this room. She'd never forget the way he had encouraged her. "You're a natural," he'd said. "You'll be the next Van Gogh." After Ricky died, Walt had allowed her to continue to do her paintings up here.

There was a lot to sort through, that was for sure. Ricky was a prolific painter with changing subjects that made it difficult to classify him in any one particular stylistic direction. And they were all here, stacked several rows thick, stashed into three closets, hanging all over the walls. The only missing painting, to her knowledge, was his final one, still resting on the easel in the Ziemny's basement the way he'd left it. She liked to go down and study it when Walt was napping. The fact that his last painting was of a weeping willow had touched her deeply.

She'd already gotten through most of the paintings from his "one color period". At first, those were among her favorites, but now she wasn't so sure. A lot of his older works on the far side of the room, mostly of the Holocaust, fascinated her. Stark images, sketched in charcoals. Or paintings in grayish and blackish oils. Ricky had told her that their grandmother, Walt's mother, the same one who had put Walt on a steamer for America, had been killed in a concentration camp, and it had haunted Ricky throughout his youth. Painting helped him release pent-up feelings, he told her, and he'd wondered aloud if it was the same for her. But they were still too pent-up for her to admit it to him.

It was late afternoon—the bar wouldn't open until seven p.m.—and she had brought up a bottle of gin to comfort her through the task. Walt had told her that she could help herself to the liquor whenever she pleased, so she'd taken him up on it. She drank these days mostly because of her persistent lies to the people she loved most. It was a burden to carry the truth around like a gunny sack of potatoes, as Walt had put it; to try to keep it hidden. She identified with Gus in that way.

Sometimes she wondered if she was an alcoholic. She doubted it, but maybe she was; just like she never considered herself bulimic even when she was sticking her finger down her throat. Things like that just happened gradually; they didn't walk in one day and introduce themselves with a big, dysfunctional label.

She took a sip from her glass beside the uncapped bottle on

the window sill. If she was an alcoholic, she handled it well, so what did it matter? She didn't get roaring drunk or anything like that; it just helped her smooth out the rough edges. No big deal.

She was distracted from her thoughts by a sudden sound behind her. When she turned, she saw Gus resting against the doorframe. "How it's going, Ahyoka?" he said. "Looks like you're making progress."

"You think so?" She smiled at him. "Wouldn't it be awesome if Ricky's paintings got famous?"

"Oh, I don't know." He came into the room, sat down on a beanbag chair in the corner. "Fame isn't such an awesome thing in my opinion."

"Maybe not." She sifted through another stack. Landscapes of every sort, from cornfields to mountain ranges. Ricky's heart wasn't in these too much; she could tell. Even his trademark flashy signature looked buttoned-down, more precise.

"So how's my friend Walt doing? I sure miss seeming him around here."

"Yeah, me too," she said. "His dementia is like a spiral. One day he seems to be in clearer focus; the next day, he's two shades worse."

"*Two Shades* worse, huh? Only an artist would put it that way." He sat and thought for a while, his thumb against his front teeth, as she rearranged the landscape canvases into the "sell" pile. "It gets like that when you're old, little Ahyoka. Sometimes our memories get fuzzy, and we rewrite our history, embellishing it. And sometimes we get a front-row seat, like a PTSD flashback, and every agonizing detail comes flooding back."

"Wouldn't it be great if they invented a pill so that we just remembered the good things?" she said.

He hoisted himself up from the beanbag chair. "That'd be

difficult to do; separate it out, I mean. Most every one of our memories comes wrapped in both good and bad."

She watched him move from painting to painting, stroking his long braid across his shoulder. "So what are you going to do when the Mazurka Inn gets sold?" she asked. "Will you stay here in Langston?"

"Not sure what I'll do yet." When he got to the end of the row, he stopped. He seemed sad today, at loose ends. Maybe just because he wasn't talking nonstop about the Kennedy assassination for a change. Ever since those men turned out to be art dealers, he seemed different somehow, quieter. "But like the song says, a change gonna come."

She didn't know what song he meant. "What kind of change?"

"You can only fight fire with fire."

"What does that mean?"

With one palm raised high in the air, his form of waving, he disappeared through the door, leaving her alone again.

Gus, like her father, was an enigma, though on opposite ends of the enigma yardstick. Puzzling over both of them, she worked for another two hours or so, sipping her gin and forming two distinct stacks: the paintings she thought they should keep on one side, the ones to offer to New York City on the other. Ultimately, it'd be Leon's decision.

The last places to sort through were the closets; she had enough time left to start with the smallest one, near the bathroom. When she opened the door, she was surprised to find a portrait of Walt staring at her, a stunning likeness from maybe thirty years ago, maybe more. He looked a little like Leon did now, without the dark brows and mustache. Somehow Ricky had managed to capture the wealth of Walt's face—the depth of his sorrows as well as his joys—no easy feat in such a treasure trove of a man.

Moving the canvas forward to see what was behind it, she let out a gasp. There was no mistaking the unforgettable, translucent eyes, painted vividly in peacock blue-green. *Mama!* She collapsed from her kneeling position to the floor. Never before had she seen her mother this close-up, only in indistinct family photos or the black and white pictures in her high school yearbooks. This portrait of her, around the time when she was Willow's age, was real enough to make it seem as if she was right there in the room with her, real enough to breathe.

Pulling the canvas out from the stack, she was amazed to find a second portrait of her mother behind it. And another after that one. And another. And another. Her mother, in every conceivable light, in every mood, every expression. The art studio pulsed with her presence.

She spread the paintings around her, sat down again on the floor, overwhelmed, bewildered, smacked with a keen awareness. She'd done it. She'd stumbled upon her own fate. She was meant to have come here to Langston. Somehow her mother had fulfilled the promise made to her in her diary, she'd found a way to stay close to her. Willow was exactly where she was supposed to be.

TWENTY-THREE

OCTOBER 1999: CONFESSIONS

EARLY that Saturday morning as Stella dressed for her day, Leon called. Mary was summoning her to her bedside, he said. Though she'd had numerous conversations with Mary since her diagnosis, this one seemed different, more purposeful and urgent from the tone of Leon's voice.

Mary's deterioration had been slow, sometimes undetectable, unless the three of them—she, Leon, and Willow—purposely paused to recall her functioning level just a week or so before. Hospice told them she was doing much better than anticipated in terms of life expectancy, but the trade-off was that the extra time allowed the pain to escalate. She was on continuous liquid morphine now, which Leon administered to her through a dropper.

As Stella mounted the stairs at the Ziemny's home, she heard nothing; no moaning or cries of misery coming from Mary's room. Maybe it would be a good day for Mary, after all, not the dire decline Stella feared. The bedroom door stood wide open, and Mary was sitting up in bed. As recently as a few days ago, she liked to have the curtains open so that she could enjoy the sunlight flooding the room. Now she preferred them closed, and it was the first thing she asked Stella to do. "Leon thinks a bright room will cheer me up," she said, "but it depresses me more."

Dutifully, Stella pulled the cord to draw them shut. Before she could sit down, Mary asked her if she would change the television channel for her too, even though she had the remote control lying beneath her own hand. "I can't stand to listen to the news, especially all that Y2K gloom and doom," she said.

Another big change, Stella thought, as she switched to an old rerun of *The Andy Griffith Show*. Mary had always been a CNN junkie.

"Do you really think the world will end in 2000?" Mary asked.

"Of course not." Taking a seat beside the bed, Stella smiled gently. "This Y2K thing is just a lot of hype. Mostly it'll be a problem with computers, but the world won't end."

"It will for me."

Stella reached for her hand, and Mary noticeably stiffened, though she allowed her to hold it as if the gesture was for Stella's sake rather than her own. Mary had never been much of a toucher. After a few more minutes, she craftily withdrew her fingers as she changed position in bed. On TV, Opie was feeling neglected as Sheriff Andy flirted with the girl who used to star on *Father Knows Best*. "Oh, just turn it off," Mary said.

Stella went back to the television, clicked the dial.

"That's better, thank you." She leaned back against her pillow. "Sometimes I feel like I'm on vacation up here. Being away from Walt, I mean. Not that he's really Walt anymore. That's terrible for me to say, isn't it?"

"Not at all. I understand what you mean." Stella sat down again.

"Do you? I'm glad you do. My husband of over half a century, and he doesn't have the slightest idea who I am. He asks Leon, 'Who's that old battle-axe over there in the bed?' He used to ask where Mary was, or talk about me as if I was still a young woman, but he doesn't do that anymore. He's forgotten all about me."

"I'm sorry."

"Yes, I'm sorry too. It's a sad thing alright, losing your husband when he's still alive." Mary turned to look at her as if she'd made some kind of faux pas. "Have I ever told you how grateful I am that you stuck by my son all these years?"

Stella was taken aback by the sudden shift in direction and the comment. "Not in so many words …"

"Well, then, I'm telling you now. I don't know where he would be without you."

"Maybe he'd be happier."

"Don't say that!" She observed the way Mary's eyes clouded, causing Stella to think it had crossed her mind too. "Leon never knew what he wanted," Mary continued. "That's always been his problem. He's that same little boy who wants to eat every piece of Halloween candy, even knowing it'll give him a terrible bellyache."

Stella tried to absorb this, but it made her uneasy. She was Leon's wife, not his nursemaid or his mother. Or his Halloween candy. What exactly was her point?

"I love you, Stella. I couldn't have dreamed of a more wonderful daughter-in-law than you. You're like flesh and blood to me."

"I love you too, Mary."

"The most important thing in the world, the *only* thing in the world—is family. My family is my heart and soul. I would've robbed a bank, if it meant keeping them safe. That's all I ever wanted—for them to be happy. You too. You're a part of my family."

Stella patted her hand. "I know how important family is to you. You don't have to tell me that. *Everyone* knows how important we are to you."

Mary stared up at the ceiling, a slow smile spreading across her face. "I spend a lot of hours here in this bed, and I have plenty of time to think. I dream about the days when my boys were small, and Walt and I were just scratching by to make a living. Those were the best days. Walt always had a good, secure job at the mills, and he'd come home tired but happy. In retrospect, the mills made him an old man before his time. Maybe they caused his dementia, I don't know."

Stella listened without responding.

"What day is today?" Mary asked.

"It's Saturday."

"Saturday." She nodded, readjusting her neck against the pillow. "I used to love Saturdays most of all. Back in those days, we used to drive to Chicago on Saturdays once or twice a year, and we'd really splurge. We'd treat the boys to a special lunch in the Walnut Room of Marshall Field's."

"We did that too." Stella grinned; it was a sweet memory she also cherished. "I loved it when our parents took us there."

"Ricky always ordered something called the Little Red Hen from the children's menu. Do you know what that was?"

"No, I guess I missed that one."

"It was breaded chicken, shaped in the form of an actual hen." She laughed. "I don't know how they did that. … As much as I loved going, I was always happiest on the drive back home again. … Everyone was still alive then. Father Chet was our priest. When you're young, it seems like everyone will live forever, doesn't it?"

She seemed totally lost in her daydreams. Stella just let her keep on talking.

"You know what I do when I lie here sometimes? I close my eyes and pretend that the world downstairs is still the same—that Walt is working, the boys are at school, and I'm just being 'an old lazybones', like Walt calls me now, just taking an afternoon nap. That's ridiculous, isn't it?"

"No, that's not ridiculous at all."

"My poor Ricky." Stella watched Mary snap from her reverie, the dramatic change in her face as she made the shift. "He died much too soon."

"Yes, he did."

"He was always my heart, you know. Part of me died with him."

"I know. But he's in a better place."

"It's hard for me to imagine a better place than Langston used to be."

A melancholy gripped Stella. "You're lucky to have wonderful memories like that. Many people don't."

Mary turned to look at her. "I'm sorry, sweetheart."

"What are you sorry about?"

Mary searched her face, a look of desperation in her eyes. "I'm sorry that life with my son hasn't been the best for you. That's what I wanted to talk with you about."

Stella sat up. Here it came, whatever *it* turned out to be.

"Stick by Leon. Please. Promise me that you will."

"I've always stuck by him. You said it yourself."

"I know, I know." Her eyes were still locked on Stella's. "And I know this year has been particularly hard for you—all the time Leon has devoted to us, instead of to you. But I won't be around much longer, and Walt probably doesn't have long either. What I'm saying is, wait this thing out. Once we're out of the picture— and we will be soon—Leon will have all the time in the world for you. Just for *you*."

Stella turned away. As she considered what Mary was saying, she realized she hadn't thought about it before, at least not quite in those terms. But her mother-in-law was right. When his parents died, Leon would be all alone.

"I know he hasn't been the husband you hoped he'd be. You're a wonderful, beautiful girl who deserved better."

It was almost the exact same thing Gene had said to her.

She glanced at Mary. Somehow she had repositioned herself to be lying flat again, her eyes upward, unfocused. Stella believed she understood what this was all about. Mary was probably doing what the hospice pamphlets called 'life review' and trying to relieve herself of the deep-seated guilt that was weighing her down. It had been her life's mission to protect her family from harm, and now she was second-guessing the choices she'd made along the way, including the fact that she had pushed Leon into marrying Stella—both before and after Noël Trudeau.

It was a load she could help lift from her shoulders. "Mary, look at me." She waited until Mary turned her head toward her. "Stop blaming yourself. I wanted to marry Leon as much as you wanted me to. Back in those days, he was the only thing I wanted."

Mary broke into wistful littles sniffles—that was all she had the strength for—and Stella enfolded her into her arms gently, amazed by how bony and fragile she'd become, like a tiny twig that could be snapped in two under the slightest pressure.

Composing herself, Mary continued. "And I'm so sorry that— *that Noël woman*—ever came into his life. She's the one who ruined it. But she's dead. Dead! ... Father Burton comes to see me regularly. He prays over me, reassures me that I've been a good, faithful Catholic, that I've earned my place in heaven. ... I'm hoping he's right. ... He tells me to make my peace with those I love. He says I need to forgive and be forgiven. Please forgive me, Stella."

"There's nothing to forgive you for. You and I have always been on the same team."

She kissed Stella's hand, no visible relief in her eyes. "Thank you, dear. I don't have much longer, you know. A few more days only."

"Is that what hospice told you?"

"No, they don't know. They can only guess about these things. But a person knows. My mother knew, and I told her she was wrong, but she died the very day she said she would. People know when their time is up."

Stella was silent. She wasn't sure what to say.

"Now, Leon … he's really surprised me these past few months. He's taking such good care of his father now, isn't he?"

"Yes, he is," Stella said.

"Who would've ever thought that?"

"Not me."

"Or me. It's funny all the things we think we know, but then we find out we're wrong. … Do you like Willow?"

"Willow? Sure. I don't know her that well, but she's been a big help to you and Walt. And to Leon too."

"Yes, to Leon too. She's been good for him. For all of us. She's innocent, you know. And I want you to like her."

"I do like her, Mary." Stella wondered why that was important to her.

"Good. I'm glad. Thank you, Stella." She kissed her hand again. "Now, would you send my son upstairs? Tell him I need to talk to him."

△△△

Mary listened to the sound of Stella's footsteps grow faint on the stairs. As she waited to hear Leon's familiar, pounding gait, she started praying. When she opened her eyes, he still wasn't there. What was taking him so long? She prayed again, this time for the strength to do what she was about to do. She could feel her life slipping away. Or maybe it was just her fears getting the better of her. Father Burton told her that everyone was afraid, but that we had to go ahead and do the things we feared the most anyway, afraid or not. That was what courage was, he said; what God expected from us. And she was too close to the grave to be going rogue now.

At last, she heard the sound of his footsteps on the stairs, stopping suddenly outside her door. He stood in the doorway, tentative and apprehensive, like that little boy who used to hang in the doorway of his little brother's room when he got sick with another one of his nerve attacks. "Come in," she said to him. "Sit down with me."

And he did. She turned onto her side so that she could have a good, clear look at him. "You're such a handsome boy."

"I'm an old man, Mom. Not a boy."

"Well, that may be, but you're still a sight for sore eyes. That's the way we used to put it, back in my day. When you were a child, I used to wonder where you got your looks from." The softness in the memory disappeared. "Then I realized you got them from my father. He was a handsome devil, you know. More devil than handsome." Leon squirmed in his chair. "Did I ever tell you that my father had lots of lady friends on the side? Mother knew it, of course, but she pretended she didn't. Pretended to everyone except us, that is. She cried to me and my brothers all the time about him—the lipstick she found on his collars, the way he smelled like a whore when he came home, what a worthless bum he was ..."

Leon got up from the chair, stood by the window.

"I won't be here on this earth much longer, you know. ... What is today?"

"It's Saturday."

"Oh yes. Stella told me that. I'll be gone by Wednesday."

"You don't know that, Mom."

"Of course, I know that! Why does everyone tell me I don't know that? Someday when you're in this position, you'll know when you're dying too."

He was making that face of his again, close to a wince, the expression that made her feel as if talking with her for any extended period of time was excruciating. She rolled onto her back again, looking at the ceiling, saying another prayer inside her head. Maybe it *was* excruciating for him. She harped on him, always had; she knew that. Even now, when she realized how much she loved him, how proud of him she was, she was still taking her little digs because that's the only way she knew how to communicate with him. "I've been hard on you, haven't I?" she said.

"No."

"Stop lying to me. I'm your mother. I know when you're lying."

He shrugged.

She motioned to him to return to the chair, and he sat. "I don't know why I'm that way with you."

"Because I remind you of your no-good, lousy father?"

"Yes, I suppose that's it. … That, and the fact that things always came so much easier for you than they did for Ricky. Your good looks. All the ladies. … Poor Ricky."

His posture drooped. He was no longer making the wincing expression, but he looked like a tire with the air gone out.

"I know it's too late," she said, "but I'm hoping you can forgive me."

"Don't do this, Mom. There's nothing to forgive."

With effort, she tried to sit up. "Can you prop up my pillow, dear?"

Holding her forward while he adjusted her pillows against the headboard, he helped her lean back against them.

"Ah, that feels good." She closed her eyes for a second. "Thank you."

"I better go check on Dad now."

"Not just yet." She drew a deep, extended breath. "There's something I need to tell you first. But, frankly, I'm afraid."

He sat down again, reluctantly.

"Do you remember when you and Stella went on that little trip to Niagara Falls?"

He glanced at his watch. "That was a helluva long time ago."

"Yes, it was. You were only married for a few months, but you'd already moved into your beautiful new home. Of course, it wasn't so beautiful back then, not like the way you've fixed it up now."

He was looking at his hands, getting bored or impatient she presumed, so she better get straight to the point before he ran off. "Anyway, I went over every afternoon, just like you asked me to do—to get your newspaper and mail. … And a letter came one day."

She waited so long to continue that Leon turned suddenly toward her as if he thought she'd died in mid-sentence. There were tears in her eyes. "What's wrong, Mom? Are you in pain?"

"Not physical pain, dear." With effort, she lifted her fingers to her face, wiped the dampness from her cheeks and eyes. "The letter had been floating around for a while. It was addressed to your old apartment at Adele Litka's house—Adele was such a prissy woman, wasn't she?—but eventually, it got forwarded to the right place, and I—."

"That trip was ancient history." He interrupted. "Why are you talking it about now?"

"Because of that letter," she said. "That letter was from Noël."

He stood up, frozen in front of his chair, an agony darkening his eyes.

She turned away. "I recognized her handwriting—it was so extravagant. I thought, why in the world is she writing to you after all this time? You were happily married to Stella, and that girl had given you and your brother so much heartache that I couldn't stand to see her trying to tear you apart all over again. I know I shouldn't have opened it. But I did."

"What did it say?"

Was his voice bitter cold as an arctic wind or had it lost every ounce of its strength? She couldn't tell which. "She wrote that she was pregnant with your child."

His eyes looked wild, crazed. "That's impossible! She couldn't have kids."

"Well, that's what I thought too. That was what you'd told us anyway. And here was this letter out of the blue, years after your divorce. So naturally, I thought she was trying to pull something, pull you away from Stella with some new trick. And if that trick didn't work, the other one would."

"Other one?"

She closed her lids, urged herself to say it quickly; it was almost over. "She said that both of them couldn't survive the birth. And she'd already chosen the baby."

"Good God, Mom!"

When she opened her eyes, she saw his fingers pressed against his cheeks as if he was holding his face together. "How the hell could you keep a thing like that from me?"

"I did it for your own good! You and Stella were just starting a new life!"

"Oh, my God!" He covered his eyes with his hands. "How could you have done that to me?"

Mary tried to get up, but she didn't have the strength.

"What did you do with the letter?"

"I burned it."

"You *what*? Oh, sweet Jesus."

Never before had she seen such a dreadful expression on his face, on anyone's face. That muscle in his cheek was throbbing fiercely. "You've got to forgive me, Leon. I thought I was doing the right thing, for all of us. I thought she was lying! I thought she was trying to—"

"None of that was your call to make!"

A spasm of pain ripped through Mary's abdomen. She clutched her pelvic area. Leon was propped up against the wall. "I know I did a terrible thing," she said. "But I did it because I loved you. I've always loved you, even when I didn't show it. And I'm so proud of you, the way you've taken care of your father. And me now too." His eyes had gone from crazed to dead. What had she done to him? "But here's the good part. The best part. The very best part. …Willow."

"Willow?" His jaw dropped; finally, he'd made the connection, she could tell. "Are you saying that Willow is my daughter?"

"Yes."

"How do you know that? Did she tell you that?"

"She didn't have to. I knew it as soon as I met her."

She watched him flee from the room, heard him thunder down the stairs. Collapsing against her pillow, she felt relief more than anything else. The poison, far worse than cancer, was finally out of her. She could have died with it inside her, but she'd chosen not to. She had to do it. For Willow.

△△△

Stella was sitting downstairs with Walt listening to Beethoven on the radio as Leon talked with his mother upstairs. She wondered if

Mary was delivering the same kind of pep talk for their marriage that she'd given to her. For the first time in many moons, Stella felt clear-headed about what she needed to do. And it wasn't for Mary's sake; it was for her own. She was going to give her marriage everything she had—one final, full-throttle shot—come what may.

Willow was lugging up another one of Ricky's paintings that she'd found in the basement, an abstract work in various hues of blue. "Look at this." She held it up to Walt. He started tracing some of the odd shapes in the air, then reached out to grab them as if they were three-dimensional objects. "What do you see?" she asked him.

"Crispy sky with no edges."

"Kind of like heaven?" Willow asked. His answers made no sense, but Willow always pretended they did.

He smiled at her. "Happy place, happy times. Let's go!"

Just then Leon came hurdling down the stairs, his thick silver-and-black hair falling into his blazing eyes. "I'm going out!" he barked. Grabbing the keys, he slammed the door behind him before either one of them could ask a single question.

"What on earth?" Stella got up and moved to the window, pulling open the drapes in time to see his car backing out of the driveway, almost hitting the trash can, and careening into the street.

TWENTY-FOUR

October 1999:
Moroccan Lanterns

LEON drove around aimlessly for hours. He didn't know where he was heading, maybe not consciously, but a definite destination revealed itself when he noticed the road signs an hour later. He was halfway to Willow, Ohio.

He tried to disentangle his thoughts as he drove. He felt betrayed by all of them—by his mother certainly; by Willow for her silence; even by Noël for lying about her infertility. Maybe it was all a lie and Willow wasn't even his child, but the math added up: She was born eight months after he'd taken Noël away to the Moonstone Inn; one month prematurely. Why hadn't he figured it out sooner? Why didn't Noël try harder to reach him? And why— oh, God, why—did she let herself die?

By the time he was on the straight, two-lane road with twenty more miles to go, his thoughts turned inside out. He no longer blamed Noël; he blamed Willow. Surely, she had to have known all along that he was her father, otherwise, why would she have shown up here, insinuating herself into every corner of their lives? Why not reveal her true identity? Did she have some sort of devious plan, yet to unfold? Was she after him for his money or for her rightful inheritance? Ultimately, though he knew it was unconscionable to think it, he blamed her for being born, for taking that life, that most precious life, away from him.

By the time he entered the city limits of Willow, his heart was swollen with the heaviness of self-recrimination. All of it, every piece of it from A to Zed, was his own goddamned fault. No one else's. While Noël's life was ending because of him, he'd been going on with his own ridiculous life, and she died believing he didn't care enough to respond to her letter, to come to her. While he was going on with his own life, gadding about Europe, Tampa Bay, all over tarnation, he'd left that forsaken little girl, his daughter, alone to flounder. Did Willow even know her mother had sacrificed her own life for hers?

It was too much to absorb; he would never find peace. Not now, not ever.

He was a fool. Ricky had known the truth about Willow all along. Even his mother had recognized her as his daughter. Not only was he a fool, he was dense and hard-headed and selfish. Unspeakably selfish. And now it was too late.

△△△

After Leon had rushed out of the house and Stella had gone upstairs to check on Mary, Willow sat stewing in the living room. When Stella came back down a few minutes later, she announced that Mary wanted to speak with her right away. Willow was dazed with dread; she had a sinking sense that Leon's hasty departure had something to do with her. Welts were popping out on her cheeks, hot and itchy.

When Willow entered her bedroom, Mary was propped up against the headboard. She looked like a different woman—there was a rawness and clarity to her face, as if a dozen rough coatings of paint had been scraped away, and this was the original Mary underneath.

She smiled when she saw Willow, reached for her hand. And then she told her the whole truth, confessing her culpability about her mother's letter. She was telling her this, Mary said, because she didn't want her to think, not for one moment, that her father had willingly rejected her.

Though Willow should've hated her for it—the whole trajectory of her life would have been different if Mary hadn't destroyed the letter—how could she? Until that moment, Willow didn't know such a letter even existed. Her mother had left that part out of her diary, probably to spare her feelings when it had remained unanswered. But the fact was, her mother *had* found him, she *had* believed in him enough to tell him the truth. And the fact was, Mary had felt threatened enough to burn the letter, certain of the choice he would have made.

Mary was sobbing now, telling her how much she'd grown to love her over this past year-and-a-half, how she'd become one of the greatest blessings of their lives, and how sorry—how very sorry—she was to have cheated them all out of more time together. Willow reached out to comfort her, and they embraced. No, she didn't hate Mary; oddly enough, its opposite stirred her heart, a deep sense of compassion for this frail, fragile woman—her grandmother—whose veneer had chipped off and revealed her to be so painfully vulnerable.

"Walt's looking for you today," Willow said as she left the room.

"He is? Thank you for telling me that, sweetheart. And here I thought he'd forgotten me." Mary lifted her gnarled fingers over her chest. "But don't bring him up here. Let him remember the Mary he's searching for. … I wish you'd known that one too."

∆∆∆

Willow was a decrepit town, devoid of any evidence that it had ever been named for the abundance of weeping willows that used to dot its landscape. A keen sense of loss gripped Leon. Other than that, it looked exactly the same, the same three-block downtown with the same buildings with the same names, just unkempt and decaying, which seemed the worst thing it could have become. It would've been less painful if he had found it different—re-shingled, repurposed, unrecognizable—but not this. Not neglected and abandoned, as he had left her.

When he pulled into the arched gateway of the Garden of Resurrection cemetery, he was deluged with memories of the few times he'd been there before. It wasn't difficult to find the Trudeau family plot. The grass had grown thick and undisturbed over their graves without one flower, one decoration of remembrance, on any of them. He read the names: her father—old, despicable Jack— had died, but the other names were no surprise; her mother, Lily, her brothers, Adam, Bo, and Monroe, her Aunt Clarissa. Noël was not there. Stupidly, his hopes soared for an instant, as if her absence meant her death wasn't real, that it was all a nightmare.

It was true what they said: Buried emotions were like live wires, and his were unearthed. As he searched for her grave, every ounce of his being throbbed with longing for her. Years ago, she had pointed out to him the general vicinity of the area in which she hoped to be buried, beneath the grove of weeping willows. But the landmark was gone, the willows long since died, collapsed in a decaying heap. He wended his way through the rows of headstones, heading in the approximate direction he remembered, scanning each marker. He hunted for over an hour, until suddenly—. He stopped. There, in the finality of granite, was her name: *Noël Trudeau: 1946-1973*.

He sank to his knees.

He stayed that way; how long was anyone's guess. He stayed

that way until the late afternoon shadows grew long and lean, until his legs went numb. He said everything he could possibly think of to say to her, but it all kept coming back to the same truth: He loved her—beyond the mountains of regrets and apologies, beyond the rivers of lost hopes. He loved her, living or dead, then and now. When the unbearable moment came to leave her, he kissed her cold tombstone as tenderly as flesh and blood.

△△△

Walt seemed to pick up on Willow's melancholy and was especially sweet all day, not an ounce of trouble or protest as she cleaned him and fed him and toileted him and played music for him. He used to like the big bands but now classical music soothed him, so she played Vivaldi, which she perceived to be his favorite composer, though probably just because it was her own.

All the while she wondered where Leon had vanished. Did he hate her now? She was wrong, so wrong, to have let the subterfuge go on for so long. Though she wasn't much used to praying, she closed her eyes and pleaded to Walt's forgiving God that her father would be okay.

When Walt was safe in bed, she went back downstairs and into the kitchen, opening her bag and taking out her mother's diary. She always carried it there secretly in the hope that one day the right moment might present itself—when she would confess the truth and show Leon the diary as confirmation. Opening it to one of the well-worn pages, she read it again:

Let me tell you about your father. He's a complicated man, very much a man whose actions speak louder than his words and often belie them. He may not say the right things, but he always ends up doing them. He's carved with so many holes inside, yet when it's

darkest, he shines through his brokenness like a Moroccan lantern.
And the light is magical.

Willow had waited long and hard for that side of him to show
up. And finally, it did. But what side would show itself now?

Stella had gone home hours ago, ignorant of what had
transpired, or so Willow assumed based on the way she was
behaving—completely perplexed as to why he had stormed out of
the house, his prolonged absence. She told Willow to call her the
moment he resurfaced from wherever it was he'd gone. *Resurfaced*,
that was the word she'd used, a cavalier choice, Willow thought.

△△△

It was pitch-dark by the time Leon walked through the back door.
He was relieved to find the house dark, quiet; he was tired as a dead
man and couldn't take one more emotion.

To his surprise, Willow was waiting for him in the living room;
he found her huddling in the corner near the front door, as if ready
for quick escape. He stared at her. Her eyes were Noël's, not so
much the color, the shade of green was more like his own, but the
shape of them. How come he hadn't noticed? She was coiling a
strand of hair around her index finger, the same way her mother
used to do. He'd pictured this moment all the way home, but he
still didn't know what to say, how to say it, where to begin. "Why
didn't you tell me?" he said.

"Stella's worried. Call her and tell her you're okay."

"Stella can wait. I asked you a question." It came out harsh; he
could hear the harshness in his own voice, and he hated himself for
it. "You knew all along I was your father?"

"Yes."

"Why didn't you tell me?"

"I was afraid."

"Afraid of what?" To his horror, she looked petrified, her eyes widening. "Of *me*?"

Emerging from the corner, she stood by the stairs, one hand on the post cap of the banister. "At first, I was afraid that telling you wouldn't change a thing. And then, later, after I got to—*know* you—I was afraid that it'd change everything."

"It does change everything."

She looked down.

Here was the crux of it. The part he couldn't forgive himself for; the part he couldn't get past. "Your mother must've hated me for abandoning her."

"Meaning, you hate me for killing her."

The comment, her sorrow, the self-loathing in her eyes, the fact that she was blaming herself for Noël's death, snapped him out of whatever contrite confusion was holding him back from her. "Oh, Willow, I don't hate you."

A sob choked in her throat.

He approached her slowly, uncertain of his next move. "Look, I don't know how to do this. Be a father, I mean. I'll tell you something else I don't know. I don't know how I got so lucky to have a perfect daughter like you just show up on my doorstep. I hope you don't hate *me* for not being the one who raised you into that person."

She couldn't fight her tears any longer, and he put his arms around her, instinctively. This was his child. His and Noël's. He'd known Willow was at loose ends, that she'd felt lost and alone, that she drank too much. His little girl, who had suffered too long by herself. But even with all that to bear, she managed to be brave and good and loving and teach him how to care for his own father. She was a miracle in every way that mattered to him.

"I've been doing a lot of thinking," he said, stroking her hair as she wept. "You have a piece of everyone inside of you—your beautiful mother, of course; your artsy Uncle Ricky; your quirky old grand-dad; and you're a deep thinker and healer like your Uncle Adam. I see them all. They're there. They're all alive again, in you. And I don't know why I was so goddamned stupid that I didn't see it sooner."

At last, the unthinkable happened, he broke down; engulfed by the power of something he'd not felt before, strange and new as it was—a father's love.

△△△

Moments later, still holding Willow in the darkness, she looked at him through her tears. "Didn't I get anything from you?"

"Of course." He smiled. "You're a smart ass."

She burst into laughter. "How do you always make me laugh and cry at the same time?" She wiped her eyes with the back of her sleeve. "But I hope I get something more than that from you. I hope I can be a Moroccan lantern too."

"What does that mean?"

"You were wrong about Mom. She didn't hate you for not coming to her."

"And how would you know that?"

He watched her go into the kitchen, open up her bag, and come back to him. "Here." She shoved a spiral notebook with tattered edges against his chest. "Read her diary. See for yourself."

TWENTY-FIVE

OCTOBER-NOVEMBER 1999: ALL SOUL'S DAY

THE phone in Stella's house finally rang late that same Saturday night. "What on earth was that all about?" she said to Leon. "Why did you take off like that?"

"You know Mom," he said. "She has a way of pushing my buttons. Even when she's dying. I just had to get out for a while, that's all."

Stella figured it was something like that. By now, she was well versed in Mary's insufferable ways. Truthfully, she wondered if her mother-in-law had also done a number on her, the same manipulative mind game. Their little talk that morning had turned Stella around 180 degrees, filling her head with a fierce determination to not only try to renew her commitment to Leon, but to make him fall in love with her again too. There was no disputing that his family soon would be gone from this earth and Leon would have nowhere else to turn. For the first time, it'd be just the two of them. Mary or no Mary, she owed it to the many years she'd invested in this marriage to give it one more shot.

All day long, she'd been looking through their wedding album, staring into her own youthful eyes as she beamed at her new husband, trying to rekindle her own lost hopes, their shared dreams, the thrill she felt when he took her into his arms on their wedding night and made passionate love to her, the same way he'd once made love to her in the back seat of a car when his marriage to Noël was collapsing; Stella's ultimate triumph. After the photo album, she'd gotten out his old LPs and played music from those early years, before Noël had infected their lives. Stella had closed her eyes, drifted off, remembering. And sure enough, her desire for Leon was reawakening.

"Come home to me tonight," she said to him now on the phone, her voice soft and low. "I've missed you so much, darling. Come home and let me show you how much."

A long pause lingered on the other end of the line; maybe it wasn't that long, but it felt that way to her; it felt like it stretched out for miles and miles, into an endless ribbon of open, empty highway.

"I can't come tonight, Stella, you know that," he said, finally. "My mother is dying."

△△△

Once Willow got back to the Mazurka Inn, she was wide awake; she couldn't even fathom trying to fall asleep. She sat on a bar stool in the dark. Over the past few weeks since Mary had taken a turn for the worse, they'd closed the place completely, and it was likely to remain so. There wasn't one taker who was interested in buying it. She poured herself a scotch. A stiff one.

Her secret was finally out. She officially had a father now; a father who accepted her and wanted to love her, whether or not he did yet. And she had a grandfather who loved her, in whatever vague way he still could, and a grandmother who cared about her too. The agony was that they were going away soon, her grandfather fading away, her grandmother dying, and her father would eventually move back home and resume his life with Stella. She'd be squeezed out. Being invisible had been safer. If no one saw you in the first place, you couldn't really lose them.

She wished she could wind back the clock to when she was a child. How would it have been to grow up in Leon and Stella's home? Would Stella have resented her the way Aunt Betsy did, or would she have been a good step-mom? It wouldn't have mattered really, because she would've had her father, her Uncle Ricky, and her grandparents, and they would have showered her with so much love that being someone, being seen, wouldn't be as frightening as it was now. She was twenty-six years old, and she had no clue who she was or where she was heading.

She went upstairs, took out a blank canvas just like her, and began painting. She mixed dark colors, dramatic colors, arresting colors, and formed wild, painful strokes across the blankness, tears pouring from her eyes as she manipulated the various brushes, fat ones and thin ones, this way and that, till there wasn't an inch of white bleeding through. Why was she crying so much? She'd spent a lifetime bottling up her tears, and now they came pouring out without warning. She had to get herself back in control. Emotions left you on a precipice, and she was in freefall.

It wasn't until dawn was breaking outside the window that she became aware that her brushstrokes had changed without her noticing, the colors too, the shading, the pressure she was using. On top of all that blackish-purplish blob of her life, there was light—bright blues and white. And hints of yellow.

△△△

Leon waited until Sunday morning, after he'd fed his dad breakfast and was snoring contentedly in the La-Z-Boy, to go upstairs to talk to his mother.

She was wide awake, a grayish tone to her face, though her

ankles, uncovered, were blotchy, red and purplish. "I was hoping you'd come back to me," she said.

"How are you feeling?" She hadn't urinated all day; her hands looked swollen.

"I'm ready to meet my maker, if that's what you mean." Her voice still sounded strong. "But now I kind of wish I could stick around for a while longer. I'd like to see you be a father."

Leon sat down on the bed. "I can't begin to know what I'm supposed to say right now, Mom. I'm feeling my way through this thing the best I can. I only wish you'd told me the truth long, long ago. Especially for Willow's sake. We lost a lot of time."

"I know that, but maybe things happen in their own right time."

He didn't reply.

"I have regrets too, believe me. But I can't change them." She inhaled a deep breath, coughed a little. "It is what it is. After all is said and done, and it has been, tell me one more thing. Tell me that you forgive me."

He closed his lids. He knew he had no choice but to forgive her. And to do it right now, this moment, or the chance would be lost forever. He opened his eyes. She looked birdlike against the pillow, sunken into it. He'd figure it out later. "Yeah, Mom. I forgive you." He hoped he sounded convincing enough.

"I knew you would." She smiled. "Now I can die in peace. And you and Willow and Stella can be a real family."

The thought jarred him. How like his mother to wrap this jumbled mess together in a neat, little bow and tie it up nice and pretty. Stella had miscarried her child, so now she could have Noël's. Done. Perfect. His mother was like a pencil, a sharp point on one end, a big eraser on the other. "Does Stella know about Willow?" he asked. "Did you tell her?"

"Of course not, dear. That's your business, isn't it? I wouldn't dream of interfering."

He tried to ignore the irony.

"But she'll understand," she said. "Stella loves you and she always will—warts and all."

△△△

Later that same night, she slipped into a coma. And true to her word about the timing of her death, she died two days later, the first Tuesday in November, on All Soul's Day.

TWENTY-SIX

November 1999: Wall of Fame

THE day after Mary's funeral, Stella informed Leon that it was time for Walt to move into their home. She also announced her retirement from the steel mills, effective immediately, so that she could assist him in caring for Walt full-time. "Willow can still help out once in a while," she said. "That way we can go out for dinner, maybe even get away for the weekend now and then." She thought it was the perfect plan.

△△△

Though it was the last thing Leon needed or wanted, what excuse could he give? He hadn't told her Willow was his daughter, mostly because revealing that secret would mean another round of endless drama, and he was emotionally reamed out. His father was a full-time job and whatever was left of him was reserved for his daughter.

A week later, Dad was transported into their first-floor den, a sunny room with French doors, just enough space for a hospital bed, a dresser, and his trusty, old La-Z-Boy. "What is this place? Some kind of snazzy hotel?" he asked.

△△△

After helping Walt get settled that first day, Willow was able to spend some time alone with Stella. Willow liked her well enough, but only up to a point, and Stella crossed over it whenever she insisted she knew best when it came to Walt's care. Apparently, Stella had called one of her friends in Chicago whose father had Alzheimer's and they were on the phone for over an hour. After that, she seemed to believe she'd acquired some kind of carte blanche to do whatever she wanted. "Agreeing with him all the time only makes him more confused," she explained to Willow. "Every now and then, you have to lay down the law to keep him in tow, just like a child."

How would she know how to raise a child?, Willow thought bitterly.

Everyone had *plans* now. Everyone, except Willow. Thank heavens, for the art exhibition.

Three days ago, a man by the name of Jorge Jimenez had made an offer on the Mazurka Inn, provided he could get the financing, and he planned to turn it into a Mexican restaurant. After that, Leon had made his own plan—he decided that the bar was going to be used one final time for a showing of Ricky's artworks to those dealers from New York, open to the whole neighborhood, as a gesture of farewell. He hired a couple of guys to help Willow ready the place—install the right lighting, hang the paintings with invisible wires, sturdy yet attractive, while saving the walls from a zillion nail holes. Willow knew it was a splurge for Leon, but he wanted to honor his brother's memory. Besides that, he'd get the money back and then some, if even a few paintings sold. In the meantime, Gus remained upstairs at the Mazurka Inn, spinning his own plans.

It was difficult for Willow to move forward when the past kept getting in the way. At least, that's how she was feeling as she mentally prepared herself for the difficult task of transforming the bar into an art gallery. Somehow, she had to summon the courage to dismantle Walt's hallowed wall of fame, picture by picture, snapshot by snapshot, of the hearty individuals who had once shaped the neighborhood.

She stood on top of a chair to remove the highest rows first. Down came the unknown Busias in their babushkas, the skinny steelworkers in coveralls hoisting mugs of beer after a hard day's shift, bygone Catholic school children standing alongside nuns in full black-frocked regalia and white paper-plate headdresses, Ricky's freckled-face high school graduation picture, and dozens of couples on their wedding day, including Leon and Stella. She stared at that photo the longest—the two of them in their white winter wedding wonderland, dressed in fancy white clothes, surrounded by white flowers, all of it happening at the same time she was growing in her mother's womb, waiting and hoping.

"There go Walt's memories." She heard Gus' voice as he came down the stairs.

"I know," she said. "It makes me feel horrible to do this. It's like a metaphor for what's happening to him."

"Did you recognize *me* in that picture?" he asked.

"No way. Which one?"

He walked over to a black and white photo in the bottom row, pointed at it. A young man, twinkling black eyes and coal-black hair with a Native American headband around his forehead, sat posing behind a full set of drums.

"You played drums?"

"Did I play drums?" Gus grinned. "You bet I did. I played all the high school dances back in the '50s. I had my own group—the Drumbeats. See? The name's right there on the bass."

She leaned in closer. "Oh, yeah. So it is."

He sat down at the bar. "When does Jimenez take over the keys to this place?"

"Leon said they're closing on the tenth of December."

"Less than a month away." As he yanked a tiny calendar out of his pocket, she noticed a turquoise ring in the shape of an arrow on his left middle finger. She'd not seen that one before and wondered if it meant something. "That's good. It gives me some time. There's going to be a full moon on December seventh."

"So?"

"So I need a full moon for a fire ceremony," he said.

"What's a fire ceremony?"

"You'll see for yourself, if you want to. You're invited to come. I think it might do you some good, Ahyoka."

ΔΔΔ

For the umpteenth time that Saturday night, Walt was howling that he wanted to go home, and Stella couldn't stand it anymore. After just a few days of this, she was already dead tired, weary to the marrow. Foolishly, she thought she'd be able to confine him to the den, but the downstairs was already overrun with his geriatric accoutrements—bags of unused Depends, dirty diaper bins, his roving commode, cases of Ensure, waterless shampoo, powder to thicken his food, and their ugly TV trays, one for Leon and one for him; not to mention that dreadful La-Z-Boy that permanently reeked of urine no matter how many times a day she changed the disposable pad or sprayed it with Lysol. Caregiving was an endless series of repugnant tasks, tasks that multiplied by the hour, tasks that sucked them dry of any shred of personal space or breathing room.

Leon had driven Walt around the neighborhood a total of four times that night, but the trick no longer worked. Walt wanted his mother, and no one else would do. "Walt, your mother is dead!" Stella snapped, at last. "She died years go."

"Mama died?" His sad, old eyes widened in grief. "I just talked with her. She was just here."

"No, you didn't," Stella said. "That's impossible."

Leon stood up from his seat, frowning at her. "No, it's not impossible. You're absolutely right, Dad. Stella made a mistake. Your mama just went out for a little while. She asked us to take care of you while she's gone."

He looked at Leon, a lost child-man, trapped between worlds. The guilt tore at Stella. "Then, Mama's okay?"

"She's fine and dandy."

"Why are you encouraging his hallucinations?" she whispered in a resentment she was ashamed of harboring—his kindness to his father versus his lack of sympathy for her. "Just give him the Risperidone."

"And why would I do that? He's finally seeing the one person he's been searching for his entire life."

It took more than two hours of cajoling to finally get Walt settled down enough to fall asleep in his recliner. Afterward, Stella brought him a blanket and covered him up for the night, kissed his forehead. There was no use waking him; he could sleep there just as well as the bed, maybe better.

"I knew moving him in here was a mistake," Leon told her. "Change isn't good for him."

"Just give him time to get used to it." She was determined to make this thing work.

△△△

Since the day his father had arrived, Leon had insisted on remaining downstairs with him at night, sleeping on the living room sofa with one eye open. He blamed her for the arrangement since Stella didn't want her inside doors ruined with all kinds of locks, but that same Saturday night, she was somehow able to convince him to come upstairs to their bedroom and get a good night's sleep.

"We have that ugly security door locked up tight, and nothing can happen to him down there. The worst he can do is roam around."

Drained as she was, she seized this as her chance. While Leon showered in the bathroom, she managed to sneak a bucket of iced champagne and two glasses up the stairs before setting them down on the nightstand and slipping into a sheer black negligee that she'd purchased in Florida a while back, never worn. Gazing at her reflection in the dresser mirror, her golden Florida glow long faded, she looked like a haggard caricature of Loretta Young.

When Leon came into the bedroom, she was sitting up in bed, holding the covers over herself as she handed him one of the flutes.

"Hmm, champagne." He raised his eyebrows. "What are we celebrating—Dad falling asleep?"

"No. We're celebrating us."

"Okay, then. Here's to us making it through another day." He guzzled the small glass down in one slug, shut off the light before he got one glimpse of the negligee, and slid into bed.

"Can I have a goodnight kiss?" she asked in the darkness.

He leaned over to peck her cheek. Gently, she took his hand and placed it inside of her nightgown, over her bare breast.

"For God's sake, Stella! I'm so tired that I can't see straight."

"You don't need to *see* to make love. You just need to *feel*. If you still can, that is."

As he rolled over, his back toward her, snoring almost instantly, a pain pierced her heart, fierce and humiliating. She scooted as far away from him as she could.

When she awoke in the middle of the night, the other side of the bed was empty. Pulling on her heaviest robe, she descended the staircase to look for him. To her surprise, she found him sitting in a chair by the stereo wearing headphones, listening to one of his old LPs, his eyes closed. For the first time since they were married,

Leon was listening to his music, the same way she'd listened to it several days ago. Was his intent the same as hers too?

A small flutter of hope resuscitated her.

△△△

In the wee hours of the morning after his father went to sleep, Leon had been reading Noël's diary. He read every single page, and was on his third reading. After listening to music that night, he sat down in the chair by the fireplace, picked it up again and held it against him before opening it once more. He read her description of the night he proposed to her on top of the Ferris wheel; he read about her decision to name their child after the resilient trees she loved; he read about their cherished friend and neighbor, Theckla Chavis, coming all the way from Alabama to be with her during her pregnancy; he read the way she described him as a "Moroccan lantern" and the Moonstone Inn as "their house by the sea", the one she'd dreamed of living in. And he wondered how she could think of that old rundown motel as a home.

He savored every last word she'd written. Page by page, he was falling in love with her, utterly in love, over and over again.

△△△

In place of Walt's hall of fame and on all the other walls too, under newer, makeshift track lighting, Willow instructed the men to hang Ricky's works of art clustered by periods—his Holocaust Period, his Landscape Period, his Abstract Period, and, of course, his Noël Trudeau Period, where Willow selected four of the most striking portraits of her mother. She had all of his best works assembled, including the ones they intended to keep, because she wanted the art dealers to see the full range of his talent. Too bad Ricky didn't live long enough to know that his creations had reached high value in the art world. Beyond that, they had deep emotional value. His work was powerful. Every single brushstroke dripped with pain and pathos, a depiction of the vibrancy and fragility of life. He liked to juxtapose them; joy against heartache, light against darkness.

A prime example was her mother's exquisite face. Though she couldn't relate to her beauty, Willow could identify with her melancholy wistfulness, captured by Ricky's discerning hand. Leon hadn't mentioned it, or Mary, or Walt, but she could tell by his paintings, and the sheer number of them, that Ricky had been in love with her too. Another story for another time, and maybe not one for her to know. There were too many other stories still in progress.

Heading over to the bar, she took a sip of the drink she'd poured herself, sat down on a stool, looked again at the portrait. "Why were you so sad, Mama?" she asked.

Startled, she heard a sound behind her.

"So now you're talking to yourself?" Leon said.

"I wasn't talking to myself. I was talking to Mom."

He stood beside her, fixated on one of the portraits. She saw the way his eyes changed as he stared at it—tender, brimming with life—and she sensed the depth of his love.

"Is it okay with you that I included his paintings of her?"

He nodded, turned around. "But I'm not okay with your choice of beverage."

Her face flushed bright red. "I don't know what you're talking about."

He went over to the bar, picked up her glass, sniffed it. "Most people have orange juice this time of morning. Not gin. We gotta wean you off of that stuff."

She was furious, embarrassed. This had come out of nowhere. "You have no right to tell me what I can and can't do!" she said. "I'm an adult."

"That you are." He sat down on the stool beside her. "But

you're also my child, absent as I've been. My only child." He looked around the room. "You know, you've done a great job with this exhibit. It looks amazing. Ricky's probably floating around in here, smiling his head off."

Leon did things like that, got her all mixed up. He'd go off on a completely different tangent while she was in the middle of emotionally processing the last one, flicking her feelings on and off like a CD player.

"You know, I caught Dad talking to him the other day," he said. "There he was chattering away like he was having a real conversation, nodding, saying yes and no, and when I asked him who he was talking to, he said it was Ricky and why the hell didn't I know that. He looked at me as if I was the crazy one."

She didn't say anything.

"I loved my brother. I loved my brother a whole hell of a lot. My talented kid brother. But he was too damned—I don't even know the right word for it—trusting? impressionable? decent?— too something-too-good for this lousy world. He thought the booze was his friend. But it killed him."

His point was not lost on her. "That's not going to happen to me. I just take a little drink once in a while to relax. Same as you do. I can handle it."

"Yeah, he thought he could too." She watched him get up and walk over toward the Abstract Period. "I'm not being judgmental. I know how things happen. But I want you to have a good future. You had a lousy past, but you can have a good future. You're a shining star like my brother was, and you owe it to Noël to use the life she gave you the best you can." He was gazing at her mother's portraits again.

"You mean *sacrificed* herself for?"

"Yup, sacrificed herself for. But, you know what?, she sacrificed herself for me too, so we're in this together, kid. That's the way she was. The way she loved. Hook, line, and sinker."

Willow tried to suppress the mountain of conflicting emotions that were building up, making her feel heavy, too heavy to move, to breathe. Tears welled in her eyes, so she turned away from him. She hated to cry; crying was weak and stupid. Not to mention dangerous. It cracked you open like a piñata.

"Willow, baby, listen to me. Your mom made a good choice to have you. The best choice. The only choice. You're the one who's carrying her into the future. She said it herself in her diary. '*You're a miracle.*' And you are."

"Some miracle."

"You're *our* miracle. Hers *and* mine."

Willow wiped another flood of tears away.

"Look what you've done for your grandpa. And for me."

"What've I done for you?"

"You woke up my right brain, that's what."

In spite of herself, she smiled.

"Ricky found AA helpful. And his footsteps aren't such a bad path to follow, are they?" He sat back down at the bar. "But that's not what I wanted to talk to you about. I want to talk to you about the future."

"Oh, that." She sighed. Here it came, the familiar lecture about how she was wasting her life.

"Yeah, that. It's time you finished your degree. And old long-lost dad here will foot the bill."

"I don't need you to do that. It's not your responsibility."

"I know I don't have to. I want to. And speaking of wants, I've been thinking that maybe it's not a nursing degree that you really want. Maybe that's been the problem all along."

"What's that supposed to mean?"

"I've seen your artwork, and it's damned good. Maybe it's really an art degree you should go after."

Her eyes lit up. How could he have known? Nobody knew that. She herself didn't know that, not in a conscious way, anyway.

"I think the Chicago Art Institute has a good school connected with it," he said. "Ricky used to talk about it, a long time ago. It's not too late to start the winter semester in January, is it?"

Too many thoughts were funneling through her brain. "I can't leave Walt."

"You won't be leaving him. You can come visit him anytime you want. Chicago's not that far away, you know."

Leon walked over to Ricky's Landscape Period, stopped in front of his last painting with the yellow boat, the weeping willow draping its branches over the shoreline. "You know, I thought about it for a long time—whether it's right to sell his paintings or not. But Ricky wouldn't have wanted his work to hide away in an old studio on top of a dying neighborhood bar, would he? Isn't that why you artists create—to share your vision?" He touched the yellow boat. "You and your uncle have a gift that will live on."

TWENTY-SEVEN

DECEMBER 7, 1999:
THE FIRE CEREMONY

I N the weeks preceding the fire ceremony, Gus had somewhat prepared Willow for what it held in store. It was an ancient Native American custom, he said. "A fire ceremony is a way to bring renewal and healing into your life, so bring something from your past that you'd like to release."

"Like what?" she asked.

"Like your old hurts, disappointments, resentments, mistakes. You know, the kinds of things that hold us back, prevent us from moving forward into our higher selves."

"And then what happens?"

"We put those things into the fire in an offering of smoke. After that, we do the same for the things we want to replace them with. And we release them to the heavens, to God."

She nodded, but she had to admit it seemed a little spooky and supernatural, kind of like the feeling she used to get when playing with her Ouija board when she was a kid, as if invoking some unseen world. When she mentioned it to Gus, he assured her that this had nothing to do with superstitious gobbledygook; this ceremony was about cleansing the soul at a very deep level. "Fire is the center of life," he said. "In Cherokee, it became the word we use for *home*."

ΔΔΔ

That Tuesday night around ten p.m., a full moon hanging in the sky, she followed him into the back alley of the Mazurka Inn. He had dressed for the occasion, a gigantic turquoise ring on every finger except his thumbs, his thick silver braid restrained neatly against his back, a white tunic shirt with a Cherokee pattern emblazoned on the front. She wore a coat, but he did not. He carried a backpack in his arms, which he set down on the gravel. Other than the luminosity of the moon, it was a dark, chilly night, a slight wind ruffling her hair.

"Why do you wait for a full moon?" she asked.

"Because that's the time when the veil between worlds is the thinnest."

She had no idea what he meant, but he spoke with such authority and conviction that she believed whatever he said. Tonight he'd transformed himself into a mystical sage. Maybe he had always been and she'd been too self-absorbed to notice.

"Ideally, we would have a wise man, a shaman, doing this for us," he said.

"*You're* shaman enough for me."

He ignored her vote of confidence. "The fire will be our teacher tonight," he said. He was humble like that, unpretentious as a river. "See that full moon up there?"

Willow stared at it.

"That's not just any moon. That's what we call in Cherokee, *usgiyi*, the snow moon. Some call it the long night's moon because it comes during the time of year when the nights are longest and darkest."

With his large, steady hands, she watched him strike a single match and toss it into the tangled nest of gasoline-soaked twigs on the bottom of the wire trashcan. She doubted that there was another sight more compelling, more mesmerizing, than a burning fire in the dead of night. As she gazed into the flames, time seemed to stop.

In his baritone voice, Gus uttered an offering prayer and Native chant. Then, he invited her to throw whatever item she wanted to burn from her past into the fire. "Don't tell me what it is," he said.

She was thinking about Walt. He didn't have the luxury of choosing which pieces of his past to burn away. His past blazed rampant, without his consent. She shared that thought aloud with Gus.

"That's why this is so important," he said. "The time to get rid of our baggage is now, while we're still able to, so that we can float into our dementia, or whatever else the future holds for us, as lightly and peacefully as we can."

It sounded like something Walt had said to her once; in fact this whole ceremony reminded her of the conversation she and Walt had while watching Reverend Schuller on TV and that's why she selected the item that she did. She stepped inside the Mazurka Inn, just inside the back door, where she'd stashed a sack of potatoes. Plenty of potatoes to represent plenty of junk—her painful childhood, her feelings of alienation and abandonment, and all the other stuff that came along with it. Ricky had found Alcoholics Anonymous; she was hoping this might be her way.

Raising his eyebrows, Gus nodded.

Hoisting the sack high into her arms, she hurled it into the flames. "This is for Walt too," she said. She hoped it burned away his Nazis, the trip to America in steerage, the pain he endured from losing his parents, and whatever else caused him sorrow. She saw Gus' lips move in a silent prayer.

The scent of burning potatoes filled the night air, and it smelled good, like baked potatoes on a grill. She watched the flames burn purple at the edges, the way they wavered into different patterns, rising and falling until they died down again, condensing into a thin line of smoke that filtered upward toward the sky in a long, straight line before evaporating.

Gus knew what he was talking about; this was awesome. She felt buoyant, peaceful, and she was hoping that Walt, wherever he was right now, (probably reclined in the La-Z-Boy) was feeling less weighted down too.

"Now replace it, little Ahyoka," Gus said. "It's time to call in your new energy."

For that part, Willow had written something down, something she'd been thinking about since Gus first mentioned the fire ceremony to her, but she'd only officially solidified her thoughts that morning while sipping her coffee. Stepping up to the wire can again, she flung the piece of paper into the fire and watched it disintegrate within seconds. Taking a long, deep breath of air into her lungs, she inhaled the newness. Afterwards, she glanced at Gus. His eyes were closed. "Your turn," she said.

To her amazement, she saw him reach into his backpack and pull out the manila envelope he'd once brought downstairs to reveal its contents to her and Walt. "That's not your assassination photos, is it?"

He nodded.

"You can't burn those!"

"Why not?"

"It's the truth in there, isn't it?"

"A truth I'm tired of carrying. Let me tell you something. There are hundreds of pieces of truth about that day floating around on this earth, not just my little pictures. Truth that no one is yet willing to hear, or reckon with, for whatever reason. What would you propose I do with these pictures?"

"I don't know." She shrugged.

"Do you want them?"

"No!"

"I didn't think so. Nor would I think of saddling you with them. So who else do you think I should saddle them with?"

She was silent.

"That's what I thought." In one fluid movement, he tossed the envelope into the awaiting fire. She watched it curl one corner and blacken it before the entire envelope burst into bright yellow-orange flames. Slowly, the fire crackled underneath layers of ash. A cloud of thick, gray smoke, images of shapes that looked like little human faces churning in it, rose higher, higher, into the night sky.

"Whoa," she said. "I don't how you could just destroy them like that."

"I didn't destroy them. I released them to the heavens, to Spirit—where all great truths are revealed in the long run. In their own good time."

She thought about her mother's letter to her father and how Mary had burned it. Maybe he was right.

TWENTY-EIGHT

December 1999:
The Great Wall

ANOTHER week had gone by in a whirlwind, and Stella felt completely exhausted. In that brief time, the Mazurka Inn sale had been finalized, the keys handed over to Jorge Jimenez, and Ricky's art showing was a huge success. The New York dealers had purchased twenty-five of his paintings outright, two of them for as much as twenty-thousand dollars apiece, and were optioning with Leon for several more.

Through it all, Walt's incessant sundowning continued, night after night. The final straw came one morning when Stella found him nestled on her white sofa, both him and the upholstery caked with diarrhea. Apparently he had awakened after they'd gone to sleep and wandered around the house before crashing on the couch, the same couch that Leon used to occupy. Not only was the sofa ruined, but a trail of fecal droppings dotted the path from the den, into the living room, and down the hallway, soiling her beautiful carpets along the way. Even after Leon scrubbed the mess clean, the odor was locked into her brain as if excrement was seeping through the walls.

"Okay, you win," she said. "Move him back into his own house."

Overwrought by the whole experience, she opted to make

herself scarce when the actual move occurred and spent the next two days with her parents in Chicago. By the time she came home, both Leon and Walt were gone. She was ashamed by how wonderful it felt.

Alone in her bedroom later on, she fought the urge to give Gene a call. This was no marriage. It was true, Leon had returned to their bed, but only to give her the thrill of hearing him snore all night long after playing nursemaid to his father all day long. She didn't know if she could hang on; she was drowning.

She ended up dialing Gene's number. Hearing his voice again was exactly what she needed to pull her out of the maelstrom; the voice of reason. "If you really feel you need to give your marriage a chance," he told her, "you're going to have to have an honest talk with him. He doesn't strike me as a very intuitive kind of guy, so spell it out. Tell him exactly how you feel."

△△△

When she arrived at the Ziemnys' house the following afternoon, Walt was sound asleep on the sofa, while Leon napped on the La-Z-Boy. She didn't even want to know how they got reversed like that or how Leon could bring himself to sleep in that smelly chair. Now was as good a time as any. Pulling the drapes open, she watched Leon sleeping for a long time before she had the nerve to rouse him. He opened his groggy eyes, squinted into the sunlight.

"We need to talk," she said.

Stretching out his arms, he yawned. "Now? I just woke up." He reached for a glass of ice water on the coffee table, the cubes melted down to tiny chips, and took a sip. "Let's go into the kitchen so we don't wake him up."

Following him, she sat down at the table. He pulled out the chair across from her, at the far end. "So what do you want to talk about?"

"Us."

He scratched his head, diverted his eyes.

"There's always something—or someone—coming between us," she said.

"Can I help it if my father has Alzheimer's? I'm not the one who caused it, you know."

"I know you're not. Of course I know that."

"Then what do you want me to do? Leave him alone, just to make you happy?" He pulled out a cigarette, lit it. Now that his mother was dead, she supposed that gave him license to ruin the place.

"You could offer one to me, you know," she said. "Gene always did."

"So now we're down to that—etiquette lessons from the Golden Grandpa." He tossed the cellophane package over to her, and she missed the catch. Bending down to retrieve it from the spill- stained tile, she lost the urge to light it.

"Leon, you're worn out. And me too. There are some very nice nursing homes out there."

"Forget it!" Cigarette smoldering between his fingertips, he held his other hand out flat in front of him as if pushing her away.

"This is consuming our lives!"

"No, no, and no. It's absolutely out of the question."

"Lots of my friends have parents in nursing homes. When I was in Chicago, I had a long lunch with my friend Sarah about her own father with Alzheimer's. She placed him in what they call a special memory care unit last year, and she said he's been doing wonderfully—there are all kinds of activities for him, and the staff is trained to understand his needs. It gave her the chance to rest and have a real life again. When she goes to see him now, they have great visits together. She can be his daughter again, not his nurse and maidservant."

"What part of *no* don't you understand?"

She took a handful of pamphlets out of her purse and spread them on the kitchen table in front of him. "Just keep an open mind. I've visited some of these places, and they're very nice. They're smaller and quieter than the rest of the facility, and they take really good care of people like Walt. My favorite is the one at Mercyville."

He wouldn't even look at the pamphlets. After scooping them up again, she tried to put them directly into his hand, but he let them drop to the floor and kicked them away.

"I give up!" As soon as the words flew from her mouth, she felt the raging dam inside of her bursting. "We're finally going to have the talk we should have had years ago!"

He didn't say anything as he put out his cigarette, bowed his head to the floor. She didn't let that stop her; in fact, it gave her the impetus to continue. "Ever since I met you, Leon Ziemny, I've been last in your book. If it wasn't your job that came first, or Ricky, or your parents, it was always something. Anything you could find to push me away."

"*Push* is a good word," he said. "Push, push, push, that's all you do."

"What's that supposed to mean?"

He pointed to the pamphlets on the floor. "I give you Exhibit A."

"Well, excuse me for having an opinion about what goes on in our lives!"

"You've got more than opinions, baby. You get everything you want. You've got that timeshare in Florida you had to have so badly, and we traipse down there every fucking year, like two old coots. And you've traveled all over Timbuktu; anywhere you stuck your finger on a map and decided that's where you wanted to go. And you've got all that expensive furniture. And that ridiculously extravagant Persian rug—"

"Which your father now ruined, I might add. Do you even realize how selfish you are? Our marriage has never been about me or what I wanted. It's always been all about you. The hell with what I felt!"

He remained silent, unmoving, his eyes still focused on the tile floor.

"A lot of that is my own fault, I know." She kept talking to the top of his lowered head, to that thick mane of silver and black. "I let you get away with it. Even before we were married, any crumb you tossed my way was enough for me. But you know what? I'm tired of crumbs."

When he looked up at her, his eyes were distressed. "As long as we're playing *Truth or Consequences*, there's something I need to tell you."

She relished the fact that he looked tormented. Turnabout was fair play. "Alright." She folded her arms. "Go right ahead."

"Willow is my daughter."

"What?" It hit her like a speeding train.

"Mom told me before she died."

"How in the world did your mother know?"

"I guess Noël sent a letter to me when we were on that trip to Niagara Falls. Mom was picking up our mail, and she found it, read it, and burned it. She'd been keeping it to herself this whole time. This whole fucking time."

Stella got up from the table and walked over to the counter, her back toward him. She tried to assimilate what he was saying. They'd taken that trip to Niagara Falls a few months after they

were married. But by that time, he'd already been divorced from
Noël for years. And then it came to her. She remembered how
he'd disappeared several weeks before their wedding, and Stella had
always suspected he'd gone to her. She wheeled around. "You mean
you slept with her right before our wedding?"

He didn't say anything.

She couldn't wrap her mind around it; too many questions
were hammering her brain. "So when were you planning to tell me
about Willow?"

"I don't know." He ran his fingers through his hair. "There's
so much going on now. I guess I thought after the holidays or
something."

"After the holidays? You say it like it's starting a diet or something. This is our lives you're talking about!" She turned away from
him again, back to the counter. The statue of the Virgin Mary
stood in the backyard. When had her nose been repaired? An inane
thought at a time like this. "Why didn't Willow tell you herself?"

"She was afraid, I guess."

"But not too afraid to show up here in Langston." Stella
returned to the table. "So what does this mean for us? What does
Willow want from you?"

"Nothing."

"Then why did she come here?"

"Because I'm her father, that's why."

"You're not her father! She's a grown woman. You're just a
sperm-donor."

He gazed at the ceiling, a baffling expression on his face. "Her
birth killed Noël," he said. "It was a choice between Noël's life and
her baby's, and Noël chose Willow."

"Oh, good God," Stella moaned. "Noël, the homewrecker has

been elevated to Noël, the saint. Now you can officially canonize her in your memory."

"Stop it."

"I don't want to stop it! I've stopped it since we got married! I'll tell you something. I was overjoyed when I heard Noël was dead and buried. And then, I got to wondering if she might be more dangerous to us dead than alive. If you had gone back to her, you would've ended up leaving her again, or her leaving you. You would've gotten disillusioned with Saint Noël or Whore Noël, or whoever she was to you. The same way you got disillusioned with her during your marriage and you ended up sleeping with me. Remember that time in the car? You were all over me. You wanted me like crazy. *Me*, not her. You just want what you don't have, that's your problem."

"Stop it, I said!" He got up from his chair, more agitated than she'd ever seen him. At first, she thought he might hit her, but he crossed over to the other side of the room, toward the refrigerator, and then back again to his chair. He was cornered now; that was what was frustrating him, the fact that he had to finally confront his own demons. In the past, he would have fled the house, but not now, not with his precious, demented father in the next room. She knew this was killing him, being forced to have an honest conversation like this. The fact that he couldn't escape was exhilarating. Finally, he was the one squirming, the one who felt trapped. Finally, she had the upper hand.

"Worship a dead woman; I don't care. Though you haven't noticed, I'm alive. I'm the one that stuck by you. And what do I get for it? You treat me like some kind of mosquito to be swatted away, a bother, a pest."

"A pest who lives like a queen."

"Some queen. You have no regard whatsoever for my feelings!"

He walked to the refrigerator again, back to his chair, another strange expression on his face that she didn't recognize. "You're right." He sat down. "I've been unfair to you all along."

She fell silent. The confession was unexpected.

"And I'm sorry." He focused his gaze on her. "You deserved better."

Finally, an apology. And the same words Gene and Mary had used—she *deserved better*—coming straight from the horse's mouth. She stared back at him in amazement. This was their watershed moment. The great wall between them was imploding; he seemed to be seeing her for the first time in years. "You don't know how long I've waited to hear you say that."

"You've got every right to be mad as hell," he said. "I did try to make you happy. I really did. I tried to cater to your every whim." He looked distraught. "I thought the past was over, but now I know you can't just nail the door shut. It has a way of opening up, all on its own, if things are left unfinished."

Rising from her seat, she came toward him. His head was bent downward again. Maybe she shouldn't have forced him to talk—he was too worn down, too tired for a conversation of this magnitude. "There's nothing you left unfinished, darling. Nothing except us. Willow just stirred up some memories, and you're rethinking something you never really had. You divorced her, remember? I'm your wife; it's me you have. It's time for you to grow up and start appreciating the green grass in your own yard." She reached out to stroke his hair.

The moment her fingers landed, he jerked away. "It's time for me to grow up alright! Way past time! But we were both fooling ourselves, right from the start. It wasn't *me* you wanted. You just wanted to be married. And just for the record, that time in the car wasn't about me wanting what I can't have. It only happened that time because I was desperate to force her out of my head. I was trying to—oh, God; oh, God almighty—she was always the one."

Her hand trembled in the air.

"Why on earth did you marry me in the first place?" he said. "Why *did* we get married?"

She felt too weak to stand up and sank into the seat beside him.

"Who knows why we got married. Was it only because it was time to bite the bullet? … And, Mom, of course … she kept pushing it. She wouldn't let it go. Pushing me that you were the right woman. Pushing when I kept changing our wedding date." He continued in what was no longer a dialogue but a monologue; because he was unable to get away, because she'd finally cornered him, the bottled-up monsters inside his head had free rein to air their voices. "And you kept pushing too. Pushing to get married. Pushing for a gigantic wedding. Pushing after I left you for Noël. Pushing after that too—you were the one who insisted we take that ride and—" He stood up, walked over to the sink where she'd been standing, his eyes distracted, plaqued. "I guess there're all kinds of reasons people who aren't in love get married. And they're always the wrong ones. And there're all kinds of reasons why people who love each other too much leave each other. Those reasons are even worse. I should never have dragged you into this. I should never have let her go. But then … oh, Jesus … I wouldn't have had Willow now."

His barrage of words slashed like razors raining down. How was it possible that two people could be together in the same situation, in the same room, in the same bed, in the same marriage, while living in parallel worlds?

"I'm sorry." He turned around, his savage little monologue

apparently over. "I should have been a stronger man. I wish I had been. Before all our lives made a wrong turn."

It took her several seconds to catch her breath enough to speak. "For what it's worth, I didn't marry you because your mother wanted me to, or just to be married," she said. "I married you because I loved you."

He bowed his head again. "I cared about you too. I *do* care about you."

"Just not enough?" she said.

He looked away, toward the window. He couldn't look her in the eyes; he couldn't answer.

She felt half-dead. All these years she'd waited for this talk, for the wall between them to tumble into dust. But she never expected that once it did, there would be nothing, absolutely nothing, on the other side.

TWENTY-NINE

2000:
Seashells

THE year 2000 arrived without any cataclysmic disaster. Except for one. After twenty-seven years of marriage, Stella filed for divorce. Actually, she'd filed just before Christmas, their final gift to each other. Leon was more than generous when it came to the settlement, agreeing to let her keep the house in Langston, everything inside of it, the time-share. He even reimbursed her the full amount for the Persian rug.

He came to wish her well the day before she left for Florida. She was packing up the car in the driveway when he appeared out of nowhere, gloveless hands stuffed in his coat pockets. "Take care," he told her. "And go get 'em."

"You mean, Gene?"

"If that's what you want—sure." He paused. "But I was talking about life in general."

"What's left of it."

"Yeah, what's left of it." He kicked at the shallow snow with the toe of his shoe. "I just wanted you to know that … I'm sorry."

"You've already told me that."

"Yeah, well … I guess I had to say it again."

△△△

Willow had left for Chicago in December, and as of mid-January, she was officially a college girl, enrolled in the School of the Art Institute of Chicago for an undergraduate degree in fine arts with a concentration in painting and drawing. Not an easy school to get into, but her portfolio seemed to have amply impressed the powers that be. Though she missed being with Walt and Leon, she felt as if life was opening up to her, and she couldn't imagine a more stimulating environment—studying the master artists of the Institute, delighting in the architecture and culture of a city like Chicago, and getting reacquainted with her brother and his wife.

She made it a point to come home to Langston at least once a week, and Walt perked up whenever she was around. Leon had hired a home health agency to help out a few hours each day, but mostly his father's care was up to him. Every time he put her back on the South Shore train to Chicago, she felt torn in two, and guilty too, for her expanding life, while her father's life—the father who made her new adventure possible—was shrinking. "That's the way it's supposed to be," he told her. But she wasn't so sure about that.

△△△

A few weeks before Stella's allotted time at the condo was up, she managed to sell her share. She had her eye on a private villa in a lovely retirement community on the Clearwater coastline and had already put in the deposit. She'd discovered it when Gene took her away to a nearby resort for a long weekend.

When she'd first come to Florida, their relationship had progressed. Gene was an unselfish, devoted lover who made her feel like a goddess. An odd switch, to be sure, to have gone from being insignificant to one man and the center of the universe to another. Frankly, she didn't covet either role.

Gene was crushed when she told him she was moving away.

Two months after she was settled into her new villa, the final divorce papers arrived in the mail. Stella stared at the envelope without opening it, then stuck it into her file cabinet under the letter "D". And that was that.

△△△

It was a beautiful April day—all days were beautiful down here in Florida—and Stella decided to take a solitary walk along the shore, where she did her best thinking. It was one of those days when her focus was sharp and things seemed crystal-clear. As she walked, she was figuring things out—better late than never—and she finally figured out the one and only reason Leon had married her. To anesthetize his pain. She'd permitted him do it; allowed herself to become the ether that let him sleepwalk through life.

But why had she married *him*? That one was harder to reckon. She'd told herself all along the same thing she'd insisted to him, that it was because she loved him, but had she really? Love was supposed to lead you deeper into yourself, not further away, like being with him had done from the start. So why had she pushed so hard, as he'd phrased it, to marry him? Because he was the ultimate challenge? Because she wanted to win the battle with Noël Trudeau? Because he had a beautiful head of hair? Because she'd let other marriage opportunities pass her by and he was her last chance?

The last reason resonated. When you're young, getting married can seem like a frantic game of musical chairs. As the clock ticked, you had to find your place quick, before all the chairs—husbands, in this case—were taken. No one wanted to be the old maid left standing. Just about any chair was better than none. Or was it something more convoluted than that? Was the pull toward Leon as innate as the 'fight or flight' response to an intolerable situation, and she had simply become the fight to his flight?

Who knew the intentions behind what made people get

together and stay together? Leon had married her with his own intentions, and she'd married him with hers, yet neither had stopped to consider the other's in the process. Since she had moved into the retirement community, she had plenty of time to sit and observe long-married couples to see what made them tick. Sure, there were some happy ones who danced in their own magic, but those seemed few and far between. The majority picked and sniped at each other, or didn't talk much at all, or seethed with resigned resentment, or gritted their teeth in martyred acceptance. She recognized them because she'd done them all. And it led her to the conclusion that real love, lasting as fine wine, was a rare commodity; the exception, not the norm. For some reason, we deceived ourselves that it was the other way around and lived disappointed ever-after.

The water was pure blue and calming, blending perfectly into the sky with no distinct line of demarcation. Staring at the tranquil sight, Stella felt an ever-deepening sense of contentment. Among the many truths she was finally realizing, this was the most liberating of all: learning to live with someone else was icing on the cake, but it wasn't the cake. Learning to live with yourself was the cake. She liked herself now. She liked the image in the mirror staring back at her. She was free, for the first time in her life, to be nothing but herself.

As for Leon, let him and his father continue their descent into the past. She had a future to get to. Picking up a seashell, she tossed it into the boundary-less horizon.

THIRTY

September 11, 2001: The Planes

THE sliver of moon looked like a piece of broken glass floating in the black sky. Walt reached up and tried to catch it between his fingertips, but the slippery little booger kept moving away on him. A wistful little tune was running through his head—he couldn't quite recall the words—but he kept on humming it anyway. He was sitting on this huge porch, not by himself, but with that nice man, the one who always hung around with him. At first he thought it was his father, but that's not who he was. He called himself Leon, and his father's name was Zbigniew. Whoever he was, he was good to him; Walt felt safe around him.

Today, two planes fell down from the sky, right across the street. Walt was surprised that the houses were still standing because the planes went right through them, and the whole kit and kaboodle had burst into flames. An awful thing to see. Just awful. A big black column of smoke chased all the neighbors down the street, running for their lives.

"Didn't those houses burn down today?" he asked.

Leon turned to look at him but didn't answer.

"Well, didn't they?"

"You must've had a bad dream," he said.

Hell, no, it was no dream. Walt knew he saw two big planes

falling down from the sky. He looked up to see if he could spot them. The moon across the street, high over the neighbor's rooftop, was a fingernail. He tried to catch it between his thumb and forefinger, and this time, he was almost successful.

It was a nice night, perfect weather. Walt liked this big porch, plenty of room. He was sitting in some kind of crazy swing from a carnival ride, and Leon was perched on the front steps in front of him. Whenever Walt tried to move his legs, his seat rocked back and forth. "So when is the man coming who'll take us up?" he asked.

"What man?"

"You know, the carnival man." Sometimes this Leon could be thick as mud. "The one that runs this ferry seat I'm sitting on."

Leon smiled. "One of my best memories happened on a Ferris wheel."

"You don't say."

A warm breeze blew across Walt's face. It felt good. He started humming again. A nice little tune, but he'd be damned if he could remember the words. Other than that, things felt perfect. He wasn't certain if it was day or night, but it was dark outside, so it must be night. That was the way it went. Time swung back and forth, like the carnival chair he was sitting in. "Didn't two planes fall down from the sky today?"

"Maybe somewhere," Leon said. "But not here."

"No, not here." Where they were right now, wherever it was, was a perfect place to be. Not the kind of place where planes flew into buildings. "You know?" Walt said. "This is a big palooka of a platform."

"Yes, it is." Leon nodded. "It's a big porch, all right."

"Didn't two planes fall down from the sky?"

"Maybe somewhere," he said. "But not here."

It was a quiet night. Nobody seemed to be around except for this Leon guy. Walt glanced around to the right, and the carnival seat started swinging again. "Is that a house next door?"

"Yup."

"Who lives there?"

"Not sure."

"Oh, I know who lives there." Walt shook his head, grinning. "Good old Stanley. He and I played stickball today. I let him win, but don't tell him that. He's lousy at that game. If I didn't let him win once in a while, he never would."

"That's nice of you."

"Nice? I don't know if it's nice, but you gotta treat your neighbors like fellows," Walt said. "Why don't you ask him to come over?"

"He's not home right now."

Walt leaned forward and gazed at the other side. He wondered who lived in that house. "So when's the man coming who'll take us up?"

"You mean, the carnival man?"

"Who else? He's the only one who can do it. You can't take yourself up."

"He's on break now. He went to have a smoke behind the merry-go-round."

"Another break? There's no good help anymore. Not even at the carnival."

Leon took a cigarette out of his pocket and lit it. "You want one?"

"Hell, yes, I want one. But don't tell Mama."

"Your secret's safe with me." Sticking the cigarette between Walt's teeth, Leon burned it up at the end. Walt blew the smoke out through his nose, the same way Leon was doing. They'd been waiting for the carnival man for a long time now. "Isn't he ever gonna come?"

"Who? Stanley or the carnival man?"

"The carnival man!"

"Maybe tomorrow."

"Tomorrow? Hell, I don't have all day to sit here and wait. I gotta get home."

"Just let me finish my cigarette," Leon said. "Then we'll go home. Are you done with yours yet?"

"Done with what?" Leon got up and pulled a sparkler out of his mouth from between his fingers. "Now, where did that come from?"

Leon shrugged. "Magic."

"Didn't two planes fall down from the sky today?"

"Maybe somewhere, but not here."

A long time went by, maybe years, and Walt was still sitting on the porch waiting for the carnival man. "I miss that little girl that used to live here."

"You mean Willow?"

"Who? No. I mean Mishka. Little Mishka."

"Yeah, I miss her too."

"*Show me the way to go home* …" Finally, the words came to him, and he started to sing. He thought he was all alone, but when he looked down toward the front steps, there was his oldest son! Walt struggled to get up from the wobbly seat to go to him, but he got himself all crooked in the process, and Leon caught him just in time before he fell flat on his face. "Where the hell have you been, Leon? You haven't been around here since there were cows."

"You know who I am?" Leon sat down beside him.

What a stupid question. "Well, of course I know who you are! You're Leon, my oldest boy." For some reason, this made the kid's eyes get wet. Walt made the bench swing on purpose, trying to make him laugh the way he used to do when Leon was just a little squirt. "I'm glad this is such a big platform. That's what Mary always wanted. There's plenty of room here, for all of us."

Leon kissed him on the temple. "Welcome back, Dad. For however long it lasts."

Walt looked into his boy's tired face. "You know something? You look like hell. You need some rest." He patted him on the knee, glanced around the tiny front yard. "I don't think the carnival's gonna come around here anymore."

"Probably not."

"Then let's you and me go somewhere else. Get out of this place."

"Like where?" Leon asked.

"Oh, I don't know. Maybe somewhere that has nice trees."

"You know, I've been sitting here thinking about that same thing."

"That's 'cause you're my boy, and you and I think alike."

Leon grinned.

"Where did that pretty girl go?" Walt said.

"Mishka?"

"No, the other one. The one like Christmas. She was just sitting there with you a minute ago. On the step. She turned around and gave me a great big smile. Just like Mama's, like the sun coming up. Where did she go?"

Leon's eyes got big as Sausalito. "You mean—*Noël*?"

Walt didn't say anything. He was no damned good anymore when it came to names.

"What's it like for you in there?" Leon asked him.

"In where?"

He knocked gently on Walt's noggin. "In there. Is it a good place to be?"

"Hell, yes, this a good place to be." Walt looked around the platform. "Let's leave it set at this dial."

"I agree. Let's leave it right here."

They didn't talk for a long time. Yapping had its place, but sometimes the quiet felt better; it gave you the space to let the water sink in. Only important things should come out of your mouth, not any damn fish. "My Mama has yellow roosters. All over the kitchen. … How come nothing's yellow anymore?"

"I don't know," Leon said. "I don't know where the yellow goes."

"It goes up."

"You mean the sun?"

"Nah, not the sun. It's nighttime. … Help me get off this crazy ride, would you?. This is a nice place, but I'm tired of it. I've been here for too goddamned long. I thought it was gonna go up, but it doesn't go anywhere anymore. Not the way it used to." He looked up at the sliver of moon and tried to catch it between his fingers. "See that moon up there? That's the last one before home, but it's just a slice. If it was a whole pie, we could find our way. Do you think we can find our way home in the dark?"

He watched Leon get up from the carnival swing. "The only thing we can do is try. We'll try together, okay, Dad?"

"I'm not your dad! Hell, you're an old man."

THIRTY-ONE

SEPTEMBER 2001: VOYAGE

THE day before, the country was besieged by a terrorist attack. The twin towers in New York had imploded, and the world was in chaos. Willow had immediately called her father and he'd sounded strange—then again, everyone sounded strange—so she tried to keep it in perspective. He'd told her that he and Walt had been watching morning TV when the whole thing had happened and that he'd shut off the set as soon as Walt started seeing Nazis again. The very next morning, Willow caught the train from Chicago back to Langston.

When she walked through the unlatched front door, she had an eerie feeling. The television in the living room was playing softly in the background, a strange car parked in the driveway, and Leon and Walt were nowhere to be found. She found them in the den, where Walt was lying dormant in a hospital bed, a plump woman in a nurse's smock hovering over him. The organ in the corner was covered with supplies—water bottles, medicines, whatever it took to keep him clean and comfortable. Leon turned around, saw her standing there. "What's going on?" she asked.

"This is Mabel, the hospice nurse," he said.

"Milly," she corrected.

"The planes are falling out of the sky," Walt mumbled. "The Nazis are everywhere."

Milly, the hospice nurse, gently touched Leon's hand. "The sedative should start working soon, Mr. Ziemny."

△△△

By the time the weekend rolled around, Walt had taken a real turn for the worse. Doc Podemski said he thought he'd had another mini-stroke, maybe more than one. Willow refused to leave. With all the terrible stuff on television, and now seeing Walt withering away, things felt apocalyptic to her. She needed to be there. There was no place she'd rather be.

On Monday morning, another hospice nurse, not Milly, but a perky one named Melissa arrived at the house, along with a CNA who gave Walt a bed bath. "It won't be much longer," she said. On her way out, she handed Leon some literature about signs to watch for as death approached.

"As if we need these." Leon sighed, tossing the booklets on the coffee table.

For the first time, Leon looked really old to Willow. Two years away from turning sixty, he'd lost more than twenty pounds in the past year, his face gaunt and lined. Willow kept urging him to eat, but like his own father, and her too, he could be as obstinate as an old Polish mule.

As she prepared his favorite dish, spaghetti and meatballs, she noticed a lidded box on the kitchen counter filled with family photographs. She brought it to the table, opening it slowly. She guessed Leon had already taken the time to sort through them, probably in anticipation of Walt's funeral home collage, because each of them was a photograph of Walt in a different phase of life—Walt as a teenager in cap and gown, Walt in his Army uniform, Walt getting married, Walt as a young father and an

older one, with each son in cap and gown—all the Walts Mary
had missed so much—along with the only Walt Willow had ever
known; Walt as an old man, standing proudly in front of his wall
of fame at the Mazurka Inn. It was strange the way death, even
imminent death, unified a life into an ageless, homogenous whole.
Already, he wasn't just one Walt and he'd soon be all of them again.
She couldn't imagine this world, their world, without him in it.

She called Leon to the table and slid a plate in front of him.

Reluctantly, he stabbed a meatball with his fork and chewed it
as if it was a lump of arsenic.

She really couldn't blame him; she wasn't the slightest bit
hungry herself. His hair was nearly all silver now, and it struck
her, just then, how precious and fleeting life was. It was time, high
time, that she said it out loud. "Le—I mean … Dad? … I love
you, Dad."

"Dad?" He smiled at her, a sad, slow smile. "Guess what. I love
you, too."

△△△

Leon had fallen asleep in the chair beside his father's bed, and he
awoke with a start. The bedroom was dim, even though it was
morning. Wednesday morning. Over a week had gone by since
9/11. He glanced at the other chair by the foot of the bed, and
there was Willow, sound asleep. Something about the expression
on her face reminded him of Noël. He'd kept trying to convince
Willow to go back to school; she'd already missed five days of
classes, but she wouldn't budge. Deep down, he was glad for her
stubbornness; her presence was a comfort beyond measure.

The light seemed to bother his father's eyes—his squinting
the only sign of responsiveness—so Leon kept the drapes drawn
tightly. Hospice told them he probably had a couple days or so left,
maybe even hours. "One is never exactly sure about these things,"

perky Melissa told them during her visit later that morning. Leon wondered if his father somehow knew the appointed time, the way his mom had been so certain. Melissa stuffed her stethoscope and blood pressure cuff back into her bag. "Have a nice day, Walt," she said, raising the volume in her voice as if Dad were deaf, not dying.

"She needs to find a new job," Leon told Willow after she left. "She's seen too many of these. She doesn't feel them anymore."

"That's the dilemma of being a nurse. If you feel all of them, it's time to go. And when you stop feeling all of them, it's time to go too."

Mostly his father's lids were shut tight, but every once in a while he opened them and uttered a few nonsensical words. "Bumpity bump," he muttered. "Stop swishing!" Willow and Leon sat on their usual chairs beside his bed, keeping up the vigil. The hours seemed to stretch on forever, each second on the clock beside his bed ticking away its own eternity. They took turns getting up to eat, or go to the bathroom, or take a little break doing anything else in the light. Coming back into that room again, crossing over the dark threshold of death, took a little more courage each time.

By evening, Dad was groaning. The liquid morphine didn't seem to be helping anymore. Why was he so agitated? Was it physical pain—the nurse insisted it should be manageable—or was it something else? They tried to comfort him, told him to follow the light like the hospice nurse had advised, gave him permission to die, but he kept hanging on, suffering, screaming out for his mother every once in a while. Hour after unbearable hour, his moans filled the house.

Willow was sitting slumped in her chair chewing on her fingernail when she abruptly shot up straight. She figured it out!, she told Leon; Walt must think he was on the ship that first brought him to America.

"Holy shit," he said. The thought that his father was reliving his most traumatic childhood memory was horrifying; the unresolved wound that was keeping him anchored to this earth. "I wish he hadn't lost that icon." He lamented.

"Oh, my God, I forgot about that!" Willow said. "I think I know where it is! I found it in his sock drawer once when I was putting away the laundry." She ran upstairs to retrieve it, then returned to the bedside.

Leon watched as Willow, his little girl, pressed the oval of the Black Madonna of Częstochowa into his father's limp palm, closed his fingers over it, and kissed them, the same way he'd told them his mother had done nearly a century ago, and Leon knew he was witnessing something unforgettable, something close to sacred; the instinctive love passed between generations.

"No! No!" His father cried out, his mouth twisting in a grimace. "Mama!"

Leon dropped to his knees in front of him. "This time, you're on the top deck of that boat," he whispered, "—in the sunshine, not in steerage. This time, you're going the other way. Your mama's waiting for you on the pier … You're going home."

His father's eyelids fluttered slightly as he turned his face toward the sound of Leon's voice. The tip of his thumb began gliding slowly over the smooth icon tucked into his hand, over and over again, a half-smile forming on his bluish lips. And then the motion stopped. Slowly, his breathing became less labored, less so, even less, no longer detectable. All sound and movement stopped. Willow sat up, looked at Leon.

Suddenly, he gasped. One deep, final breath in, but no air came out. Nothing, but stillness. It was over.

As Willow wept softly, Leon stroked her hair. He couldn't help but think about all those nights, all those times, when the only thing his father had wanted was to go home, and he realized it was about more than just the Alzheimer's; it had been a lifelong refrain. No more tricks, no more lies, no more driving around the block endless times. His father's forever-frozen face still had the trace of a smile. At long last, Walter Casimir Ziemny was home again.

THIRTY-TWO

OCTOBER 2002:
THE GARDEN OF
RESURRECTION

IT had been a year and a month since Walt died. When Leon had first told Willow his plan after the funeral, she was worried about him. "This neighborhood has nothing left for me," he'd explained. He wanted to move into her mother's old home in Willow, vacant again. "I need to go somewhere new."

The problem was, the town of Willow wasn't new, it was an old, dried-up place from the past, and Willow had feared it wasn't healthy for him to go backwards like that. Until, that is, it turned out he had a mission all his own.

After arriving in Willow, the first thing her father had done was to visit the office of the city planners and secure a permit to begin reseeding the weeping willow trees throughout the town. "I figure if the trees were important enough for your mom to name you after them, they're important enough for me to replant them," he informed her during her first visit.

Willow trees, she soon learned, were fast growing, reaching a height of ten feet in just a year's time. They were willful, adaptive trees, not terribly picky about the type of soil they needed in order to thrive. That first year, her father spent a lot of time planting and pruning, adding compost to the soil, and fertilizing them. And within a span of just a year, the little town was starting to look picturesque, not quite yet the way her mother had described it in her diary, but give it ten years.

△△△

From time to time, while relishing her second year of art school in Chicago, Willow thought about Gus, wondering what had happened to him and forever grateful to him for the life-changing gift of the fire ceremony. She didn't drink anymore, and her other fire ceremony hopes were on the horizon.

Come November, she'd think about Gus even more. That was the time of year when the deluge of Kennedy assassination TV specials made their annual appearance, spouting the lone-nut conclusion as cold, hard fact, not the cock-and-bull myth she knew it to be. Most of all, she hoped that Gus, wherever he was, had found peace.

And she missed Walt. Oh, how she missed him!

Leon had given her the icon of the Black Madonna of Częstochowa, and she hung it up on the wall over her desk where she could stare at it when she studied. More times than not, she found herself taking it down, curling it in her hand, rubbing her thumb over the smooth surface again and again.

△△△

She enjoyed her frequent visits to see her father. He had quite the routine. He'd walk to the little downtown each morning, have breakfast at the Seashell Supper House—a stupid name, given the fact that it was open all day and nowhere near the sea—and later he'd have a chocolate soda in the old ice cream parlor in the back of Rose's Drugstore. The people didn't seem drab and colorless to her anymore. The men he hung out with were mostly older, like Walt, telling their stories in varying stages of forgetfulness, and some younger guys too, her father's age—they liked old time rock and roll and reminiscing about their hot rods.

Willow saw how much Leon looked forward to his daily hike to the Garden of Resurrection, where he brought red roses to her mother on a pretty-regular basis, keeping her grave and the graves of her family neat and pruned, like little gardens unto themselves, then trekked back to town again. All that walking kept him young, he said.

In his spare time, he had refurbished the entire house except for the half-finished attic—he tore down a wall between the kitchen and the dining room, ripped out the carpets, restained the floors, put in a new brand-new kitchen. The rest of the walls were covered with Willow's paintings and Ricky's too, including his final landscape of the weeping willow, and two portraits of her mother; the most beautiful one over his bed and the other, his favorite, hung on the opposite wall. "She's my sunrise and my sunset," he told her.

He liked to read on the back deck, Louis L'Amour novels and car magazines. In the evenings, he enjoyed having a drink or two with his pals at the Turning Point Tavern. And as of the beginning of summer, he got a dog—a black lab named Spike.

All in all, Willow was both relieved and moved by the life he'd created for himself out of ashes.

△△△

On that particular October weekend, Willow was joined by her brother Adam for the visit, who came without his wife, his first trip back to Willow since he was nine years old. Adam wept when he visited their mother's grave. Afterward, he showed Willow and Leon the ballpark where he played on his first softball team and pointed out the empty lot across the street from the house where he used to practice.

Leon treated both of them to a special dinner at the Seashell Supper House. Amid the quaint collection of sea shells lining every nook and cranny of the place, Willow listened intently as he and Adam shared their memories about the Chavises, Uncle Adam, the town, their one Christmas together that Adam hazily remembered, and of Noël, of course. Once the recollections started coming out, Adam gushed like a fountain. Later in the evening, he presented Leon with a complimentary ticket to attend a post-season game at Comiskey Park and Willow fought a snicker when Leon told Adam he'd be there with bells on. She knew he was a diehard Cubs fan.

As the dinner was winding up, Adam surprised both of them by announcing he was planning to retire from pitching at the end of the year at the age of thirty-eight.

"You going to stay in Chicago?" Leon asked.

"Probably. But my wife is a small-town girl and kind of tired of Chicago. She's six years younger than me and wants to have a baby. Maybe we'll end up moving back here, who knows? Stranger things have happened."

△△△

After Adam turned in for bed that Saturday, Willow and her father sat out on the deck sipping hot cocoa, ever-faithful Spike curled up beside his legs. It was a cool autumn night; the time of year when the leaves were just starting to turn. The October full moon was high. *The Hunter's Moon*, as Gus would have called it; the only night in the month when the moon was visible in the sky all night long. Winter would be here before they knew it.

"I wish the weeping willows didn't have to look so dead in the winter," she said.

"They'll revive again," Leon replied. "Your grandpa used to say that we need winter to make us strong." They sat in silence with their own thoughts for a time. "You know, your mom was right to name you after those trees," he added. "You're just like them. They grow up fast, with deep roots. And they're beautiful."

She smiled. "Do you ever get lonely here?"

"Nope," he said. "You'll see. When you're young, you think you're on a linear path, heading farther and farther away from where you started. But it's not like that. Life is a circle. And I'm just going around."